Redman in White Moccasins

Books by Glenn R. Vernam

INDIAN HATER
PIONEER BREED

Redman
in
White Moccasins

GLENN R. VERNAM

DOUBLEDAY & COMPANY, INC.

GARDEN CITY, NEW YORK

1973

All characters in this book are entirely fictitious, without relation to anyone living or dead. While most of the incidents described are based on factual happenings, they are so altered, compounded, and dissembled that any resemblance to actuality is purely coincidental.

The following chapters adapted from short stories:
Chapter 3, "When Outcasts Meet," *Open Road for Boys,* December 1941.
Chapter 8, "I Saw the Black Ram of Thunder Canyon," *True,* December 1942.
Chapter 14, "Indian Sign," *Blue Book,* March 1947.
Chapter 20, "One-Man Horse," *Blue Book,* April 1952.

ISBN: 0-385-07448-4
Library of Congress Catalog Card Number 72–84950
Copyright © 1973 by Glenn R. Vernam
Printed in the United States of America

TO RAMONA

Whose long-held belief that my tales of the old days would be equally interesting to others led to the writing of this book.

Redman in White Moccasins

CHAPTER 1

"Why, the dirty old coyote! Hey, look at that!" I jerked Ben Duane around by the crook of his elbow.

The tail of my eye had caught the motion of old Pinchpenny Schwenn throwing a fist at the kid's face. They had just finished loading out Schwenn's string of beef cars. The engine was already bucking the slack out of the train, coughing up little curls of gray smoke into the late September air as the drive wheels grabbed at the rails. Ben swiveled toward my pointing finger in time to see the fat Dutchman's fist swing a second time. It looked like an unskinned ham that had been dragged through the feed corral. The boy got his face out of the way this time, but the blow chunked into the side of his neck to send him skidding headfirst across the cinders.

Ben was already loping toward the train. I was only a step behind. Old Pinchpenny half-lifted a manure-daubed boot in the young Indian's direction before he saw us coming. I guess maybe it was Ben's double-barreled yelp that made him change his mind, swinging his foot on across to catch the bottom step of the caboose, as the locomotive whistle bounced a long wail against Squaw Butte and jerked ahead. Characters like old Pinchpenny seldom hankered for arguments with Ben, especially when his bristles were up and they could see open country in the other direction.

Now, he ducked inside the caboose, like a barn rat dodging a lynx cat, as the train picked up speed a dozen rods ahead of us. I doubt if he even heard what Ben yelled about his ancestors. Anyhow, he was used to having his pedigree read by everybody more than half his size. Nor did he ever seem to pay it any mind so long as it didn't cost him anything.

The train was clanking through the last switch, well out of the yards, by the time we got over where the kid was piled up, a wadded

1

heap of ragged clothes and bloody brown skin. We rolled him over. He was about the sorriest chunk of human I'd ever seen.

"Pinchpenny's Indian!" I said absently, scratching my mind for some overheard remarks about Schwenn hiring a drifter from over on the Reservation.

"Who else?" Ben snapped back. "Name's Tom Little Bear. 'S the only kind of help old Schwenn can get any more." He wiped some blood out of the Indian's mouth and ran a surprisingly gentle hand over the bony shoulders. "And the old devil don't even deserve that!" He spit sidewise like he'd bit off a gall bladder.

I didn't ask him how come he knew so much about the Indian. It didn't seem like a good time to crowd him with questions, the way he was stirred up.

This was in the early days, back at the front end of the century. Northern Wyoming was still a pretty new country. Plenty of people around that neighborhood hadn't shed their raw spots about Custer getting tangled in his own loop while trying to put store pants on old Sitting Bull. In such minds, any live Indian was sort of an insult to a noble cause. They naturally didn't waste much thought on what might happen to a Reservation stray that got fouled up with old Pinchpenny.

Ben Duane, however, seemed to have a different slant on things. He worked on the idea that everybody deserved an even break, whatever the breed. Maybe that's why he salvaged me, Curly Brent, out of a gyp horse-trader's camp at Miles City the year before, staking me to an honest job with the Broken Arrow. I never did ask him the way of it; I was satisfied to just be there. I reckon I more or less figured that anybody with a heart as big as his didn't need to explain his actions. On the other hand, like a lot of outsize, square-jawed, easygoing jaspers, he could be as ringy as a rump-shot grizzly when he ran into a raw deal. Now, he sounded like the wrath of God as he bawled at me to get some water out of the stock-pen tank before the fellow died and I turned into his gravestone.

"Want to tell us about it, kid?" he asked, after I had dumped my second hatful of water over the Indian's head. "Schwenn's reason for unloading on you like he did?" And I couldn't help noticing how all the iron had gone out of his voice as he helped the wobbly victim to his feet.

The Indian rubbed his face with a grimy hand, shaking the water out of his hair. He was still some groggy. He sagged over against Ben, feeling of his neck while he got his voice working.

2

"No pay me t'ree moons," he finally mumbled through a pair of split lips, already swelling out of shape. "Plenty hard work make haystack, build fence, feed cows'n ever'thing. Now he go with train to stay long time." The Indian gulped a couple of times and sucked in some fresh wind before going on: "Now winter come pretty quick. Me have no money for live. I ask he pay hones'. He say no good, me fired. Owe me no'ting. Beat like I'm squaw an' tell me go Reservation, where I b'long."

The looks of that blood-smeared face, coupled with the halting explanation, had me pawing the dirt from the start. The Indian wasn't any older than I was, around eighteen, and I knew plenty well how to feel for him. I was trying to find something helpful to ante when I heard Ben bite off another gall bladder.

"Lousy old cutthroat!" he rasped. "Should be dogged up a tree and let starve!"

The Indian slid out from under Ben's arm and pulled himself slowly up alongside the loading chute. He was still plenty shaky, but you could almost see his native toughness fighting to throw it off. And from the way his black eyes reflected Ben's outburst, I was glad it wasn't me that had suckered him out of his wages.

"Schwenn, him forked tongue," the puffy lips went on in a tone that fit the warpath gleam in the beady eyes. "All time robber thief! Some day catch him an'—"

"Take it easy!" Ben broke in, slipping a hand under the one dangling arm. "Just let things ride for the present. We'd best get you cleaned up now."

We were in Neka, that day, for a load of winter supplies. We had left the partly loaded wagon out back of the Neka Trading Company store while we went to dinner and rounded up a few extra odds and ends. It was on our way across from the blacksmith shop, with a bag of horseshoes, that we ran into the ruckus with Pinchpenny and the Indian. Now, Ben swung the kid away from the loading pens to head up the street, leaving me to shake the rest of the water out of my hat. Left there like that, it didn't surprise me a great lot to see him turn his head, a minute later, to tell me I was elected to check over the load and get the team out while he was gone.

What did surprise me was Tom Little Bear's looks shortly afterward. When Ben brought him back to the wagon, where I was hooking up the lead team, I thought for a minute he'd been swapping Indians. The kid was all slicked up and stepping proud as a four-hundred-dollar show horse. He was rigged out in a new pair of boots, Levi's, with store creases still in them, a red-checkered shirt, and was packing a new sheepskin coat over one arm. With his face shining clean under a pearl-gray Stetson, he had little likeness to the ragged wreck we'd pulled out of the cinders.

Ben must have seen my mouth drop open like a trap door. At any rate, he hurried to say, "Tom will help you, Curly, while I settle the bill for this stuff. You two get the outfit ready to roll, time I get back. The day's shrinkin' fast."

I pulled my face shut enough to say, "Sure, Ben!" and tossed the Indian a jerky nod. I half-hitched the lines around a wheel spoke and invited him to help heave on the rest of the canned goods. And he turned out to be a right good hand, even mauled up the way he was. He seemed to have the knack of being in the right place at the right time, and not anyways bashful about a good-natured waggle of his head, one way or the other, whenever I spoke to him. By the time Ben came back, we were making out like a pair of strays that had found each other, although he still acted like he had talked himself out for that season.

I remember how he sat propped up against a sack of sugar, like a cigar-store cousin, the whole twenty miles out to the ranch. He apparently never moved a muscle all that time. Neither did he pay any attention to Ben and me, up on the seat ahead of him, hashing over everything from the price of steers to the Widow Scanlon's latest run-in with Matt Grunning's sheepherder.

It was a plumb perfect afternoon, one of the kind you never see except in the high country during the few weeks between the first frost and real winter—we called it the Season of the Short Blue Moon. And that was a good name for it. The whole country suddenly took on sort of a bluish cast at that time. The scraggly sage had melted into soft, bluish-gray clumps, loading the air with that good fall smell. My lungs couldn't seem to get enough of it as we wound out across the flats. I lay back in the seat to watch the spooky blue shadows that hung in the canyons and draped down over the far hillsides like lacy shawls. Some fleecy white clouds were drifting like sheep's wool across the deeper blue sky above Warbonnet Mountain. A bunch of antelope peeked at us over a rimrock ridge before flashing their white rumps above bluish backs as a signal of more important business in far places. Even the gashed-out brakes of the badlands, angling off to our left, had taken on kind of a gauzy blue softness to hide their naked dark slopes and weathered bluffs.

I'd always thought Indians were great nature lovers. The books all tell you that. But if our new hand appreciated any of this, he kept it a tight secret. His wooden face was still staring at nothing when we topped out on the rim above the ranch just at sundown.

As we started down the grade, I noticed the black eyes come alive for the first time on the trip. It made me think of somebody suddenly running a windowshade up in a dark room.

"Yours?" he said, prodding Ben's elbow.

At Ben's nod, he shifted over for a better view. Then he went into another trance. But this time, there was no blankness in his eyes; he was really seeing things.

I didn't blame him. The sight of Ben's Broken Arrow layout, looking down from the hill road, always twisted a knot in my gizzard. It was a picture to fan your imagination: the low, rambling log house set in the pine grove under the flank of Warbonnet Mountain; the bunkhouse, blacksmith shop, sheds, barn and corrals drifting out in a kind of a semicircle among the cottonwoods crowding against the bend in Rope Creek. The creek itself always made me think of a rope looped around the place to anchor it against the foot of the mountain. The whole spread nestled down into a basin-like widening of the valley, like something the Lord had set aside for a favorite son, under the sheltering bulk of old Warbonnet. The string of tree-fringed meadows along the bottom looked like so many green flags tied to the twisty rope of a creek carelessly tossed down between the hills. Altogether, it was the kind of a setup to make you feel like you'd come to the end of the trail, if you ever had a dream. Now, with the last slant of sunshine glancing off of each bend in the creek, and the cook's supper smoke climbing up through the pines in a lazy spiral, it was enough to crack the shell of even a wooden Indian.

Old Doc Crowley put the feel of the place into words one evening, suddenly throwing the spurs to some of his drinking language, like he occasionally did. Old Doc had brought a whole corral full of fancy education with him from someplace back East, but he seldom exposed it unless he got some kind of a burr under his saddle. That particular evening he had stopped at the ranch for supper on his way back from sewing up a horn-ripped puncher over at the Box C. He never missed a chance to have a good powwow over a full bottle with Ben. They were a lot alike in the way their minds tied onto things most of us never even thought of. This night, I'd just come over from the bunkhouse to get a fresh bucket of water, when the two of them came out on the porch, still going on about something I couldn't make head nor tail of. However, I'll never forget how Doc stood out there under the stars, slowly wagging his shaggy head like some old mossy-horn bull daring anybody to spring an argument.

"A shining beacon in the great sea of mediocrity," he barked through his bristly mustache, swinging his arm as though to take in the whole ranch. "Only a spirit come down from Olympus could have brought forth a golden Isle of Hesperides amid the drab forest of stoicism."

His words were too far off my range to make much sense, yet, for some reason I could never figure out, they somehow gave me about the same feeling that always boiled up in me every time I looked around the place.

I guess something similar happened to Tom Little Bear. The way he would sometimes stand just looking at the valley, when his eyes weren't trailing every move Ben made, would make you think of a lost dogie that had finally found its way into the feedyard in the middle of a blizzard.

The only dry spot in the skillet was the way the other boys all edged away from him, like he was something the dog had dug out from under a rock.

CHAPTER 2

As I've said, this was a long time ago, when most people still took a pretty dim view of Indians in any form. Our bunch was no exception. Old Baldy Peters never looked more like a little, bandy-legged fighting rooster that had just lost most of its tail feathers than when his eyes fell on the Indian. Baldy had never quite got over the time old White Owl's boys had tied him up to a war post in their camp and let the squaws ride him bareback with a cactus whip. Blondy Evans wasn't prodded by any sour memories, but he sure acted like he was afraid everything he'd heard about bloody Indians might rub off on his fancy red shirt or taffy-colored hair, if one got close enough. Even Charley Norris, who always reminded me of a reformed eagle with a hankering to help scratch out worms for the neighborhood ducks, had a way of pulling his long, craggy frame up to its full six and a half feet and staring straight ahead whenever Tom appeared. Jed Hart did the best he could, rolling his big, round blue eyes and letting his tongue run loose, like he'd been appointed to take up where General Miles left off, but he didn't ease things much. They all took to calling Tom the Red Maverick, like he was some runt dogie not worth branding. It shaped up into a pretty tough go for the Indian.

As a matter of fact, I didn't do much to help things most of the time. My general opinion of Indians was about as hidebound as anybody's. A person seems to get that way unless he is bright enough to cut his own trail, instead of following the herd.

It was Ben's actions that finally pried a corner of my mind halfway open. Ben was something special in my eyes, when it came to picking a man to tie to. When I managed to get it through my thick skull that his outfitting this uncombed maverick was only the opener in setting him up as a steady hand, I began looking under the lids of a few things I'd been taking more or less for granted. I knew Ben wasn't any hand to bet on a lame horse. The fact that he had brought the Indian into camp, and was making a stab at treating him the same as he did any of the rest of us, started my mental windmill trying to pump up some definite answers.

But I was three jumps behind, as usual. A chunk of what he had up his sleeve dropped on my head without my even knowing it. It was a long time before I saw the whole pattern; then, only after it had taken shape.

Ben's first move was to put me riding stray hunts with the Indian. I give him credit for having the results of that already figured out. My earlier guess about Tom's age was on the button, making us both a little past eighteen. And what two kids of the same age could work very long together without pairing up more or less? Too, the older hands kind of left us to ourselves, which gave us something of the feel of a couple stray pups snuggling up to each other for extra warmth. Anyhow, we got along fine in spite of our natural spookiness toward strange breeds.

As time rocked along, we fell into sort of an easy friendship that fattened on itself from day to day. Further acquaintance showed that we had much the same dispositions, while I soon discovered he came as far from fitting the lazy, no-good picture most people had of Reservation Indians as I did of shaping up like a bank president. And when it came to honest pride and natural-born dignity, he was cards and spades above a lot of noble white citizens I could name. I suppose that's what comes from having a long line of chiefs for ancestors. Bloodlines show up in a man, same as a horse.

"You mean to say Iron Lance was really your grandfather?" I cut in on a story he was telling one afternoon. The country was full of legends about old Iron Lance. The famous Sioux war chief had been as high rated for his leadership as for his fighting skill with that magical Spanish sword captured in the long-ago time from some wandering explorers. "Then how come you belong to the Crows?" I demanded.

"Plenty Horses other grandfather," he said, as if explaining two times two to a weak mind. "He steal daughter from Iron Lance; give to son, Yellow Bear, for wife. Me son of Yellow Bear. Grow up Crow . . ."

"I see!" My fingers combed idly through my horse's mane while a flock of half-buried stories struggled for air.

Plenty Horses had been top dog among the Crows in the old days.

According to legend, he had cut about as many notches in his coup stick as anybody in that country. Yellow Bear had swung about as much weight until the army starved him into settling for the Great White Father's blessings. That put Tom Little Bear right up among the high-collar class on his own range.

What puzzled me was why, with a background like that, he had walked out to take the kind of a raw deal most whites were aching to give him. I said as much.

We were hunting strays up on the head of Piñon Creek that day. Tom had spent most of the afternoon trying to map out his ambitions in a mixture of mangled English and sign language. I couldn't talk his lingo, while he was dead set on learning to make himself understood in mine. It kind of complicated things.

Anyhow, the story he told me was probably the same one that had persuaded Ben to stake him to an outfit and a job. It all sifted down to the fact that he couldn't see any future in being penned up like a park buffalo. He wanted something better. After a stretch of pow-wowing with the big idea, he decided the only answer was to quit the tepee and get out where he could learn white-man ways firsthanded. He figured a few years' wages and experience would put him in line to set up for himself, with a halfway decent chance of success.

I had to hand it to him. He had real nerve. To even think of making such a climb from where he stood, put him out in Never-Never Land, where Indians just didn't go. Yet, the way his ordinary whipped-out, underdog look sort of melted away, as he talked, his body seeming to square itself a half bigger inside the new clothes, I suddenly got the feeling he would be hard to stop.

I had been halfway tinkering with a similar idea that summer. A wool-gathering dream of someday having a spread of my own was a thing to keep my mind off of corral dust and long hours of pounding leather. But that's all it amounted to, a plaything for a kid to moon over. Now, however, Tom's dreamy talk seemed to weave some sort of a spell that painted visions all over the landscape. I can still feel the way the sunshine suddenly brightened up while funny little chills ran all the way up my backbone.

"It'll work out," I mumbled goofily, talking as much to myself as to him. "Wanting to is half the battle."

We just sat there for a minute, staring out over our horses' heads across a hundred miles of open rangeland to where the Shoshoni

Peaks started climbing toward the sky. It seemed like what we both wanted was really lying out there, waiting for us.

"Maybe we can work something out one of these days, the pair of us together. Our ideas seem to match up top hand." I didn't more than half realize what I was saying. It was Tom's thin, brown hand suddenly covering mine on my saddle horn that finally brought me back to something like clearheadedness.

"Good!" he said. "Two pair moccasins make better travel."

I nodded. At least it was something nice to think about while we shoved our little gather of strays down to the ranch.

Night, however, has a way of cooling off high-flying gas bags. Looking out on the cold, gray light of a frosty October morning, all I could see was a couple of half-baked, forty-dollar punchers looking through a jewelry store window. Screwed back down to normal size, I realized just how little chance our speculations had in reality. Maybe Tom felt the same way; I don't know. But he didn't talk about it any more for quite a spell.

Still, talk or not, we knew in the back of our minds that we were both looking through the same knothole, when the chips were down. It made kind of a chummy feeling, at that. I enjoyed his company a lot, riding with him the rest of the fall. And he taught me a whole raft of things I was glad to know. I'd always been quite a hand to pick up any tricks of outdoor life that might help ease a man over the rough spots that cropped up out in the tall uncut. Tom Little Bear knew them all. His backlog of long-ago stories and old Indian legends was also something I never tired of. I was always digging at him for this and that. To kind of even things up, I did what I could to help him learn white-man ways and how to wrangle our language. He was clever at tying onto the little twists that made for a good personal appearance. Coupled with his natural good sense and enough of Bobby Burns's cooking to push his hide off his ribs, he was soon looking like somebody you wouldn't be ashamed of in any company.

The only snag in the whole deal was the bullheadedness of the other boys about loosening up toward him. As I sided Tom most of the time, they even started freezing up toward me. They couldn't seem to get on top of the notion that Indians were all alike, that trusting any of them was as bad as getting careless with a mule. The idea sort of spraddled out to include any white man foolish enough to ride with one of them.

Baldy Peters handed it to me right off the griddle one evening, cornering me like a misguided pup, down by the horse corral. "Yo're a right nice kid, Curly," he growled over my shoulder, trying to keep his raspy voice down. "Ever'body's been a-leanin' on yore rope ever since Ben signed yo' on here. But yo're crazier'n a hoot owl iffen yo' figer yo' kin throw in with that Injun 'thout ridin' fer a fall. Injuns jest ain't no good fer nobody." He whittled a fresh chew off of his Horseshoe plug and ran his tongue along the gummy edge of his knife blade before wiping it on a pant leg. "I'll admit," he went on, "that this'n don't seem as bad as most, but that's jest the surface. You keep on hangin' around with him an', first thing yo' know, he'll either clean yo' to the bottom of the pot or leave yo' with yore neck in a noose over some whingding yo' wan't nowise to blame fer. It's jest that cussed Injun nature. They can't run straight, never!"

"Tom will!" I cut in stubbornly. "He's different. When you get next to him, you'll find—"

"Awright, be a jug-headed fool an' cut yore own throat. I'm jest a-tellin' yo'," he threw back over his shoulder, as he waddled, still sputtering, off into the dusk.

I figured I knew Tom pretty well by that time, so Baldy's blowoff made me kind of sore. Much as I liked the old jasper, I saw no call for him to ride the Indian into the ground. It looked like dirty pool. Still, Baldy had had a lot of experience with Indians. And he was as wise as a three-toed coyote. The talk he made kept me straddle of a rail most of the next day. On one hand, I'd see the Indian whetting his knife to square up for his granddad's hard luck; on the other, he was just a hard-working misfit trying to claw himself up out of a hole. I felt like I was in the middle of a two-headed horse.

My wits were still tangled up, like a cayuse's mane after a hard winter, when I ran into Tom that afternoon. He was hazing a bunch of long yearlings out of Juniper Canyon as I came down the main trail with the stuff I'd picked up. I needed no telling to know he had done a good day's work, and a hard one. It was no picnic to comb that mess of scab-rock brakes and brush thickets running up into the Thunderbolt Hills. His offer to take on that section, while I covered the easier territory up on the open benches, would have made even an Indian-hater feel good. By the time I'd thrown my gatherings in with his and swapped chin music for a mile or so, I had pretty well pushed Baldy's crepe-hanging back out of sight and got both legs back on one side of the rail.

That's the way things rocked along the rest of the fall. Tom ate

11

with the rest of us and slept in the bunkhouse, but the boys made it pretty plain that they liked his room a lot better than his company. Baldy came up with another anti-Indian sermon or two, trying to cut me back into the main herd, when he saw the outfit was beginning to look at me as though I'd voted for old Crazy Horse for President. I had my hands full, trying to hang onto my ideas.

Only Bobby Burns, our cook, seemed to go along on an even keel. Baldy claimed that was because the cook's head didn't work too sure any more. I knew Bobby was a little off; anybody could see that. Still, he had a lot more sense than some people gave him credit for.

Bobby's trouble was a relic of his last Texas trail drive. A badger hole had downed his horse in front of a stampede one dark night, and he wound up, crippled leg, twisted spine, addled head and all, as a grub wrangler. He was a good one, too, even if some silly clowns did claim the steer that stepped on his head had shoved its foot on through, taking everything with it. But stepped on or not, the steer hadn't got away with any of the Scotch canniness. Some of Bobby's little speeches packed wads of dynamite. Now, he seemed to take kind of a devilish delight in treating Tom like the flower of the flock, especially when the others were around. Any slam against the Indian was sure to bring his head around like a cocked six-gun, his bright little eyes throwing sparks out from under the scarred eyebrows. Then he would put on his lop-sided grin and remind everybody that, "Dee'll the duf'rence, red, white or blue, a mon's a mon fer-r-r a' that," before running off into a woodpeckerish burring that nobody could understand.

This kind of straight-out backing brought the old cook into Tom's camp right from the start. The Indian didn't say anything, but you could see it in his eyes, if you had a mind to look. At first, I thought maybe he didn't know Bobby had been stepped on too hard, but time showed me that it wouldn't have made any difference to Tom. He took people as he found them, and said nothing.

It was much the same with the other boys; he just went his own way, paying no noticeable attention to their sidestepping or backing up on their dignity. So far as you could tell from his actions, he was plumb satisfied with everything. He did his work well and never made a wrong move that I could see. Yet, I couldn't quite get out from under all the warnings that had been dropped on my head.

I tried to talk it over with Ben one day. Ben was usually easy to talk to. But this time he just looked off up the mountain with that unblinking stare he sometimes used to blanket his thoughts.

I was beginning to get a little red behind the ears when he finally turned around and said shortly, "You'll just have to figure out your own friendships, Curly. I'm only hiring you to work."

That left me still up in the air. And I'd probably have dangled along in the same fix until something broke down, if it hadn't been for that Shoshoni horse. You wouldn't think anything like an ornery old outlaw stud could break trail for a bunch of fogged-in humans. I know it's not supposed to work that way, I'd have doubted such a thing happening myself, if I hadn't seen it all fall into place like a jigsaw puzzle. There are some things you just can't figure.

CHAPTER 3

We got Shoshoni the fore part of November. I went along to help bring him home. He was one of the handsomest things I thought I had ever seen. A dark chestnut with light mane and tail, he stood a full sixteen hands high and shone like a sunset on Looking Glass Lake. He was extra deep in the chest and fitted out with the kind of long-muscled, clean-cut legs some artist might have carved. The high-arched neck, topped by that calendar-picture head, needed only a suit of shining armor to complete the image of some ancient war chief daring the world. I guess he was some sort of a throwback to one of the old Arab or Barb horses the early Spaniards first brought to America. Individuals of that nature occasionally showed up among old-time Western horses. And like with some super specimens amongst the human breed, outside influences often decided whether they wound up at the head of the trail or down at the end of some back road.

Shoshoni had gone the wrong way through no particular fault of his own. The Rafter Four, over on Paintbluff, raised him from a colt, and a jugheaded bronc peeler ruined him when he was a three-year-old. A man with any decent amount of horse savvy could have broken him out without too much trouble at that time. Unfortunately, this peanut-brained twister didn't know anything but to rawhide a horse plumb into the ground right off the bat. The idea that Shoshoni was the kind that wouldn't stand for rawhiding, never entered his head. The whole deal had wound up by making the horse into one of the wickedest man-killers in that territory. He had sent two men to the marble orchard and half-ruined three others before they gave up on him. The only reason they didn't kill him, and have done with it, was that nobody had the heart to bump off such a horse raiser's dream of a stud.

When Ben heard the Rafter Four had decided to get out from under any more mishaps by selling the big chestnut, he wasn't long in swapping them a check for their prize headache. He had been nursing the idea of breeding up a special strain of saddle horses that would put the Broken Arrow on the map. Shoshoni had the kind of goods he needed to do it. Ben claimed he intended to keep the big killer strictly at stud; he wasn't going to have anybody getting hurt trying to ride him. However, I knew the boss well enough to see he had some loco idea of unkinking the brute in the course of time. Real horsemen will go clear to the end of the rope in the belief they can make something out of a good horse that has been spoiled; the better the horse, the surer they are that they hold the winning hand. Ben was a horseman from the ground up. I was all set for some interesting observations.

Like most of the cards that fate deals off the bottom of the deck, though, my observations didn't work out nowise like I'd figured. Ben took Tom and me along to help bring the horse home. The Rafter Four held out over in Paintbluff Valley. The trail over there forded Splitrock River just above the mouth of Rope Creek, then snaked around through the foothills to Paintbluff. We got there just as the cook was pounding his triangle for dinner.

It was a nice fall day. Their cook was at least half as good as our Bobby. Thus we were all feeling pretty good as we shoved back from the table and went out to the corral. Shoshoni was there to meet us, handsome as ever. But you could see by his eyes that he didn't have any better opinion of us than he did of anybody else. Circling the corral, he snorted a couple of war whoops and waved his fists at us a few times to let us know what he thought of us. But when Tom and I got him stretched between us, our ropes snugged up tight on either side, and Ben moving in from behind, he had sense enough to see it our way without too much fuss. Fighting a losing battle wasn't his style. But once when I slacked off my rope, just to see what he would do if he thought I was getting careless, his muscles suddenly bunched as he skinned back his teeth to make a grab for Tom's leg. I didn't need any more showing about what he would do, and how quick he could do it, if he had a chance. That hair-trigger hellishness scared me a little, even though I got him snubbed back into place almost at once. And I didn't try any more experiments, especially after Ben unloaded his barbwire opinion of nitwits monkeying with dynamite.

Having my hand called that way by both Ben and Shoshoni left me with kind of a scaly feeling the rest of the afternoon. I was still dragging my chin when we rode into the river ford just before sundown. If I hadn't been so busy feeling sorry for myself, I might have been alive enough to dodge the ducking I got. Anyhow, when my horse stumbled over a rock in midstream, I didn't really come to until I was soaked from boots to hat crown.

It had started clouding up shortly after noon. By the time we hit the river, the sky was lost behind a dirty gray overcast, while a raw, biting wind had sprung up from somewhere. It looked like the makings of a spell of squaw winter was building up in the northwest. After I came out of the water, it built up all the faster. And a November wind whipping down out of the northern Rockies can be the coldest thing short of the North Pole. By the time we got to the ranch, I was shaking like a dude's shirttail on a bucking mule.

Ben saw I was in trouble. As soon as we corraled the stud, he hustled me into bed with a couple of hot rocks and some kind of a drink that felt like the lightning had struck. Then he forked a pile of blankets onto me till I nigh smothered.

"No call to play hospital," I chattered through my dancing teeth. "Get thawed, I'll b-be aw right b' m-m-mornin'."

"Let's hope so!" Ben measured out another one of his fireballs and poked the blankets tighter around me. "Hate to have you rattlin' the dishes out of the cupboard."

I'd put up a holler about him taking me into the house, instead of my own bed in the bunkhouse, but he just grunted and shoved me through the door. Now I was kind of glad; I didn't feel too good. And it was more cheerful there with him and the blazing fireplace, not that either one registered for very long.

I must have gone to sleep right after that second shot of devil's brew hit my stomach. However, I kept waking up every little while, kind of drowsy like and lightheaded. My chest seemed to be shrinking down again my breast bone, like a wet cowhide over a barrel, while my head felt like it was about to start off somewhere on a trip of its own. I remember Ben poking more hot rocks into the bed from time to time. Again, he would be fighting me back down under the blankets when I got to throwing my arms too wild. Blondy showed up alongside Ben about that time—or maybe it was later. I kind of lost track of time. Anyhow, I know I could see the light from the window glancing off his yellow hair and red shirt. Ben was saying something to him about Doc Crowley and hitting the high spots. The way they pulled over by the fireplace, when I threw my head around,

16

made me think they might be rigging up some sort of a joke on Doc, something I wasn't supposed to know about. I couldn't make much sense of it. Anyhow, it didn't seem to matter a great sight. My head had started floating around again about that time, so I slacked off and let myself go to sleep.

When I finally woke up, the first thing I noticed was snow on the windowsill. Canting my eyes farther around, I saw everything outside was covered with six or eight inches of the stuff. It looked like we'd had quite a storm in the night. I tried to lift my head to see better, but it seemed to be tied down to the bed. I tried to sit up, but that didn't work, either.

A shuffling noise pulled my eyes around to see Bobby Burns limping across the room from Ben's big chair. He patted my shoulder awkwardly as he shoved the blankets back up under my chin. About all I could see of him was the two tufts of hair sticking out over his ears and the old scar that made him look like he had been branded Lazy Z over one eye.

"I'll hae yer noosebag ready in a minute," he said, showing a full-size grin. "It's a'ready on the stove."

The blankets felt like they weighed a ton. I tried to push them off, but made a poor do of it.

"Ben says ye mustnae do ony stir-rin' aboot till he gets in," he went on, shoving the covers back in place. "I'll fotch ye a bit o' br-r-roth in a minute. I've been keepin' it hot on the back o' the stove."

"But I'm gettin' up," I muttered. I tried to scrape the fuzz off my tongue with my teeth. "I—I—"

"Ye'll do nae soch thing!" He shoved me back down. I was kind of glad of it. I seemed weak as a new calf. It was a funny feeling. "Joost re-relox, loddie. 'Tis a vurra seeck mon ye've been. We can nae take ony chonces the noo."

Sick? I stared up at him. My head felt like a feather pillow, when I tried to think. Still, there was some kind of a fuzzy picture floating around in the back of my mind. It was more like a dream: Ben and Doc Crowley and Tom Little Bear and somebody else, all mixed up together till they looked like a four-headed man, had been staring at me like they would at a downed steer. And Doc had made me swallow something that tasted like it came out of a slop bucket—and smelled worse. I remember sputtering about how it was ranker than Ben's gullet scorcher. A few other scenes began to come back, like

17

snapshots in a fog. Then I looked out at the snow again. It was kind of pitted, as though the sun had been working on it for quite a spell.

"Just how long have I been knocked out?" I asked, when Bobby finished spooning broth into me and wiped my chin off with a dishrag.

"A motter o' some ten days," he told me, easing my head back down on the pillow. "An' a vurra sick lod ye've been. Hooever-r-r, the meeracles o' Doc Cr-rowley hae presairved ye fer fur-rther-r sins an' tronsgroosians. A' thot r-remains is tae lie still, keep war-r-rm an' obsorb noorishment till he says ye micht once mair-re make a ra-re gilly o' yersel'."

The next time I woke up, Tom Little Bear was leaning over the foot of my bed. Ben was across the room, backed up to the fireplace. Both of them looked like they might have been carved out of pine stumps. But their faces lit up like the shine of new saddles under a full moon, when they saw me roll my head over in their direction. They acted as though they were as glad to see me alive as I was to be there, even if I did look like I'd been pulled out from under a rock right after a spring thaw. It would have crowded me to weigh a hundred pounds, while I felt like somebody had swapped my backbone for a cord string. My head had cleared up some, but it was just too much work to lift it off the pillow.

"You made it over the hump, like a top hand." Ben's voice floated across the room ahead of him as he walked over to look down at me. "You had quite a tussle, but you made it. Now, it's only a matter of building up some strength. I reckon Bobby's soup will take care of that in a little while."

"But what really ailed me?" I asked. "I never had a cold hit me like that."

"It wasn't just a cold. Doc had a four-dollar name for it, but the main joker was as stiff a case of double pneumonia as I ever want to see."

I caught a glance that passed between him and Tom, and suddenly knew I'd been to a place where only the all-out efforts of a bunch of bighearted men had kept my slippery feet from skidding through the Pearly Gates.

"You're out of danger now, long as you stay in bed and keep warm," he went on. "But no getting up till Doc blows the whistle. That's orders! You've been hard enough to salvage; we don't want any complications now. You'll have plenty of time to rattle your hocks when you're fit to make a hand."

18

"Me watch. Mebbyso shoot, you no mind Ben." Tom broke in, his grin spreading out till it threatened to make an island out of the top of his head.

So that's why I didn't go to the Thanksgiving dance over at Sid Andrews's Bent Triangle. Neither did Ben go. He claimed he didn't dare slack off on his job of close-herding me, now that I was beginning to feel a little oaty. Of course, that was just his cover-up. I was still plastered to the bed, and he knew I was really too shaky to do much more than feed myself. But that was Ben's way, always shaping up an excuse for doing what he figured was right.

Anyhow, that's the way things stood, just Ben and me and Tom Little Bear left to hold down the ranch. Tom had stayed, too, more or less as a matter of course. The way the boys felt toward him, there weren't any of them about to be caught ringing him in on a neighborhood party. And I doubt if Tom ever had an idea he might be included, especially with Ben and I not there. It was just one of those open and shut deals that both sides shuck off as the natural thing, without bothering to wonder why.

So far as I was concerned, I didn't even waste any thought on how I was keeping either of them away from the dance. I was too busy feeling sorry for myself about having to stay in bed, when everybody else was having a good time. My craw didn't have enough grit to grind a kernel of wheat as I hunkered down under the blankets like a frazzled-out chunk of rope.

The Bent Triangle dance was the annual fall blowout for the whole country. To miss it, was as bad as losing both legs at one time. I'd been figuring on it half the summer, then wound up in bed.

Tom tried to prod a little spirit into me by talking about how nice it would be to be alive when spring broke, but I wasn't interested in spring right then. He finally saw it was a losing game, and drifted outdoors, leaving me to chew on my own gall.

"No wonder he can be cheerful," I told myself. "Dances don't figure in his life, nohow." It never once dawned on me that his honing to live like a white man might include some of the lighter things we all enjoyed.

I've often wondered since if this whole deal wasn't some kind of a little blindfold game fate had rigged up specially for the three of us. Such things are too deep for me to figure out. Anyhow, at that time, I was too sunk in my own bog to think of any fate besides the one that was keeping me roped to the bed.

I didn't even bother to watch the boys ride off, with old Bobby Burns cutting didos on his pinto mare. They left right after dinner. I had already turned my back to the window to cut off sight of the dying drift of smoke from the bunkhouse chimney. It was about the only active thing to be seen outside: it and the catlike walk of Shoshoni milling around the corral Ben had turned over to him.

Piled up on my stack of pillows all week, I'd not had much to do daytimes but watch the horse fiddle around. It helped pass the time. The corral was directly across from my window, giving me a grand-stand seat. And Shoshoni was really something worth watching, if you could manage to forget the war hatchet he was always packing against the human race. It always needled my blood just to see him. Every move was like he was walking on steel springs, while his mus-cles rippled like snakes crawling under his shiny hide. It had snowed more while I was getting back on full feed, making a spotless white background that set him off like something you might see in the movies. When he'd bow his neck and throw his head up to whistle a challenge at the world, silvery mane tossing in the breeze and tail cocked up like a prize rooster heading for battle, you couldn't help think of some old blue-blooded king out to take over everything this side of somewhere.

But it would have taken more than a pretty horse to spur my in-terest that evening. I didn't even want to see him, after the boys left. In fact, I wanted to shut out everything, even Ben and Tom. They finally quit trying to haze me out of the hole I'd crawled into and drifted off by themselves.

Ben had been breaking Tom in on how to dodge traps on a check-erboard while they sat around nights, riding herd on me. Now they left me to fight my own head while they pulled chairs up in front of the fire and settled down for a good game. They were still at it, humped over the board like a pair of ravens eyeing a crippled prairie dog, when I went to sleep.

I woke up sometime around midnight. It came all of a sudden, like somebody had yelled me out of my sound sleep. I lay there for a minute, trying to get hold of what had jolted me awake. Then the tail of one eye reached over to meet the glare in my window. My mind first grabbed the idea of a full moon peeking over the hill, but let go of it just as suddenly. Full moons didn't pop up in front of west windows. Anyhow, what there was left of the moon's backbone had already been working on the other side of the house for an hour or more. Groggy with sleep as I was, something right down frightening yanked my eyes full open and jerked my chin up over the windowsill. One good look outside was all I needed. Sleep disappeared like a blown-out lamp to leave me rared up in bed with both eyes popped out like walnuts.

"Fire! Fire!" I was yelping like a scalp-hungry Sioux. "Ben, Tom, the barn's afire! Fire-r-r-r! Barn's burnin'!"

CHAPTER 4

The blaze had already gnawed out through the hayshed roof. Great hungry tongues of flame twisted upward in showers of sparks from a dozen places. One whole wall of the barn was starred with winking red eyes, its windows bigger crimson splotches outlining crazily dancing figures of red and black and gray. I heard a horse scream as one corner of the building exploded in a burst of fireworks.

That horse scream jarred me into some more yelling. I wasn't too weak to be scared. I knew what it meant.

In those days we didn't do much winter feeding of stock. Most horses wintered on the range, same as the cattle. A little hay was scattered out for them, if the snow got too deep or was crusted; otherwise, they were left to rustle for themselves. The Broken Arrow followed pretty much the same pattern. The only stock we barn-fed was enough saddle horses to go around and a little bunch of special brood mares Ben was bent on coddling through the bad weather. If Shoshoni hadn't been so cussed ornery, he'd have been in the barn with them. As it was, he was prancing around his corral, like a blind man in a watermelon patch, squalling his bloodthirsty warnings to the mares and three or four saddle broncs trapped with them.

I guess it was the mares that were riding point in Ben's mind. He had set a lot of store by them for the year's breeding. At any rate, my howls were still batting my eardrums when I saw his red drawer legs explode out the back door, and, churning between boots and flying shirttail, lope across the yard. He was yelling for Tom as he ran. The last I saw of him was when he grabbed a saddle blanket to twist around his head before disappearing into the barn.

I don't reckon I'll ever forget that night. The barn was built with stalls along one side, the rest being one big hayshed from ground to rafters. The fire had evidently started somewhere along the back side of the feedway and crawled up the face of the hay pile, where it spent some time chewing out through the roof before the draft got hold of it. There wasn't any wind to speak of, but when Ben opened the door it was like you'd turned an air hose on a locomotive firebox. Great wads of flame-shot black smoke suddenly blossomed out of the roof to swirl across the corrals in a shower of charred shingles. Inside, a bucket of pine pitch or kerosine couldn't have made it flare up brighter. Horses were screaming their heads off, their feet sounding like gun shots as they tried to kick their way free of the stalls, while burnt alfalfa and red embers drifted down on their backs. I heard sort of a muffled crash back in there somewhere, like one of them might have knocked a partition down.

Tom wasn't more than a dozen rods behind Ben, but the suddenly increased heat set him back on his heels when he made for the door.

I was flattened up against the window pane, trying to get sight of Ben. I hadn't seen him since he went inside the barn. Washed out as I was, I had wits enough left to know he had no business in there, not for any amount of horses. Then, all of a sudden, I saw something that really plugged the breath in my throat. The roof had started to sag. The ridge line showed clear against the sky, its middle settling lower by the minute.

I clawed my fingernails into the window casing and yelled at Tom. I knew he couldn't hear me, not over the roar of that fire, but a man does a lot of locoed things at such times. I guess he feels he just has to do something.

And who is to prove that some of these things don't work out under certain circumstances? Tom always packed the idea of spirits sometimes carrying thoughts between friends or guarding them with the same medicine. He tried to explain it to me a lot of times, but it was away over my head. All I know is that this time, before I even got my mouth shut after yelling, I saw his eyes lift up to the barn ridge. He saw the same thing I did.

An instant later, he dived headfirst for the barn door. He made it inside, but the heat knocked him back like he'd been kicked by a mule. His second try was no better. He turned his face to brush the singed hair out of his eyes just as a flaming two-by-four let go under the barn eaves. The whole north wall was starting to melt down gently into a tangle of blazing timbers.

Maybe the son of a long line of chiefs has more backbone than ordinary mortals; or maybe a less civilized mind can spit in death's eye easier. I wouldn't know. But whatever was behind it, Tom Little

23

Bear suddenly flipped his coattail up over his head and disappeared into that hellish furnace with a flying leap. All I could think of at the time was that he didn't have a thing in the world except his life; a maverick kid stacking his whole pile on a boss who had only dealt out a little ordinary kindness. I wouldn't have bet a nickle on seeing either of them again.

Yes, you guessed it—Ben was down, back there in that scorching smother. I didn't learn till afterward how Tom had caught a glimpse of him during that second try for the door. Ben had been caught under that falling partition, down and smashed flat. And the partition was all on fire.

I wasn't able to see any of that part from my window. All I knew about the next few minutes was holding my breath for what seemed like all night. I sagged down like a poleaxed steer when I saw the Indian finally backing out of the swirling smoke. He was dragging a big, bloody bundle by its two arms. He had thrown a piece of half-burned tarp over both of them, but their clothes were afire in a dozen places. What I could see of Ben's red drawers was a smoking black char.

They weren't any too soon, at that. It seemed like they hadn't much more than cleared the door when the building suddenly folded in on itself, belching up a geyser of reddish smoke and blazing embers as it collapsed.

Everything went pretty hazy for a while after that. I guess the excitement had burnt me down to the grate. About all I can remember was seeing Tom drag Ben into the house on a horse blanket. The Indian seemed top hand except for the black holes in his clothes and a face blistered red as a beet. The smoke he had swallowed didn't show, and he kept his hands out of sight. Ben was in bad shape. One leg hung out at a crazy angle and the smell of burnt flesh was strong enough to pull my stomach up against my chin.

I laid back down and pretty well lost interest in what was going on for a spell. I probably blacked out altogether. At any rate, the next thing I knew, Tom was poking me in the ribs. He said he'd got Ben into bed and fixed up the best he could.

"I make fire to hol' good," he grunted, dragging Ben's chaps down off the peg beside the door. "Ben covered plenty warm. Go for Medicine Doc now. Here, mebbyso t'ree, four hour. You sleep now. Ever'thing safe."

24

"Hunh?" My head jerked up like a turpentined tomcat. "You mean get Doc Crowley in three, four hours? How?"

He wasn't kidding me! Not with all the horses on the place perfuming that pile of smoking ruins. Doc Crowley hung out in Neka, twenty miles away, while the nearest neighbor wasn't much closer. Gabbing about twenty miles and back, half of it on foot, in three or four hours was a pretty lame joke. I told him so.

"No walk. One horse left." He slid into the chaps without looking up.

The flat statement caught me between wind and water. It took a split second to grab its meaning. Then dawning realization pulled my eyes around to the window facing Shoshoni's corral.

"What?" I yelped. "Can't nobody ride that locoed snake!"

"Must do. Walk too slow. Ben die." His thin face never looked more like a tomahawk, fire-blistered cheekbones highlighting it as though daubed with war paint.

There were no ifs, ands or buts about it, so far as he was concerned. It was just something that had to be done, and there was nobody but him to do it. His voice sounded like fate reading the score to a man with both feet in a bear trap. And we were really caught in the bend of a rope. I remembered that whiff of burnt flesh; a man with burns as bad as that didn't last too long without proper treatment. Besides, there was the busted leg, soon to start swelling as soon as life came back into it. The Indian was right: something had to be done! And time was the kingpin.

But Shoshoni wasn't the answer! Anybody could see that! Another man killed or crippled wouldn't help us any. And that's what would happen if Tom tried to ride the big outlaw to town. Hadn't the brute already knocked down the ears of five of the valley's top riders? What chance had Tom? He wasn't even in the bronc-twister class, so far as anybody'd ever heard. The idea of him sticking his neck out, like a green sprout of rhubarb, didn't begin to make sense. Even a dumb Indian ought to be able to figure that out. We needed help, not more trouble.

"Forget it, Tom!" I snapped, trying to sound like old Judge Moss. "That big devil'll have you under his feet in ten seconds. Then where'll Ben be? I can't even—"

The rest of my lecture bounced off the slammed door. The quick pound of boots down the walk told me that the gods now had all three of us squatting in their laps. It was a fair guess that they had

25

us already checked over the rimrock. Otherwise, they'd never have put such an idea in the Indian's head.

My stomach clamped down on something that felt like a keg of horseshoes, as I watched him drag a saddle out of the shed and trot over to Shoshoni's corral. The broken-backed moon had climbed up high enough to chase most of the shadows out of the corners. A million stars, such as you never see outside of the high country, blazed down almost within hand's reach. The red glow and little dancing flames from what was left of the barn added a few highlights. All this, shining against the snow, had the place lighted up like a stage setting in the Palace Theater at Cheyenne. I saw I wasn't going to miss any details of the performance, though I'll admit I'd have felt a lot better watching something else right then.

CHAPTER 5

Tom was working like an old hand with the rough string. It kind of surprised me the way he seemed to have every move figured out ahead of time. And he wasn't taking any chances. Instead of bracing the big killer on foot, inside the corral, he shook out a careful loop while still on the ground, then swung a leg up over the fence from the outside. His appearance on the top rail, squalling like a cougar, brought the big stud across the corral, his ugly yellow teeth all set up for a chunk of Indian meat.

But Tom disappointed him. He dabbed his rope over the stud's head at a dozen feet. He jumped down on the outside of the fence a split second later, hauling in his slack and snubbing the rope around a post. It all went slick as a whistle.

It sounded like a boulder on the loose had smashed into the corral, when Shoshoni hit the fence. I'll swear I felt it flatten the window pane against my nose.

The horse had swung his head high in that last screaming lunge, the slobbery, chomping teeth reaching out for the slim figure that had mocked him from the top corral pole. He saw the Indian disappear just in time to pivot his body broadside against the fence. It staggered him for a moment, but only a moment. Then he was squared around, fighting the rope like a trapped wolf. His bared teeth and maddened eyes shone like the Devil's dice in the moonlight.

Tom, however, was still calling all the plays. As the horse tied himself in knots, bawling his hate toward everything on two legs, he slid inside the corral with another rope. Shoshoni was fighting the rope on one end and kicking holes in the atmosphere with the other. The Indian had his loop ready. A moment later it snaked out to snare one hind foot. A quick dally around a post on the opposite side of the corral finished the business. Caught off balance, the stud went down

27

like an upset garbage wagon. Tom jerked in his slack to hold the downed horse stretched out like a flopping catfish.

Though still chomping his teeth and threatening murder with his eyes, the chestnut had sense enough to ease off on useless battle when Tom got a gunny sack over his head. Not able to see where the enemy was, he let the Indian rub his hide in a few places and slack off the choking rope without doing anything but twitch a little. He was still full of war talk, however. He came alive with one big lunge when he felt the saddle slide across his back. He could tell what it was without seeing it. His whistling snort was loud as a bull elk's bugle as he caught his feet to stand braced and panting.

Tom didn't waste any time. His hands moved like a striking rattler as he hauled the cinch up and pulled a bridle over the brute's head. Then he was across the corral and, with a single rolling twist of the wrist, loosened the heel rope so the foot could step free. An instant later, I saw a knife flash in his hand as he forked the stud and eased himself into the saddle. The knife kind of puzzled me, until I saw him reach forward and slide it under the neck rope; then a quick slash before he sailed it over the corral fence.

"Good boy!" I heard myself yelling. "You'll win by a mile!"

He deserved to win. That kind of headwork had put him in the driver's seat without any unnecessary risk. And he hadn't wasted any ammunition doing it. By the time he jerked the blindfold off, he was already screwed into the saddle and had his stirrups. That was a whole lot. The fact that he hadn't poured out what was left of his fire-scorched energy in the first round was one of the biggest marks on his score card. I began to perk up.

Yet, I found my breath still coming ragged as I watched the horse stand there for an instant that seemed long as an hour. The pair of them reminded me of a horse-and-rider statue I had once seen in some city park. However, no sculptor could ever have got that perfection, or made it seem to float in the moonlight like something straight out of the Arabian Nights.

I reckon it was only the space of a heartbeat that they stood like that. It couldn't have been much longer, or I'd have wilted down for lack of breath. Then the picture suddenly exploded against the sky-line in a twisting tornado of man and horse. It was like somebody had touched off a box of giant powder under them. Shoshoni went up in the air, a bawling red cloud, and came down like a lightning bolt. Next minute, he resembled a prairie twister gone wild—hugging the ground, climbing the moon and trying to swallow his tail, all at the same time. If you ever saw a mouse get up inside an old maid school ma'am's petticoat, you'll know what I mean.

Tom Little Bear was riding with everything he had. He needed every bit of it, too! Nobody had underrated Shoshoni's ability. It wasn't exactly the fanciest ride in the world, but I'm here to tell you it was one of the most wonderful ones. When you figure the Indian was playing a lone hand, with nothing between him and the undertaker, if he made one slip, you have to give him credit for a lot of something most of us are short of.

The whole thing was like one of these moving pictures, when something goes wrong with the machine and everything starts flying every which way, like a skillet of popcorn. Tom was still glued to the saddle. You could almost see his muscles straining like rawhide strings as he met each unpredictable explosion of the volcano under him. Shoshoni had gone plumb loco, murderously, killing mad! Head bogged between his knees and back bowed like a steel hoop, he sunfished, swapped ends and pulled off the crookedest series of piledriving spine snappers any horse ever dreamed of. Then he headed across the corral, fence-rowing savagely, screaming at every jump. You couldn't mistake it for anything but what it was, the vicious determination of an educated killer. No ordinary outlaw bronc ever went at it that way.

I caught a glimpse of Tom's face as they whipsawed toward me. The moonlight was bright enough to show a big red smear spreading across one cheek from his nose. How much longer he could stand that wicked battering was the pay-off question. I knew from experience what each pounding wrench was doing to him. A man's insides can stand only about so much—even an Indian's.

But he was still on top. Then, the next instant, a snaky twist slewed him sidewise in the saddle. I thought he was a goner. My heart battled my windpipe for a moment before he hauled himself back in place. Having one hand twisted in his rope strap was all that saved him. I found myself wanting to cheer, trying to pray, and wound up being glad there was nobody around to see how sappy I could actually be in off moments.

My eyes jerked into focus again as Shoshoni suddenly paused at the end of a jump to throw himself straight up on his hind legs, like a released spring shooting off at an unexpected angle. It was a surprise shift, deadly in its swiftness, the old killer trick of going over backward in hopes of crushing the rider underneath when they landed. But the Indian's medicine was still working. His loaded quirt butt smacked down between the chestnut's ears to set the old hellion back down on all fours, still shaking his head.

I heard my wind come back with a funny little grunt, almost a whinny.

But the horse wasn't through. He tried the same thing again, twisting crazily out of a sunfishing dive. It was a trick I'd never seen done; and I'd need to have seen it to believe it possible. Tom was still on the job, though. He met the stud's ears as they passed his face, his quirt butt pounding them down to somewhere near level.

With a wild bawl of rage, the snaky head doubled back, slobbering teeth striking like a prairie rattler at the chap-covered leg behind his left shoulder. Tom's foot shot forward at the same instant.

I can't say that hard-driven boot toe, cutting into the tender nostrils, changed the horse's ideas of murder in the first degree, but it did change his style of action somewhat. His devilish squall promised the Indian everything but decent burial, as he quit the ground in a long, twisting sidewise contortion that carried him plumb up against the skyline.

I'll swear I could see the whole top pole of the corral fence under his belly, when he flopped on his back, like a cat, and let go all holds. There was no doubting his intentions; it was plain first-degree murder. And he wasn't particular what happened to himself, if he could take that stubborn little wad of humanity with him in the process. It must have been while he was coming down, all four feet batting the air, that I chewed that hole in my tongue.

I'd have sold the Indian pretty cheap right then. It looked like curtains and slow music. However, I hadn't seen it all. His medicine was working overtime that night. Though he and the horse came down in one bundle, he contrived to roll sidewise out of the saddle on the way down. How he managed that acrobatic twist that landed him in the clear, six feet away from the sprawled horse, I'll never know. It was plenty hard to believe, even seeing it. And when Shoshoni got his feet under him again, he came up with the Indian's legs clamped around his lathered ribs and that quirt going like a carpet beater.

But that was the last hard round. Though the horse came down still fighting, to cross the corral in another spasm of high, snaky gut twisters, you could see his boiler had lost its big head of steam. That fall had knocked most of his wire edge off. I guess it was a good thing. The way Tom humped down in the saddle, hanging on with both hands, to keep from flopping like a rag doll, showed that he was about ready to call it a day. I knew just how every nerve in him was begging for a chance to ease off, while his insides got themselves sorted out and settled back in place. A ride like that can pretty near take a man apart under his hide.

And here was the Indian with his job only half done. He wasn't any nearer town than when he started. Yet, pounded up like he was, it looked like he aimed to finish what he set out to do. I saw how he managed to unfasten the gate with one toe, when Shoshoni at last gave in to a ragged trot around the corral. The horse spied the opening when he came around again. I reckon he thought that opened up some fresh possibilities. At any rate, it didn't take any guiding to bring him out in the yard. There, he immediately bogged his head and came unhinged all over again.

It was right there that Tom really went to work on him, quirt and spur. The Indian was probably getting tired of being the fall guy, or maybe he had the horse savvy needed to know that this was the one moment in Shoshoni's misguided life when a man might have the chance to straighten out his warped thinking. I don't know. Neither do I know where he got the strength to rawhide that big chestnut after all he'd been through that night. It was enough to make a believer in Indian medicine out of anybody. And it was sure making a believer out of Shoshoni. Tom's spurs were raking that murdering old son-of-a-gun from shoulders to flanks while his quirt lifted hair at every jump. He had got to where he was riding like a bag of meal, but I'm here to tell the whole wide world he was doing a piece of riding that would do to write home about.

I guess some inkling of what it all meant finally soaked into the stud's skull. At any rate, he suddenly broke into a wild, head-long run, as if he wanted to start a fresh life in some far place—and do it quick. The last I saw of them, bobbing against the skyline before they disappeared in the darkness, Tom was still herding the horse in the general direction of Neka.

I was melted down under the blankets, pretty well washed up from all the excitement, when I thought I heard Bobby Burns's cracked voice drifting through the quiet house. It turned out the boys had all got back from the dance a couple hours after Doc Crowley's sidebar buggy came buck-jumping into the yard, with Tom trailing along behind on the reformed outlaw. I roused up enough to hear old Bobby giving the rough side of his tongue to somebody out in the other room. He was throwing out the same words he always used in taking Tom Little Bear's part:

"De'll the duf'rence," he yelped, "red, white'r blue, a mon's a mon fer a' that!"

I guessed that pretty well said it all, so I sagged back down on the pillow. Anyhow, I couldn't think of anything to add any heft to it.

CHAPTER 6

"I see where a wolf crossed the crick in the second meadow this mornin'." Baldy Peters balanced a stack of gravied spuds on his knife as he took advantage of a hole in the conversation. "Some traps might pay off there under that yella bluff, Tom."

Tom Little Bear looked up with a quick grin. "Good!" he agreed. "Set trap t'night. Mebbyso come back."

We were all up to our chins in Bobby Burns's daily harvest that night. Bobby's big table was a prime place to be, when the snowbanks piled up deep and the bottom dropped out of the thermometer. With everybody spouting good nature, their coffee cups sending up little spirals of steam, stacks of juicy elk steaks and Bobby's sourdough bread lined up alongside of big bowls of butter and jams in the center of the table, I couldn't think of any nicer place in the world. Looking out over my last half of a big steak, banked up against a drift of spuds and brown gravy, I took the measure of a slab of crusty apple pie and wondered how a backcountry stray ever landed in such a lush pasture.

I sawed off another chunk of steak as I slanted a glance across the table at Tom. "How rich did you get today?" I asked.

"Two coyote. One mink." He was right proud of himself.

"Mony a wee bit makit a muckle," Bobby advised from the kitchen door. "Ye'll nae regroot this bit o' oxtry wor-r-rk when ye sit in yer ain hoosie."

Tom's grin spread like a winter sky opening up to let the sunset through. I guess he was thinking along the same line as Bobby. That was what had prodded him into spending his spare time on a little string of traps, instead of donating it to seven up and bunkhouse poker. It was working up into January. There hadn't been much to do around the place since before Christmas. With half a dozen hands to put out a little feed for the stock, there was plenty of time for every-

33

body. Tom used his to the best advantage he could figure. He was still chasing the idea of building up a stake for what he called his "Someday Ranch." What furs he picked up was just that much more toward the big day.

It made good sense. I'd been pawing over the notion of joining up with him in the interests of my own "Someday." I even had Charley Norris bring me out a bunch of traps the last time he was in town. Unfortunately, this last storm had come along about that time, augering Ben into putting the hobbles on me. He claimed a critter that had been flattened out like I was had no business crowding his luck. Besides, he needed me as a handy man. It had been hard for him to do much up until just lately. He was kind of old maidish about chores that needed doing around the house and keeping the place set to rights. So, while he was laid up, he made a house hand out of me, though I figured it was mostly an easy excuse to keep me in out of the weather.

But now things were beginning to look up. My strength had built up a lot in the past weeks. I figured I would be plenty able to get out with Tom as soon as the weather broke. Ben didn't need me half the time, now that he'd thrown away his crutches a week since.

The burns he had collected the night of the big fire had all healed up in good shape, after keeping everybody on edge for quite a spell. They had been pretty bad; the one under his right knee a real stinker. Every time Doc Crowley looked at it, the first three weeks, he'd shake his head and act like he'd be glad to sell out cheap.

Doc knew well enough that he'd bought in on a tough job, when that old sidebar buggy came banging into the yard just as daylight was breaking, his lathered buckskins blowing like a pair of tied-down steam whistles. Tom had made it to town on the big chestnut—both of them still alive—and back home shortly after Doc rolled in. The Indian had told him enough that he knew about what he was up against. He thought a lot of Ben, and you could tell he was plenty worried when he barged into the house, peeling his coat as he came. However, I guess it was even worse than he had counted on. Some of the things he said made me wonder why Ben wasn't already dead.

Whipped out as he was, Tom stuck around the house long enough to help set the broken leg and get Ben moved over onto some clean blankets. Doc had messed things up a heap, cutting off the burned drawers and plastering the raw spots with some of his concoctions. It had been a nasty job for both of them. And a tough one! After they'd finished, Tom headed straight for the bunkhouse, while Doc practically fell into a chair by the fireplace. He must have set there for a full hour, resting, wiping little drops of sweat out of his bushy eyebrows every now and then.

After a long time, he kind of perked up and started firing questions at me about what I'd seen out the window during the night. I must have told it pretty well, the way he hung forward, half out of his chair, all the while.

Then I had to tell it all over again, when the boys moved in on me with a fresh set of questions. One look at the barn and Ben and Doc Crowley was enough to settle any doubts about that end of it. But they had to go out and hold a powwow over the hoof gouges in the corral and the dried sweat streaks on Shoshoni before they would believe my story of the ride. Jed Hart wouldn't even be satisfied till he took a gander at Tom, still asleep in the bunkhouse.

"Blood'n blisters all over his face!" Jed's big voice rolled all the way back from the bunkhouse. He waved his arms, still looking like a kid who had caught Santa Claus stuck in the chimney. "Spurs full o' hair an' clo'es all over blood an' horse spit. An'—an' him an Injun! Hell, fellers, it's plumb unnat'ral!" His mouth flapped like a back door after the folks had all moved out, the round, blue eyes goggling at me as though I was to blame for it.

Once the facts of the whole deal jelled in their minds, however, their spookiness toward Tom melted like snow in a Chinook. He was no longer an outcast. In fact, you'd have thought from watching them that he was something they'd birthed themselves. What with saving Ben's life and all, I reckon they'd have gone clean around the circle with anybody foolish enough to auger otherwise. As for Tom himself, this being treated like he belonged to the outfit kept him lighted up like a rainbow had landed on his head.

We were what you might call a right happy outfit by the time the Holidays wound up. Tom was all right as soon as his stiffness wore off and a few burns healed, while my sashaying around that night hadn't seemed to damage anything in particular. I got up in another week or so to start packing feed and water to Ben. He was up and around on crutches in time for Christmas. Doc said he was shaping up for a complete recovery, in spite of all the rules of God, nature, and medical science.

Even Shoshoni was a reformed character. He still had all his starch and vinegar, but he seemed to have decided there was no use wasting it on a little thing like a man on his back. In fact, he acted like he was plumb proud of himself every time he and Tom started out together. The Indian rode him quite a lot in tending his traps.

I was all fired up over the trapping proposition. Tom had rounded up almost a hundred bucks' worth of fur since the first of December. That was important money in my scheme of life. Why couldn't I do the same? It would be a simple way to match his pile when he got lined up to stake out that ranch. We talked it over some, and he said, "Good! Soon's you be well 'nough."

I figured I was already well enough. I rared up above the table to announce to all in general that I guessed I'd put out a few traps next week.

I heard Ben's chair scrape, and hurried to add, "I'll rustle wood of a mornin' an' keep up the other chores."

He nodded, his tongue chasing a piece of pie crust down over his chin. "Can't say I've much need of a nurse any more. But," he went on, as sort of an afterthought, "you'd best let the weather loosen up a bit before you start. Make it easier to get broke in."

I caught Tom's eye and we moved over to the fire to kind of sort things out and map a few plans. I knew I'd have to take it a mite easy for a few days, and I didn't want to horn in on any territory he had staked out.

But there was nothing to worry about. Everything worked out fine, though I was kind of disappointed at first. Trapping looks like a plumb simple proposition—just set out some traps for the animals to put their feet into, then pull off their pelts. I managed the first part all right, but getting the critters to step in the right place was something else again. I like to ran myself ragged getting nowhere, till Tom took me in hand. He proved to be a good boss. He showed me all kinds of tricks that I would never have thought of. A lot of it looked like foolishness, but it usually paid off. In the course of time, I was bringing in a pelt every once in a while.

I remember it was the third Sunday in January when Charley Norris cracked one of his long silences at the supper table. "Why don't you boys take a shot at a real fur territory?" he asked. "I'll bet you'd clean up."

We both popped up, like ground hogs out of a hole. "Where's that?" I wanted to know.

"Down Splitrock Canyon." He stopped to bury a half slice of bread in his face, then went on: "I was huntin' wild horses over on Dead-

36

man Crick a couple years ago. I'd worked my way almost down to the big canyon before the crick gulch pinched out into a brush-choked gash I couldn't very well ride through. I had no reason to go farther, anyhow. But there was a little skifft of snow on the ground, and I noticed a scad of tracks all through there—wolf, fox, mink, marten, and the like. It stands to reason it would be the same, if not better, down in the main canyon, where nobody ever goes. A man could get in there on the ice this time o' year."

Tom and I looked at each other. I guess it struck us both as funny we had never once thought of that place. We heard Baldy Peters say, "A body'd be crazier'n a hoot owl to go down in that hole, even when she's froze up," but it went over our heads.

"Oh, I dunno," Blondy put in, running a spoon handle through his yellow foretop. "Ice should be as solid inside the canyon as out. Maybe more so, the way the sun scarce ever gets in there."

The proposition sashayed around the table half a dozen times, everybody taking a whack at it as it went by. I was digging inside myself for everything I'd ever heard about the place. Tom sat hunched over, his elbows straddle of his plate, while whatever he was thinking followed a far-away look in his eyes.

The canyon was a sixty-mile gash through the Elkhorn Mountains. Splitrock River washed the base of its sheer one- to three-thousand-foot walls nearly the whole distance. The river raced through there like some hell-bent monster trying to chew itself up, leaving nothing but odd bits of shoreline here and there. The walls were practically unclimbable, while nobody with half sense would think of riding the stream itself. About halfway of its length, the Indians' old Medicine Trail came down Skull Creek to ford the river in a stretch of slack water. That was the only way into the gorge, that I ever heard of, except up at our end where Rope and Oven Creeks emptied in on opposite sides, shortly below The Narrows. The high cliffs and pounding water made its whole length a pretty spooky place. I doubt if any white man had ever been all the way through it and lived to tell the story. The few who tried it, so far as I ever heard, never showed up at the other end. Not many had ever been into it, aside from crossing at one or the other of the two fords. It looked to me like any furbearers in there would still think they owned the world. And if Charley saw sign enough up on Deadman to shake the kinks out of his tongue, he could not be far wrong in reasoning there would probably be more in the canyon itself.

"I've heard there's hot springs down there 't keep the river open for a stretch all winter." It was Jed Hart, his china-blue eyes rolling like a couple Easter eggs in a washpan. "Sh'd a man git caught in a place liken that—"

"There's no law says a feller's got to float his carcass every time he sees open water," Blondy broke in. "There's such a thing as turnin' back before he goes over the edge. That is, if he's not plumb loco."

Jed sat there waggling his head, like he'd just been let in on some great discovery, while Baldy opined, "The hull idee is crazier'n a hoot owl!"

It was Tom who put more or less of a clincher on the deal, when he suddenly lifted his head to say, "My people hunt bighorn there before white man put on Reservation. Medicine Trail cross river at Skull Canyon. Many bighorns for kill both ways from ford."

Tom Little Bear's people had been in the country since the misty long-ago times. He seemed to know everything they'd done and how they got there to do it. He could usually tell it, chapter and verse, as he had learned it from the Old Ones. If he figured the canyon was a good bet, I was plenty willing to string along with him.

"We could rig up a light sled to haul our outfit," I suggested, with all the brilliance of somebody inventing the first wheel. "It would pull easy on the ice and beat back-packing."

Tom reached over to pat the inventor on the shoulder, while everybody except Ben and Bobby went on arguing about our chances of shaking hands with Saint Peter.

"Sled's the t'ing!" he agreed with a grin.

Bobby finally cracked his whiskery smile to remind his listeners that, "Only the bra' an' vaintooresome wear-r-r the fine r-robes o' threeft an' glor-r-ry befair the mooltitude."

That "brave and venturesome" part roweled me the length of my spine and put the bit in my teeth.

CHAPTER 7

Ben kind of brought me back to earth a moment later, leaning back in his chair while he packed his pipe. He scratched a match under the seat of his chair and thoughtfully squinted at a curl of smoke twisting up from the bowl. Then, speaking around his pipestem:

"I'd like you boys to help raise the frame for the new barn before you set out to corner the fur trade. Getting those big timbers up will be a job for all hands. It won't take long, once this cold snap breaks enough to let us get at it. Then, if you're still in the notion, you're welcome to a few weeks off. The canyon would be a nice trip, anyway."

There was nothing unreasonable about his wanting to hold us until the heavy work on the barn was finished, even if his owly idea of us walking into a bonanza did stick out a mile. The boys had cut out the logs and poles needed for the barn frame at odd times, when the weather was favorable during the earlier part of the winter. Getting them up in place and fitted together, however, would be a job that called for all the hands in sight. That he was generous enough to let us off then, without waiting to finish the boarding-up and shingling, was stretching things in our favor a whole lot. And the fact that he wasn't throwing out any hair-raising boogers waiting for us in the canyon was a heap of encouragement. I knew he would have had us tangled up in enough snarls to last till hot weather if he'd thought our chances were half as slim as Baldy tried to make out. The whole deal left me wound up like a salty horse on a frosty morning.

But the way things panned out, I might as well have saved my steam for later, when I really needed it. Happenstance plays funny tricks sometimes. Tom always claimed such things were planned schemes laid out by certain spirits. Maybe he was right.

Anyhow, the weather seemed to take a spiteful delight in holding us up. Then we ran into some trouble with the barn framing, using up more time than we had figured. Consequently, it was reaching up into February before we finally got off. Fortunately, though, it had stayed cold, sealing the river even tighter under its solid blanket of two-foot ice. As the Splitrock seldom broke up before late March, we figured we would have plenty of time to get all the furs we could handle. There wasn't a single spot on my rose-colored glasses, when we finally cinched our outfit onto the sled and waved goodbye to the boys left to finish the barn.

Neither of us would have swapped places with the plushiest nabob in Wyoming, as we dropped down to the mouth of Rope Creek and headed into the gorge. The sled slipped along over the ice as though our outfit might have been a bundle of feathers. The sun was friendly, even though it didn't have much heat, while the canyon walls shut out the chilly wind that had been pecking at the upper country all morning.

As soon as we got through The Narrows—the rock-walled gut, where the river was jammed into half its normal width before plunging into the canyon—we found ourselves in a regular picture-book world. Almost at once, the cliffs began reaching for the sky on both sides. Some were bright Indian-red, while others flashed their gaudy pinks, yellows, and orange; many of gray or brown or black were spotted with bluish-green outcroppings or streaked with all the many assorted colors of a dude's necktie. Weather and time had chiseled out spires, columns and all sorts of fancy images in places where water and frost had gouged the face of the smooth walls. Here and there, the canyon widened out into little pockets, leaving small sandbars on one side or the other of the stream. These were sometimes spotted with brush, to make sort of an oasis before the gorge pinched together again. Stunted jackpine and juniper showed as green paint dabs in crevices and crannies along the upper ledges, or stood like stubby fingers stuck up over the rim. Looking up at the snowcapped rim, outlined against the silky blue sky, two or three thousand feet above our heads, I felt like I'd maybe wandered off over the edge of something one of these moon-eyed book writers might have dreamed up. Even the throaty bellow of the river, clawing its way along under the ice, didn't call for much imagination to make you think of dragons and water demons slavering for the taste of human meat.

But I enjoyed every foot of it. We both did. It made a man feel so kind of all alone, like the first person in a brand-new world, where anything might happen. Jobs and money and bosses and two-legged coyotes trying to hamstring some of their own kind for an easy meal, all seemed a million miles away. And the best part of it was being there with Tom. He was a natural part of the whole set-up; you could see it in his eyes, in every move.

We drifted along easy-like, taking all the time we wanted and stopping for everything that looked interesting. After the first mile or so, we saw game every little ways. It seemed like every brush pocket held a few deer. Partridges and grouse played leapfrog with us, as we went along. All kinds of little animals had littered the snow with tracks. We even spotted a nice bunch of bighorn sheep, outlined for a minute against the upper cliffs.

"Plenty good!" Tom tossed back over his shoulder. The shine in his black eyes was all Indian—a happy Indian on his own stamping ground. "As my grandfather spoke of it. Ever'thing!"

"Your granddad hunt this far up?"

"Plenty times in canyon. Go many places. Mebbyso here. But mos' from Medicine Trail."

That made sense. Anybody wanting to hunt the canyon would likely pick the Medicine Trail as the way in. This trail was as old as time itself. The Indians had used it for generations before the white men came. Even before that, according to Tom, it had been the ancient trail of some unknown people who had disappeared long before his tribe came along. Apparently, they used it as a route to their ceremonial medicine wheel, outlined in rocks on top of the mountain, a place as mysterious to the modern Indians as to the whites who still puzzle over it.

Anyhow, it was still a good trail into the canyon, coming down from the north to follow Skull Creek down to the ford. There, it climbed out through a narrow gulch and up over some steep benches to reach the top on the opposite side. It was the only crossing in the canyon, making the chief cut-off from the Buffalo Plains in the east to the upper Yellowstone. Occasional trail-wise pilgrims still used it in cutting across country. I'd been over it a few times myself, noticing how the gorge widened out a bit there, allowing a smidgen of shoreline along the stream. How far this extended, I didn't know. There was no seeing past the bends, and I was never curious enough to leave my horse and explore it on foot. Anyhow, it all fit in with Tom's grandfather story. And I guessed if the old man could make out to hunt the canyon, we should be able to do the same. I said as much.

"Is good!" he agreed. "We make fine trap for fur."

From then on, the place seemed more friendly, as though it might be the ballywick of Tom's people and I'd been made welcome. It's hard to put into words. But the walls took on sort of a close, warm feeling, like a house you'd built yourself. The way the after-dinner sun painted a long, golden welcome strip on the ice around the next bend below us cinched everything down tight, so far as I was concerned.

That all-right feeling was still building up when we made camp the second night. We had just dangled along, investigating everything and prowling some caves whose smoke-smudged ceilings spurred my imagination into a high lope. This dallying had probably brought us less than a third of the way down the canyon; more likely, less. We never did know exactly where we were; nor did we care. Just being there was enough.

Anyhow, it was around three in the afternoon when we drifted around a bend to see this little cove set back a ways from the river. The place was made to order as a camping spot. We both stopped in our tracks for a better look. High water and drift had built up sort of a bench above the stream. It was bigger than any of the skimpy sandbars we had seen, spread out like a big front yard in front of the cove. Piles of dry driftwood cluttered the lower edge, while a good stand of brush covered most of the top. Circled back into the cliff, as it was, the walls shut off the heft of the wind that sucked through the gorge, making it as snug as a five-dollar blanket. Shelter, firewood, and the sunrise rim facing us across the river! It was a plumb natural. I even shot a nice spike buck that tried to sneak out the other side of the brush while we were looking things over.

We unloaded right then and there. Tom took off for a little look-see down the canyon while I dressed out the buck and made camp. He came back, shedding good news like a duck does feathers. Though he hadn't gone very far, he said fur signs were scattered thick as skunk tracks in a henhouse. We patted ourselves on the back the rest of the evening.

"Big cleanup here, Curly," he promised. "We trap good."

I found he wasn't talking through his hat, by any means. The next few days were something to remember. The river below us, for several miles, seemed to be a natural hangout for the canyon critters. Without any humans around, they had apparently all settled down and raised families. For the same reason, they had never learned to dodge traps and hide hunters. After the first day, it kept one of us busy skinning and stretching pelts while the other tended traps. I went plumb fur crazy. All that wealth piling up, worked on me like a free-running still would on a booze-hound.

It was the run-in with Tom's spirit ram that finally gave my one-track mind something else to chew on.

This all started one evening after getting outside of an early supper. Dusk was building up down where we were, but the tail end of sun-set was still splashing along the upper cliffs across from us. The whole canyon wall was lighted up so everything stood out clear as the bib on a granger's overalls. I'd been watching the swath of light, how it was gradually shrinking up from the bottom, and thinking how handsome it was. I had reached around for the coffee can, taking my gaze off the cliff for not more than a half second, when something that hadn't been there before caught the tail of my eye.

I froze. It was past believing, till I got my head up for a square look. But there was no mistake! Where it came from, I'll never know; but there on the peak of an outjutting pinnacle, where there had been absolutely nothing a second before, stood the biggest chunk of big-horn ram I'd ever seen wrapped up in one hide. He loomed up like he'd been carved out of the pinnacle itself. Outlined against the orange-red face of the main cliff, you could see every line of his body and almost count his whiskers. He looked big as a cow!

And what struck me even harder than his size, was his color. In-stead of the ordinary brownish hair all bighorn sheep commonly wear, this critter's was black as a fresh-shined boot, from hoof to horn. And those horns pulled the eyes half out of my head; they were immense! They looked like oversize rolls of polished steel. Seeing him perched up there, like some sort of a statue, with a last streak of sunlight highlighting him against the ancient time-scarred cliff, you'd swear he was the top range boss of the whole sheep world. I couldn't help thinking for a minute how he seemed a living part of the canyon itself—big, wild, unconquerable, and still untouched by man's weak little scratchings on the face of nature.

Then everything dropped suddenly into place, and I reached around for my rifle.

CHAPTER 8

From where I sat there by the campfire, it wasn't over two hundred yards across the canyon to where the buck stood. He was a perfect target. What a trophy to take back to the ranch! My heart kicked like a mustang colt as I swung the rifle to my shoulder.

Then imagine my feelings when Tom landed straddle of me, knocking the gun galley west!

"No, Curly! No shoot! It is the Old One. To harm him is—"

I kicked loose and clawed for my gun, but he was swarming over me like a starved bear on top of a garbage can. By the time I got my long legs untangled enough to shake him off, the ram had disappeared into nowhere.

I was mad as a dog-bit peddler. I'd lost the top prize of a lifetime. I was half a mind to use the gun on the Indian, even if his head wasn't any prize.

Before I did any damage, though, something in his obsidian eyes sort of threw a half-hitch on my raw edge. Then, after I'd cooled off somewhat, curiosity teamed up with what I used for reason to screw the lid down on my sputtering. It wasn't his style to make that kind of a tough play against anybody, unless there was a mighty good cause for it. And what was that crack he'd made about "The Old One?"

"What stuck a bur under your saddle?" I bellered, some of the red in my face dripping off my ringy tongue. "You lost me the best sheep head anybody ever dreamed of."

"That medicine ram; not for shoot." His voice was low as a prayer, and I noticed his hands make a few funny motions that I couldn't make any sense of. "He belong Great Spirit. Live here since long before my people, mebbyso always. No one must harm. It is so spoken."

"What?" I yelped, my eyes and mouth trying their best to make me look like Jed Hart. I finally pulled my jaw back into place and aimed a finger at him. "You mean to sit there with your face hangin' out and tell me that sheep dates back to before old Plenty Horses was born, after claimin' your granddad died at ninety-two four years ago?"

"What are years to such a one?" he countered, never batting an eye. "Medicine beings not have age. An' he jus' like I hear it spoken by our old men."

I shoved some burnt pole ends farther into the fire and squatted back on my bedroll. This setup had me grabbing leather with both hands. There was sort of a strange, far-off look in Tom's eyes that told me I had met something plumb off the regular range. The spooky, lonesome twilight seemed to be suddenly crowding me back against the canyon wall. It gave me the feel of a bronc discovering itself trapped behind a closing corral gate. The stillness had somehow thickened up till it seemed you could almost cut it with a knife. Over all, hung a kind of breathlessness, as though everything in the canyon had stopped to listen. All I could think of was that time had jumped back a thousand years and the rest of my breed hadn't showed up yet.

Tom Little Bear had a way of making me feel like that, when he came unwound on his old tribal legends and beliefs. Common sense told me such stuff was mostly a bunch of heathen moonshine. I was sure of that. Yet, there was something about the way he laid it out just as surely left me feeling of my scalp, till I got back out in the fresh air by myself again. It was a funny thing. And here, in the bottom of that canyon, where there wasn't any other world, and a man naturally felt like a lone ant in a haymow, it got under my hide more than usual.

I can't begin to tell it like he did. Neither can I give you the feel of it. The feeling was a big part; and nobody could get that unless he had squatted under a circle of half-mile-high cliffs glowering down over his head, all alone except for a half-civilized partner who had temporarily laid aside the civilized half. But, anyhow, here's the backbone of the story, the best I can remember it!

It seems that back in the long, long-ago time, before any palefaces came out of the rising sun, Tom's people had a legendary belief in an overgrown, coal-black bighorn ram that hung out in the cliffs along Splitrock Canyon. This critter was supposed to be a medicine animal set aside for some special purpose by the Great Spirit. With such a background, the ram wasn't anything to monkey with. Instead, he was one of the sacred things which brought forth dreams, dances and a lot of thoughtful pondering. Just to see him, all but guaranteed a year's good luck; to harm him was like putting your neck on the chopping block.

"Did you ever know of any of these good or bad things actually happening?" I asked.

"Do happen," he insisted, maybe dodging my question a little. "Save lives when my great grandfather was young man."

The old story-tellers, Tom went on, could tell of many times when, in the long-ago, the ram had shown its great spirit powers. It was history no one doubted. But what really cinched the deal in his mind was the story of his own great grandfather's run-in with the ram. He had heard it many times in family councils, and once from Plenty Horses, who had been with his father, Spotted Bull, at the time.

This particular affair took place one time when a band of Spotted Bull's people were on their way home from a spring hunt over east of the Elkhorn Mountains. They came back by way of the old Sioux Trail, part of which was still used by cow outfits trailing their stock up into the high country. This trail, after it came down off the west side of the mountain, angled off to the left to hit the main ford at the mouth of Badwater Creek, a dozen or so miles above the mouth of Splitrock Canyon. It was while angling across the flat, that lay between the river and the base of the mountain, that Spotted Bull's band discovered a bunch of buffalo shortly above the mouth of the canyon, on the opposite side of the river. The sight of so much fresh hump roast evidently warped their judgment. At any rate, instead of going on around by the ford, they peeled off to the right and made for the herd head-on. This sashay landed them on the riverbank just above The Narrows.

The Narrows, as I've said, was just a narrow, slit-like gash through the mountain into the canyon below. It was a tough proposition in any man's language, when the river was up to full spring and summer strength. The narrow gut, something over a mile long, was well studded with broken boulders and crooked as a gambler's soul. The high rock walls jammed the stream in to a half or third of its normal width, dropping it down through the steep sluiceway in a churning mass of spray-crested foam.

For a half mile or so above this bottleneck, however, the river widened and sort of piled back on itself in a fairly quiet stretch, building up strength to force itself through the pinched-in crack. This slack water made you think of some murdering old character trying to hide behind a Sunday-school face. I was to learn a lot more about the place later on, but that's another story.

To get back to Spotted Bull's mishaps, his outfit didn't give themselves time to think about anything but fresh meat. A couple of young bloods rode straight on into the river, swimming their ponies on across. They made it without any trouble. That encouraged the rest to follow as fast as they could. By that time, there were plenty of hunters to take care of the buffaloes. Consequently, a few of the men, including Spotted Bull, decided it would be safer to ferry the women and kids across on a driftwood raft they had roped together.

Whether something went wrong with the outfit or they started the crossing too far downstream, or what, Tom didn't know. Anyhow, the little band somehow lost control of their awkward raft out in midstream. Before they could get the contraption out of the drag of the current, they found themselves being sucked into the funnel-like Narrows like smoke up a chimney.

The river went through there like the milltails of hell, the narrow slit of a channel forcing it up into a humpback monster, with spray in its teeth and a foam-flecked mane. How that unmanageable raft, loaded with seventeen people locked together like a swarm of bees, ever held together was anybody's guess. Their medicine must have been working overtime.

Below The Narrows, the river widened out some, but it was still a runaway hellion. The exposed heads of ragged boulders knocked their bundle of logs into a dozen different shapes, each time spinning them back into the bucking current, still in one piece. Crosswise, endwise, hind end to, half on edge and twisting like a pilgrim's straw hat in a whirlwind, they managed to stay right side up and dodge a flock of fool killers as they swooped around kinky bends and dived through boiling rapids.

They finally hung up, straddle of a big rock that headed a sketchy sandbar, somewhere down the canyon. The raft went to pieces a minute later, but they all made it to solid footing under the west wall. Nobody had much idea how far down the canyon they were, but that didn't seem very important. The main thing was that, though half frozen and scared green, they had cheated the hungry river devil. It was pure pleasure to stomp the chill out of their joints and give thanks to whatever spirits they figured were most interested in live Indians.

Unfortunately, this good feeling soon faded out to a glimmer. The fact that they were still a sizable stretch from being over the hump wasn't long in staring them in the face. Their grub and equipment had all gone with the raft and they were afoot at the end of the line. The rocky little sandbar, where they stood, was the only foothold in sight. Everything else was claimed by the water, right up to the base of the walls. The walls themselves looked like a proposition that nothing short of an able-bodied fly would be interested in tackling. It seemed like a plumb deadfall windup to their successful voyage. They made a little medicine in the interests of wishful thinking and bedded down among the rocks for the night.

They were evidently still in pretty good standing with the better-class spirits, for one of them found a narrow crack up through the lower wall the next morning. This little fissure, kind of a shallow, open-faced chimney, had escaped everybody's notice the night before. Some claimed it hadn't even been there before. But however that part was, Spotted Bull figured it looked more hopeful than that bare sandbar. He, accordingly, managed to worm his way up through the crack, coming out on a set-back ledge halfway up the wall. Here, he found, on both sides and above him, a mess of rock pinnacles and broken ledges weathered out of the upper cliffs. While he was sprawled out there, trying to get back some of the wind he had lost during the climb, he happened to look up and find himself almost muzzle to muzzle with a bighorn ram that seemed half as big as a buffalo. It was a monster, jet black and wearing horns as big as tepee rings. He recognized it right off as the sacred ram spoken of by the old record keepers.

Here was a full-size decision for a husky man twenty-four hours behind mealtime. Too, there were sixteen equally empty stomachs down below, all in the mood to heap honors on a good hunter. Spotted Bull's mind jumped in both directions at once. Medicine beings were not supposed to be killed. On the other hand, perhaps the Great Spirit had sent this big meat animal as food for his hungry children. What if it was meant to be so used? Why else would it be perched out there on the lip of the ledge, with no way off except over the Indian's body? A rock heaved against the beast's knees would easily dislodge the slim foothold and send it crashing to the rocky bar below. Why should he refuse what was so plainly a gift?

Still, he hesitated. Everyone knew the power of medicine beings. Terrible things could happen to one who offended them. Yet his people were facing starvation, without food or weapons or even any certain way out of this death trap. His fingers wrapped themselves instinctively around a jagged chunk of rock. He half-raised his arm. Surely this was the right thing to do. His glance lifted, to see the ram staring him straight in the eyes. Spotted Bull's arm dropped back to his side. Something in the ram's eyes spoke of the teachings he had received from the Old Ones, of the straight trail one must follow if he would be a man. Only cowardly weaklings tried to dodge the Great Truths.

With nobody knows how much mouth-watering, he got to his feet and stood aside while three hundred pounds of rich roasts brushed past him to disappear around a rock shoulder.

Maybe he hated himself a minute later, when his stomach began asking questions. But if he had any such thoughts, he soon shucked them. It was some ten minutes later, while he was sizing up the cliffs for some way to get to the rim, that he saw the ram suddenly walk out on a ledge running across the face of the wall above. The sheep stopped to look down at him, then went on around the corner, still climbing, and disappeared. Spotted Bull could see no way up to the ledge where the ram had been, nor anything better farther on; but mere sight of the animal had set him straddle of an idea that could have been furnished only by the Great Spirit himself.

He scratched his head. The ram had gone back around that red-splotched rock shoulder. Minutes later, he had popped out on that ledge. His tracks would surely show how he did it. And the fact that he was still climbing, looked like he was headed for the top over a route he was acquainted with. Spotted Bull began yelling at the others down below.

It was a rough trip. The empty stomachs didn't help any. It took them half the forenoon to work their way back through the tangle of broken rock and locate the rough little cranny which led up over a smooth upthrust to the ledge where the bighorn had shown himself. From there on, it was mostly worse. They had to do a lot of guess-work. The sheep had left little sign on the smooth rock. Time and again, they found themselves balked by making the wrong turn. And at the best, they had to fight their way over broken ledges or up slanting crevices, where only nubbins of toe and finger holds made climbing possible. Much of it was a case of boost up the leaders and haul up the drags. Still, it was a way out—the only way, apparently.

And there was no question about who was the main squeeze in the deal. Every time they came to what looked like a dead end, somebody would catch a glimpse of Old Blackie off in one direction or other, still climbing. They couldn't have found all that wandering string of stairsteps in a month of Sundays, if the ram hadn't showed up like a guidepost about every so often. The last time they saw him was just before they topped out on the rim.

"So you see, Curly," Tom finished up, "why I no let you shoot. To respec' the Great Ones is mos' wise. It is spoken."

He just about had himself a believer, there for a while. The way he told it was like the river or the canyon walls or some kind of an ancient voice out of an unknown time had done the talking. It had me half-expecting to see something dressed up in a wolf hide and packing a stone ax pop out of the shadows any minute. That spooky, far-away look in his eyes, when the jumpy firelight danced across them, the hoarse-voiced river muttering some kind of a heathen chant under the ice at our feet, the age-old walls crouched around us, like fabled giants about to pounce, all added up to pretty strong medicine for a green country boy.

I slept most of it off pretty well, though, after funny shapes quit dancing in the shadows and I went to sleep. Looking a new sun in the eye, I was glad there was no one around to remind me how spooked up I'd been the night before. Laughing at myself was bad enough. By the time I'd finished going over the trapline, I was all white man again, properly fitted out with a nice practical mind.

I guess it was thinking about the big ram and the superior intelligence of civilized people that kept me from paying any attention to the wind that had been blowing through the canyon all morning. Oh, I noticed it, like anybody would in a country where the wind blows more often than not. However, I never gave any real thought to what it might amount to, in my particular case. If it had been Tom's day to run traps, he would have probably caught the drift of things right off, and saved us a lot of trouble. But back there in that sheltered cove, busy all day at fixing up our pelts, he missed the threat completely.

The whole deal stacked up to squeeze us out the little end of the horn. It was a hard way to learn something. It cost us plenty, too.

That part, however, was still in the unborn stage when I headed back to camp shortly after noon. The wind had gained a little heft the past hour, and it had warmed up some. I laid the extra warmth to the sun's making things feel like a spring day. And there was nothing surprising about that. Rocky Mountain weather often hands out a week or so of spring-like softness at odd times during the winter. I just unbuttoned my coat and enjoyed it.

I was drifting along up the canyon, soaking up sunshine and speculating on how much we stood to make out of the trip, when something pulled my eyes up to an offset ledge across the river. I dropped the sled rope and squatted right there.

It was the same old ram perched up there, just like he'd been the evening before. He looked as big as a corn-fed steer, a jet black image outlined against the red and gray cliff. He was watching me, too, staring down and out from between his wheel-size horns. What a trophy! And what a chance!

You can believe it or not, but Tom's grandpappy yarn never entered my mind at the moment. As a matter of fact, I had assayed the whole deal as superstitious bunk and tossed it overboard long before noon. I'd not given it another thought. Now, as I brought up my rifle, the only live thought I had in my head was how I would look pulling in to the ranch with that pair of horns on top of our load.

Yet I never did squeeze the trigger to send that 170-grain bullet on its way. Don't ask me why. It's beyond me. I certainly intended to get myself a sheep. And I had him dead center in my sights. But something—I'll never know what—froze my trigger finger midway of the pull. Laugh if you want to. It's all right with me. But I'll swear that's as far as it would budge.

Yes, you may be right in claiming it was just a hangover from the night before, some twist in my brain flopping my wits upside down. I won't argue. A man's mind plays funny tricks sometimes. Especially, when a bunch of million-year-old cliffs nod at each other over his head in the early dusk, whispering back and forth in a way that no puny, little, two-legged insect could ever understand.

All that I really know for sure is that I suddenly lowered the rifle and let the hammer down—slow and easy. The ram hadn't moved a muscle all that time. Maybe he knew the answers better than I did. It's all over my head. Anyhow, he was still standing there, staring down the back of my neck, as I hightailed on around the next bend.

Something that felt like a spring-thawed snowbank trickled down my backbone as I single-footed around a couple more bends in the canyon. I didn't slow down much, even then. It wasn't that I was really scared; I knew that sheep wasn't about to jump me. But the whole creepy, other-world atmosphere, crowding in on me from all sides, had me feeling like a stray gutter-pup that had wandered into a high-class dog show and wasn't sure what was going to happen next.

Imagination? Well, you can call it that. All I know is that I was straddle of something I couldn't put a name to. It was like riding with a busted cinch.

My back hair, however, had pretty well settled back down by the time I got to camp. In fact, I was beginning to feel a little ashamed of how I had knuckled under to such a sappy feeling. That's mainly why I backed off from telling Tom anything about it. I figured I'd let it ride till morning. Maybe by that time I'd have it pawed over so I could make a halfway sensible talk for myself. As it turned out, morning gave me something else to think about.

Though it never disturbed us back in our hook-shaped cove, the wind must have been busy all night. The first we knew about what was really going on was when Tom went down to the river to open our hole in the ice and get a kettle of water. I was down on all fours, trying to wheeze some life into the breakfast fire, when he came loping up over the bank, like a scared antelope. He didn't have the kettle, either.

"Chinook! Chinook!" He was howling at every jump. "Wind blow bad. Ice sof' a'ready. Get out quick!"

He started grabbing fur stretchers with both hands. His voice was going like a full chorus about the wind and soft ice.

I stood there, batting my eyes like a conked owl, for a minute or so while his words soaked in. "Chinook! Chinook!" I had to repeat the words a couple of times in order to knock the chock out from under my wits and start the wheels turning again.

CHAPTER 9

A Chinook is a peculiar sort of a hard wind that occasionally sweeps down over the northwest and northern Rockies in late winter or early spring. While by no means hot, and sometimes not even warm, it can melt snow and ice like a cook's skillet does butter. A few hours of it is enough to turn snowbanks into gully-washers and make swimming water out of an ice field.

This one had already been blowing once around the clock. And judging by the amount of wind down in the sheltered canyon, the lid must have been plumb off out in the open. My civilized mind was finally shaking off its hobbles. It was easy to picture the dozens of creeks and little washes dumping the sudden overflows into the river. That couldn't last long without the ice breaking up. And a forced breakup always meant an ice-jam in the rock-walled Narrows at the head of the canyon.

I'd seen one such ice-jam. It piled up to plug the bottleneck of The Narrows tight as a drum. This backed the whole river up, making a great lake of swirling water and grinding ice cakes. From then on, it was anybody's guess how long the jam would hold—a few hours, maybe, or possibly a day or so. But it had to go! Sooner or later, like the time I saw it, the sheer weight of all that water couldn't help forcing the ice-plug out of The Narrows. Then everything let loose at once. The whole dammed-up body of water went through the canyon, like a wad of shot through a shotgun. The idea of what would happen to anything caught in the depths of that gorge, at such a time, was what had my heart trying to climb my windpipe. I didn't waste any time helping Tom throw things onto the sled.

Twenty minutes later, we were headed back upriver. The mouth of Rope Creek was the nearest way out. And the only one, so far as we knew, short of the Medicine Trail, which we guessed to be considerably farther downstream. We figured we could make it to the creek by sundown, if the ice held. We had plenty of encouragement to hurry.

Sometime before noon, we began meeting little stretches of water on top of the ice. It was mostly just a skim, but every now and then we'd hit a place where the ice had sagged toward the middle, giving the overflow a chance to tinkle along in a merry little stream. This was particularly noticeable in the bends, where a warming sun reflected against a west or north wall. Those polished red rocks could bounce a lot of heat down onto the ice; I could almost feel them leer mockingly at us, as each hour added to the sun's weight.

The farther we went, the more pindling our future looked. We had been making a lot of fast tracks, but I was beginning to have a hunch they weren't adding up to the right figure. That old sun was really pulling the frost out of things; and there was a heap of river up in the open country for it to work on without any trouble.

We talked a little, from time to time, when the going wasn't too tough. Tom was mighty decent about my dumbness the day before; he claimed he'd probably not have noticed the makings of a Chinook, either, not expecting such a thing. If he had any other ideas in the back of his head, they were wiped out when I told him about meeting Old Blackie. The bouquets he handed me on that score snowed in all the other shortcomings I ever had. It kind of looked like he was right, too. If there was anything I didn't need on that sled, it was a hundred pounds of mountain sheep head.

For the ice was sagging lower in the middle all the time. And the sag was packing an increased amount of water. In places, it was actually surging up out of the river through a hole in the ice, then running for quite a stretch before going down through another thawed opening. We stayed over on the out edge as much as possible. Still, even there, the ice was getting more and more honeycombed by the minute. Water was beginning to show up clear over against the wall, in a lot of places. It was easy to see who held all the trumps.

"We'll make it all right," I said an hour or so later, trying mainly to stir some sand into my own craw. "There's a lot of good ice underneath."

"Good now," Tom answered shortly. "Pretty soon break someplace. Ever'thing go whoosh!" He was a great one to face facts.

Not long after noon, we both faced them. We were following a string of short, snaky bends. I was hunched down, watching my feet make the best time possible, when Tom suddenly grabbed my arm and spun me around. He was pointing out across the ice.

"Look!" he grunted. "Not good!"

I looked. He hadn't said the half of it. "Whole thing'll give way any time," I told him. I stretched my wobbly legs out another notch.

The thin stream running down the center of the ice had nearly doubled in size since the last time I'd noticed it in particular. And it was still growing. You could see it inch higher every minute, sagging the ice down more all the time. It didn't need very bright eyes to savvy how much it raised and spread while we were covering the next two hundred yards. Thirty minutes later, it was lapping at our shoe soles and showing quite a current.

"How much farther d'you figure to Rope Crick?" I wheezed, pausing to glance back over one shoulder.

"No can tell. Mebbyso t'ree hour—"

My yell broke him off short, as we both spun around. A fifty-yard stretch of ice directly behind us had let go with a soggy crunching sound. It was already heaving drunkenly in the open, bucking current. A moment later, the released river was hungrily chasing the twin furrows our sled runners had left in the rotten ice.

I never knew my legs had that much action. It was quite a discovery. But we soon stopped to get our wind. Even a scared man is good for only about so much.

Dragging that loaded sled through the mushy ice was a breath-cutter. Anyhow, the fall of the canyon kept the river from backing up very far over the ice. We counted our luck, then started wondering where it would let go next. There was no reason to think it might not drop out from under our feet any minute, or disappear in a swirl of water around the next bend ahead. The question would have made a right interesting betting proposition, if we hadn't been the chips in the game.

Everything continued to hang together, however. Our hopes built up a few notches as we covered maybe half a mile. I was slogging along as fast as my run-down legs would drive, head down and shoulders hunched against the sled rope, when Tom's yelp brought me up standing.

"Look!" His finger was leveled at the flooded center ice. "See, water go down. Somet'ing hol' back. Mebbyso ice dam up."

One glance was enough. The water had gone down a lot. It pulled back even farther as we watched. Both of us knew what was happening: only a big ice-jam in The Narrows could shut off that stream.

I suddenly felt like a salted snail. My backbone all but ran out of my ears. Dollar-bright memories of a break-up at The Narrows, the spring before, went through my head like a flight of bull bats. That jam had pulled my scalp up to a peak, just to watch it. When the forty-foot pile of ice let go with a bang, spilling forward like a four-story building pitched over a cliff, it had sent the whole mass of backed-up water plunging down the canyon in a solid wall, bucking and bellowing like a herd of stampeding buffaloes. Lurching ice blocks and boiling foam rode the ridged back of its twenty-foot crest. Uprooted trees rolled end for end, like so many matchsticks, while even wagon-sized boulders staggered against each other like a bunch of drunks out to take the town apart. It had been a pretty savage performance. Now, it looked like I was about to see it again—and not from the bank.

I knew it was only a matter of time. The jam might hold for a day or more—or maybe an hour. In the meantime, here was a pair of bright young men who had suddenly discovered that being rich was something they didn't have much use for right then. We might have been jerked by the same string, the way we cut loose from our fur fortune and broke into a high lope.

It felt pretty good to be running free, now that we'd cleared our minds of golden rainbows. I hadn't realized how much that load of furs, traps, guns, grub, and bedrolls had been holding us back. With all that out of the way, we could now think of something important. That stretch of open water behind us and the high, unbroken walls on both sides had us on a one-way track till we reached Rope Creek. It was our footwork against how long the ice-jam might hold. I wasn't betting either way at the moment.

I still sometimes wake up in the night, hearing that slap, slap of our feet on the soggy ice. There was no other sound. Everything seemed to have shut down, close and threatening, like the lull before a storm. The water had entirely quit running over the ice. The ice itself was gradually settling lower in the center, settling without a whisper. I had the queer feeling the canyon was alive, something deadly, crouched and breathless, just waiting to spring. Goose pimples played leapfrog up and down my spine as I stretched my ears for any break in the unnatural stillness.

That was maybe why I was first to catch the heavy rumbling noise. It sounded like a freight train back behind the hill. My wheezing croak brought Tom up short. His eyes met mine as he canted an ear into the breeze. His face suddenly looked like he had shed a lot of blood.

For a moment we just stood there, like a pair of owls on the same fence post. Then, with all the ambition of a hungry sod-buster chasing a fat rabbit, I legged it toward where the river had piled up sort of a little rock bar against the wall in the bend ahead. It was only four or five feet above the ice, but it was something.

Tom was at my heels as I stumbled up over the water-scoured rocks. The roar was getting louder by the minute. It bounced against the canyon walls like the roll of summer thunder. I must have looked like a trapped coyote, scratching at the wall for some way to get myself above what was coming. The roar had increased. It filled the whole gorge, rising and falling like the voice of doom.

High or low, I couldn't locate even a fingernail hold on the smooth rock face. I thought I'd go loco. Then I heard Tom yell at me from a dozen feet to the right. He had found a crack in the wall, just sort of a narrow crevice with edges notched out by time and weather. It angled up the face of the cliff toward somewhere. I didn't examine it too close. He had his toes in it and was inching himself upward when I got there.

Now, I was a plumb washout at risky climbing; always have been and still am. Getting up in the air any higher than a horse's back always wilts me down to the roots. Yet I went up that crack like a snake up a sapling. How? Your guess is as good as mine. All I know is that I suddenly found myself sprawled out beside Tom on a narrow little ledge under a jog in the upper wall. I was wet as a dishrag, and just as limp, so I reckon I must have done my own climbing.

We weren't any too soon, at that. I'd scarcely got squared around when the flood hit. That's another picture that still sneaks up on me at night. That solid wall of water looked as high as Ben's new barn. Its face was a tumbling jumble of driftwood, ice cakes and dirty white foam. It jumped and boiled like a wind-chased prairie fire, as it hammered against the stubborn canyon walls and clawed its way two-thirds up the crack we had climbed. I shrunk back against the cliff, listening to the monster beller about our dodging its teeth.

It was only a few minutes, then the crunching jaws were gone, bawling maddened hate up at the echoing walls on down the canyon. Still, the racing torrent of churning water and tossing ice that followed, throwing spray halfway up to where we crouched, was about as bad. That kind of viciousness would curl anybody's hair.

Tom's flat statement of facts, a moment later, wasn't any particular help. The way he saw it, we'd simply swapped a quick check-out for a long and disagreeable one. All our grub and equipment was gone; the river would close the canyon to foot travel till another winter; the cliff rose in a solid, smooth wall above us. It looked like we'd won ourselves a front seat at the end of the trail.

I was ready to sell out cheap. Looking around at the fix we were in, the price dropped to bedrock. This little ledge we were on was maybe three feet wide in the broadest part, tapering off at both ends to pinch out to nothing against the cliff face. Time and weather had carved the higher walls into rough pinnacles, broken ledges and jagged outthrusts, but down where we were there was only this little ledge, tucked back under the overhanging bulge of rock which rose, smooth as a lawyer's tongue, some fifty feet above our heads. Our chances looked as hopeless as an old maid's dream. My ears picked up the chant of a rising wind droning around our perch. It seemed to carry sort of a funeral-hymn tune.

My gaze switched back to the yellow-green flood below. Maybe it would go down enough by night to expose the rock bar. Starving to death on a pile of boulders would beat being hung up there on the wall for buzzard bait. At least, the rocks would be out of the wind, while furnishing enough room for a man to move around without falling overboard. Tom agreed on both points, but I could see he didn't think I was adding any shine to the picture.

I squirmed around inside my clothes; there wasn't room to do any squirming outside of them. I reckon Tom was just as miserable. The sweat we had worked up in climbing was beginning to turn into frost. The wind seemed to have us targeted dead center. And the idea of climbing back down that skimpy crack in the wall made a few shivers of its own.

CHAPTER 10

My mind was still exploring the grave-digging business when Tom's excited, "Look, Curly!" pried my face up out of the crook of my arm. "He is here. For us!" One hand was clawing into my shoulder.

I screwed my neck around in the direction he was staring. His black ice eyes had pulled his whole face forward, making it look more than ever like an ax blade. I probably looked just as funny, when I located what he was gazing at. I rubbed my eyes and looked a second time. No, there was no mistake. It was Old Blackie, sure as I was a foot high!

The big ram was standing on the rim of the wall above us, maybe a dozen yards to the right. All we could see was the head and fore-parts; the rest of him was still behind an outjutting rock. He had stopped halfway around the rock and just stood there, giving us stare for stare. Then, when he saw he had caught our attention, he walked slowly across the rim of the wall above us to disappear behind a reddish pinnacle off to the left. The whole thing was like he had spoken to us with his eyes, inviting us to follow. It was enough to spook a dummy. How or when he had got this far up the canyon still has me asking questions of myself. I knew he had been across the river and miles downstream twenty-four hours before. And I know that rim had been as empty as a congressman's promise a few seconds earlier. I have only Tom Little Bear's beliefs to fall back on when I think about him appearing at that particular moment. Otherwise, I am as empty of ideas as a stone churn.

"The spirit being!" Tom's tight voice rubbed on my ear like a whisper in church, or out in the dark after the shooting stops. "He come show the way, like for my grandfather's people. Is good you no shoot, eh, Curly?"

I guess it was. Something had hold of my windpipe so I couldn't talk. I did manage to nod, though, as I wiggled up onto my knees against the wall.

Tom had popped to his feet like a bee-stung pup. "Ram say this way." He was already edging along the ledge toward where it seemed to pinch out against the wall at its north end. "Come! It is spoken."

I came. It didn't make sense, none of it. But I was past looking for sensible things. With hope overbalancing any real faith I had in such crazy goings-on, I glued my face to the overhanging bulge and inched my feet along the way he was headed.

Tom's medicine, however, sure came out of the right bottle. Where the end of our skinny ledge faded out at what we'd thought was the end of the road, we found a sharp shoulder that hid a little backset in the rock. A couple of rough knobs, big enough for toe-holds, and a few finger-deep cracks in the rock above, carried us around the corner.

I don't know how a fly feels about crossing a window pane. Maybe he lacks feeling altogether. But I know I'm not like that. I'll swear I lost ten pounds, five years, and enough heart action to power a steamboat before I got across that six feet of space hanging between the river and the great blue yonder. I found two buttons gone from my jacket front and half the skin rubbed off my belly, when I got to where I could look things over. My backbone didn't quit trying to crawl out through my hat for the next twenty minutes.

And that wasn't all. I soon discovered we were still behind the eight-ball. When my teeth quit sounding like beans in a medicine man's rattle and most of the sweat had dripped off my chin, I found we were directly under the rim where the ram had been standing. It tied into the jutting rock that hid his hind quarters when we first saw him. The rim broke off short just back of the rock. How the ram got there was another part of the puzzle I never could figure out, when I got around to study on it. Right then, I had other things to think about. Being more or less suspended in midair, like a pair of leftover Thanksgiving partridges, I wasn't thinking about too many other things at the moment.

Our first heat had landed us up against a smooth rock face that stretched up like the side of a barn for eight or nine feet. Tom got both feet jammed into a crevice, one on top of the other, and one arm hooked around a knob of rock, pulling himself slowly upright. I was spread-eagled against the wall, hanging onto his belt. He paused, studying the rim above his head. I guess he saw what he was looking for. Anyhow, he reached around and pried my fingers loose from his belt, moving them over to a grip on the rough edge of the crevice. Then he got his legs anchored the best he could and hunched himself upward a couple feet. He was just able to hook his fingers into a break below the rim.

"I hold. You climb," he told me, jerking his head upward. "Go quick!"

My toes had been trying to bore deeper into a frost crack a foot back from the edge of nothing. I hated to swap that much security for the kind of a shaky deal that Tom proposed. But when my eyes pulled a whizzer on me by straying down over that God-awful emptiness below, getting upstairs was all I wanted to do. A moment later, I was shinnying up over Tom's wiry frame.

I knew I had it made as soon as I got one knee on his shoulder. The rim seemed to have been made by the upper cliff breaking away at the spot. That was probably where that rock pile down in the bottom came from, though I wasn't wasting any time on cause and effect at the time. All I was interested in was the scattering of broken rock ends that had been left sticking up when that chunk of cliff broke away. One good heave shoved my body over the edge far enough that I could jam both armpits down over a pair of rough knobs and lock my hands together. Tom came up over my dangling legs, like a squirrel up a tree. We were both winded and wobbly as a new calf when we finally stretched out on the rim to tally up our luck.

Tom had another name for it, though. "All time come from medicine ram," he said shortly. "Spirit work; not luck."

"It looks like you win the deal," I admitted, too shaky to start an argument, even if I'd wanted to. "Something besides us seems to be runnin' the show. And it is kinda funny about Old Blackie shapin' up as the ramrod. I hope he stays with it."

"He not far. Show plenty good way to go."

Tom never batted an eyelash. You'd have thought the sheep told him all the answers while I was busy with the shakes. He got to his feet with all the confidence of a brand-new town marshal and headed off in the direction the ram had gone.

It began to look like he was right, too. The ram's tracks led us around behind that red pinnacle, where the broken rim made a sharp bend and went out of sight. We followed it to where it butted up against another blank wall. It looked like the end of the trail again. I was beginning to have some fresh thoughts about buzzard bait.

Then Tom's belief in the future led his eyes to where a little rock had been kicked lose, its dirt-stained side winking up at us in the sunlight. He pounced on it like a cat after a mouse. I had no more than joined him before I spotted an angling ledge that ran up to a higher shelf. It was another stiff climb, that gave my belly skin a fresh rasping and stirred up a whole new case of the shakes in my in'nards, but it took us up over the cliff to where we could drop down for a little breather among some tumbled boulders.

And that's the way it went the rest of the afternoon. Most of it was bad; the rest was worse. The bulk of it is still pretty foggy in my memory. I was too scared a good share of the time to watch or think of anything but Tom's backside. I know we hung on by fingertips and eyelashes as we inched across dizzy heights that overhung an unreasonable amount of thin air. We clawed our way up over wind-polished rock faces that seemed plumb anxious to swap one careless slip for a through ticket to Saint Peter's home range. We jumped from scaly perches to more scaly footing, when faith in Old Blackie's trail blazing was all that kept us going.

I sure envied that old sheep for the way his legs and feet handled things over that kind of going. To me, it was wheeze, grunt, and another spell of heart failure, where he had seemed to go without a quiver. Sometimes I thought he was just having fun with us, yet it didn't take much of an eye to see that, crazy as it was, it stood as the only way a human could have got up that cliff.

And he never short changed us by quitting on the job. Every time we got in a bind, he would show up, somewhere above us, to set us straight again. Or, if he wasn't in sight, we'd find his tracks somewhere about, always leading off in the right direction. Time after time, we came up against dead ends, where there seemed no possible out for us. Then one of us would spot a footprint or catch sight of the big sheep off to one side or the other, usually standing still and patiently staring at us, as though waiting for the poor dummies to get straightened out. The ram acted like our future was all up to him, and he knew it. And there was no doubt about his being headed for the top; every move was up. I'm still not sure what I'd have done alone; but following Tom's lead, my bone-tired mind soon let go of everything but him and the big ram.

I'd got so used to seeing the bighorn every little while that I felt like an orphan when he suddenly disappeared for good. That is, I guess he left suddenly. I'm not sure. He had been watching us from the top of a high shoulder, up ahead, when I started scratching for toe-holds around a bulging rock face. When I got across to where I could look around without scaring myself half to death, he was gone. Everything was open and clear above, but there was no sheep in sight. Neither of us ever saw him again; nor did we find any more tracks. The whole deal was like one of these dreams that are stagged off at both ends and don't make much sense. It left sort of a funny feeling, though, like a lot of something had happened without anything being there.

But I guess the sheep knew he'd worked himself out of a job. Anyhow, we didn't really need him any more. Our last hard scramble had brought us out onto a steep sliderock slope running up to the rim. We topped out just as dusk was closing in. Another night would see us back at the ranch—and there wouldn't be any water chasing us. We felt pretty good.

I stopped there on the rim for a last look back down the way we had come. Even if the sight did make my stomach try a last jump for my wishbone, I couldn't help hoping for a goodbye glimpse of Blackie down there somewhere. I had a hankering to salute the old boy. But I guess he had melted back into his private nowhere. There was nothing to be seen of him.

"Medicine being!" Tom reminded me shortly. "See only when big trouble come. All gone now."

He probably knew what he was talking about. He savvied such things a whole lot better than I did. Anyhow, I let it go at that. My stomach was talking to my feet about getting over the mountain and down to the ranch. It had been a long time since yesterday's supper.

I've wished ever since, though, that I'd paid more attention to both Tom's and the ram's actions that afternoon. There might have been something there that would have cleared up a lot of guesswork, one way or the other, if I had let my civilized mind slip its hobbles. The way it was, I'd passed the sheep off as simply an overgrown, flesh-and-blood animal; such things as spirit beings running around as big as life in this common, everyday world of ours, had been too crazy an idea for me to swallow. Yet, looking back, there is no getting around that funny way he appeared and disappeared, like somebody had pulled him out of a hat or waved him away with a handkerchief. And he had most certainly led us over the only possible trail up out of the gorge, just like he did with Spotted Bull's outfit in the long-ago time. None of it adds up to any logic.

63

Then there was one more joker that puts the kibosh on all the logical thinking I've been able to drum up. I know this was real; I saw it with both eyes. It was that bunch of bone beads lodged in a crack on one of those shaky ledges halfway up the canyon wall. There was no doubt about their being handmade beads. I remember noticing the odd-shape holes in some of them, where they stuck up out of the dirt. The carving on them, too, showed up plain and clear, picturing queer-looking human heads and animals such as nobody ever saw. And they'd not got there by themselves. That was a sure thing. My wits, however, were too frazzled right then to latch onto what they might mean. I just passed them off as something somebody had lost, the wind later pushing them over into that crack running antigodling across the ledge. But looking back, I know they could only have been Indian-made beads, and they had been there a long, long time. When you shuffle them in with Tom's great-grandfather story, along with their strange, ancient carvings, and the fact that Indians seldom made bone beads after the white traders showed up— Well, you can figure it out to suit yourself. I'm just telling how it happened.

Anyhow, I've been asking myself the same questions for more years than I like to remember. Coincidence, destiny, luck, or God? Maybe it's all the same. I wouldn't know. But whenever I think of that old black ram, I feel a big surge of respect for the other fellow's beliefs, whatever they might be.

CHAPTER 11

If anybody had ever told me I would wind up cross-legged in a tepee, helping myself to the family stew as a member in good standing, I'd have started going through his saddlebags to see how far down he was on his second quart. Yet, here I was, an adopted son of old Yellow Bear and blood-brother to Tom Little Bear, a knife cut in my arm, paint still itching my face, and a name as long as a piece of rope. All the locoed things don't happen to somebody else.

The whole business sort of sprouted up from the run-in Tom and I had with that old bighorn ram down in Splitrock Canyon, a couple months before. Tom claimed the medicine animal had voted me into the lodge right after I backed down from taking a shot at him. This, he said, was why the critter had spirited itself up the canyon to where he knew I was going to need something more than good wishes in order to get back where I could draw steady wages. And that was the way he told it to everybody who would hold still long enough to listen. He tried to make out that his part was just sort of an extra something that got dragged in off the sidelines, through being along with me. He wouldn't have it any other way.

Then he'd usually throw in a whole wad of stuff about how I had practically walked up the face of that cliff, like a lizard up a stone chimney, taking him along. My tie-in with the ram, and how my kinship with spirit beings had saved both our lives, was the clincher. It built up into quite a yarn, the way he wrapped it up. By the time it got over on the Reservation, and the other medicine dreamers got hold of it, I was shoved right up in line with old Spotted Bull himself. And the more talk I made about shut eyes and rattling teeth being a long stretch from brotherhood with a spirit sheep, the sillier it made me look. I finally gave up. It was easier to just go stick my head in a hole till somebody changed the subject.

Our outfit augered Old Blackie clear across the board, after we showed up somewhat worse for wear and told what happened. I guess, though, none of them put much stock in the idea of a spirit sheep hanging around the canyon for a hundred years, on our account.

They all used our story as a big joke, but Baldy Peters was the only one to really bow his neck and hoorah the whole thing as "Crazier'n a hoot owl! If you'n him'd been ridin' double in this here speerit business," he went on, "how come he didn't hook hisself onta that sled an' fetch out yore two hunnert bucks worth o' fur at the same time? Or how come he made yo' do all that climbin', when he might just as well o' packed yo' out on his back?"

Bobby Burns was the only one that took it different. Bobby always gave everybody benefit of the doubt. And he hated arguments. Now he jumped in with one of his pet reminders that "The guid Laird still pairfoorms his woonder-r-rs in str-range ways tae behold. In this case, who is tae say they micht nae loor-rk inside the hide of a sheepie as wull as under-r-r the veestments of a beeshop?"

The backwash of it all kind of left me dangling in the wind. I couldn't discount the ram as part of the unknown something that had salvaged us from the flood and pulled us up the canyon walls. Yet it was hard for me to swallow something that every kind of logic ruled out of the game. If that handful of carved-bone beads hadn't pointed so directly toward the trail taken by those trapped old-timers Tom told me about, I'd probably have shucked the whole thing off, in time, the way most people do when they tangle with questions that can't be answered.

As it was, I found myself bouncing back and forth, like a dried hog bladder, between white man logic and Indian beliefs.

The fact that I had been spending the bulk of my time with Tom kind of added a little weight to the Indian side. He never gave in an inch. The whole deal was as clear to him as a goose-egg-size diamond would be to a promised bride. Spirits were part of his world; what more mattered than that they should drop a loop on his partner when the chips were down? I guess maybe the teaching he grew up with, worked on him something like Sunday school does on white kids. Anyhow, by the time the snow went off, he had it all shuffled in with the old legend and ready to hang up in the medicine man's lodge as a recorded chapter in tribal history.

He had talked with me a time or two about my going with him

66

for a little visit with his folks. He thought it was something we really should do. The lives of his people were all tied in with assorted spirit workings. He knew our black ram affair, hooked up as it was with the century-old experience of Spotted Bull, would call out the big drums and the old men who painted the records of important events on tanned hides. He wanted us in on it together. He figured there would be some honors dished out, which he claimed wouldn't pan out right unless I was there to share things with him. Besides, he was pretty sure I would enjoy such a wingding, just for what fun there was in it. He seemed a whole lot anxious for me to meet his family, too.

It was crowding up close to April when I finally decided to brace Ben for a week or so off, before we got wrapped up in spring work. The more I thought of it, the better I liked the idea of a trip over on the Reservation, especially with Tom Little Bear. Sided by him, I would have a chance to sit in on some real tepee life, instead of standing around like a goggle-eyed foreigner. In those days, the Indians didn't put out much warmth toward uninvited white strangers. You couldn't blame them for it, not after the way they'd been whipsawed. Still, being stared at like a poor relation who would look better buried, when you went among them, wasn't a thing to build any brags on. However, with Tom along, it would be another matter. His friendship would unlock a lot of doors that wouldn't even show a crack otherwise. And his stories had hazed my interest around till I was plumb fired up to see what was behind it all. I found Ben agreeable to my taking off for a while, so we aimed to go the following Monday.

It didn't work out that easy, though. It seemed like something was always popping up to send us the long way around. It was like old Bobby had the way of saying every now and then, "The best laid plons o' mice an' men gang aft aglee!" We sure found things had "ganged aglee" right enough before we got through with this blowup.

It all started when Sid Andrews dropped in the next afternoon. Ben and I were the only ones at the ranch that day. Baldy and Jed had gone up on the mountain after a load of wood, right after dinner, while the others had taken the day to put a new roof on the Pipe Spring line camp. Ben had kept me home to help him repair and oil some harness for the chuckwagon team. He liked to have all the loose ends caught up before spring roundup started.

My hammer plumb missed the rivet in a breeching strap, when Sid suddenly opened up about half a dozen geldings disappearing out

67

of his saddle horse remuda. I stuck the skinned thumb into my mouth and started flapping my ears.

Ben wiped some grease off his hands and looked up from under the corner of his hat.

"How long they been missing?" he asked.

"Hard to tell—a week or a month." Sid pulled thoughtfully at the lock of straw-colored hair that always hung down over his left eye. "They were in a bunch we've had up Cache Creek since the snow went off. They were on good feed, so nobody paid any special attention. Chuck Wheeler happened to be up that way yesterday, and found we were six head short. He spent the rest of the day combing both ways from the creek, but couldn't locate any sign of 'em. It plumb looks like a liftin' job, as it's nowise common for a few head to quit the bunch they've been runnin' with all winter."

You could tell from the way he bit his words off that Sid was pretty much on the prod. Good-natured as he usually was, it didn't take much pushing around to make his Scotch-Norsky disposition paint itself up to match his bristly yellow hair.

Ben shoved his hat over to one side and scratched his head. "Seems likely," he said, his nose kind of pinching down, like it always did when he got upset about something. "Horse thieves are kinda like mushrooms, seem to spring up overnight about every so often. I'm glad you tipped me off on this. Gives us a chance to maybe help stop something before it makes too much headway. We'll let you know if anything suspicious shows up over on this end. Meanwhile, just holler if we can help any over your way."

"Thanks, Ben. Will do!" Sid pinched out his cigarette and slid his bean-pole frame back into the saddle. "Best have your outfit go heeled," he said over his shoulder. "Should you happen onto anybody with the wrong horses, it'd be sense to have something to back your play."

Ben's nod showed he felt the same way. I let my eyes run over the old 44-40 Winchester shoved under Sid's leg and the six-gun riding low on his hip. I had a quick hunch that neither one of them would be slow about knocking the spots off of any misguided characters caught with stolen horses.

Still, Ben didn't say anything. He just reached over and picked up my knife and started reaming out his pipe. He was quite a hand to hold off on war talk till the whole tally was in. Now he just stood there, working on his pipe, while Sid rode off. He knocked the crud out of the old briar on the heel of his hand and tossed my knife back onto the bench. He was staring off up the creek with one eye pinched half-shut. A minute later, he squatted down on his heels to start drawing little lines in the dirt at his feet. I could see he was mapping out the country and getting everything straight in his mind before going any further.

The thing was still itching his thoughts, a few days later, when Charley Norris met Ed Ross, a Keyhole A hand, over on Coyote Bench. Ed was looking for a half-Thoroughbred mare and a roan gelding that had disappeared mysteriously out of their horse pasture. He said the Seven Up had lost three good cowhorses about the same time, and in the same way. Also, the T L thought they were short a few head, the last he heard. The whole thing looked like Sid Andrews was right about branding it a planned raid on the valley's stock. Charley and Ben had quite a powwow over it that night, judging by the length of time they stayed penned up in the house together. I guess, however, they decided to keep it all under their hats till they saw more daylight.

At any rate, I never heard anything about it till Ben called me over to the house the next evening. The minute I went in, he hauled me on into his office and kicked the door shut. I was still perched on one foot, with my teeth hanging out, when he told me to drag a chair up close to his desk and sit down. His face was kind of pulled in at the corners, leaving his mouth only about half size, the way he did when he wanted his voice to fade out against whoever he was talking to. He had a sheet of paper in front of him and was lacing a pencil through his fingers. I sat up straighter as he leaned across the corner of the desk and started in on the story Charley had got from Ross.

"It sounds like more of what Sid told us the other day," I said, when he'd finished. "Somebody must be workin' the whole country."

"Looks that way. And it means they'll hit us sooner or later."

"You got any idea where the stuff might be goin'?"

Ben finished loading his pipe. I could see worry riding heavy in his puckered gray eyes. He dragged a match slowly down the burnt trough in his desk-top, half hiding the flame in his cupped hand till he got the fodder burning.

"It could be somebody working out from the badlands, over south," he said at last, squinting through a fan of smoke. "The idea being to play for small bunches that wouldn't leave much sign or stir up a real war party, before they got a good haul together and were ready to move out. That's been worked once before. Somebody might figure it worth another try. On the other hand, it might just be some local scissor-bill snagging a few head at a time for a quick run to some night owl corral over in Montana."

"Which way does Ross lean?"

"Neither!" Ben's scowl slid past me to hang itself on the ceiling. "In fact, I don't think he even considered either possibility. The way Charley got it, both the Keyhole A and Seven Up are riding their bets that it's an Indian job."

He had been running his pencil over the paper while he talked. Now he shoved the paper over toward me. He sucked thoughtfully at his pipe.

"Those boys could be right, too," he went on. "See how all these places that have lost stock make a rough half-circle from southeast to northwest, facing the Reservation." He jabbed his pencil down hard enough to break the lead. "An ambitious buck could tap any of them and get home in a day or so. Small hauls cause little disturbance and move fast."

"Then you think—?"

"No, I'm still on the fence. It could be anybody. At the same time, there are always a few young bloods who like to count coup as well as they like horses. We've had touches of it, though never on this scale. Usually, a youngster or two gets to feeling oaty and starts dreaming about how Granddad got to be a warrior. First thing you know, they talk themselves up to where they have to go steal a couple steers or a few cayuses, just to prove they can. It's more of a game than anything else. When they find it's harder work than drawing rations over at the agency, they ordinarily pull in their horns, and that's the end of it."

"But this has been going on for maybe a month," I broke in.

"Exactly! And that's why it shapes up in my mind as more like a professional operation than ordinary Indian raids. But whether white or red, we've got to tie it down. We've been luckier than the others, but that can't last. Our being backed up against the river on the east and Warbonnet on the north is probably all that's saved us this far."

I did some agreeing to that, while he squared around in his chair and started lacing the pencil through his fingers again. His voice had dropped another notch when he straightened up to throw the whole business in my face.

"I've got a job for you," he said flatly. "It's important! Nobody but you is to know about it. And you've got to sit on it like a ton of rock till I tell you different. You willing to take it on, playing my hand till the showdown, without any foolishness?"

I told him I was. His picking me for something special, whatever it was, hit me like a drink of brave maker. I felt ten feet tall.

"Fine!" He nodded and went on: "What we need right now is some definite idea about whether or not the stolen horses are being taken over onto the Reservation. Otherwise, the way folks are stirred up, some hot-head might up and shoot an Indian on suspicion. And that would mean big trouble, all around. I'd like to shunt off any mistakes like that by knowing where we are headed before we start."

He paused for me to "Unhunh!" then finished laying out his plan.

"You and Tom are all lined up to go over there for a visit. Nobody will think anything about it, after all the build-up you've been giving the notion this last month. Consequently, you should be able to give that territory a pretty good look-see without stirring up any suspicions. You'll have forty miles of trail to ride, just going over there. Any unusual amount of horse tracks should show up somewhere along the way. Then Tom will want to show you off to his friends, more or less, giving you a good chance to see most of the Reservation and what all is going on. The way Tom swears by you, nobody's going to blow the whistle if you poke into a few dark corners. Altogether, it offers the best chance we've got to pin down this Indian angle, one way or the other."

"You wouldn't figure on me doing anything but look?"

"That's all. You're just a scout. If you see anything off-color, or worse, we'll plan how to act later; if not, we'll have a club to help hold off any itchy fingers till we do locate the thieves. Meanwhile, I'll try to hold the lid down till you get back with your findings."

His whole idea made good sense. My scouting around among the other Indians couldn't hurt Tom or his folks. In fact, if they had any bad neighbors, about to make trouble for the tribe, they would no doubt be glad to have them taken care of by a clear thinker like Ben, before the lightning struck. On the other hand, if the Indians were in the clear, they'd like as not appreciate my proving it. It looked like I maybe stood to do everybody a good turn. And along with having this good spring vacation, I was feeling pretty salty about the whole affair.

"Tom doesn't know about these last raids." Ben shoved back his chair and stood up. "So you keep that under your hat. You had planned to go in a few days, anyhow. I'll just tell you both in the morning that you might as well head out now, before something unexpected turns up. That'll make it all seem natural and leave no pegs for any backfires to hang up on. Savvy?"

I savvied! "Can do," I said. "There'll be no hole for suspicion from him or anybody."

It all worked out as easy as shooting fish in a barrel. When the two of us headed north, the next morning, all I needed was a badge on my vest to feel like Bill Tilghman, John Slaughter, and Yellowstone Kelly, all rolled into one. My imagination began picturing a whole string of fresh horse tracks every time we neared a fork in the trail. I had it figured out just how I would fix my face, real innocent-like and not noticing anything special, when I spotted any of the Indian boys riding valley horses. I would be looking mainly for Keyhole A, Seven Up, T L and Sid's Bent Triangle brands, though I might run into any one of half a dozen others that ranged farther south. I began wishing I had brought along a pencil and notebook, so I could record my findings in proper style.

The only trouble was, I didn't find anything to record. The trail was empty as a bootlegger's conscience all the way. Nowhere did it look like it had been used since the snow went off. Then, after we got over among Tom's people, I couldn't spot an off brand on any of the hundreds of horse I met up with. Tom took me all over the country, visiting this one and that one, from the river to the agency and west to where the Reservation butted up against a string of dryland nesters on Sage Flats. But it was all the same—not a sign of anything I could mark up as a trophy. I began to see why sheriffs and stock inspectors always looked like somebody had poured horse liniment on their hotcakes.

However, I did have a good time. Everybody treated me like one of the family. Most of them would start fixing up a big feed the minute we showed up. Sometimes, they would throw a dance or have all the neighbors in for a big powwow. The younger ones would usually stir up a game of some sort or have a few horse races, anything for a good time. It seemed like we were in the middle of an old home week most of the time.

CHAPTER 12

A lot of people think Indians are about as unfeeling as a load of buffalo chips. I reckon maybe they do look that way to some of the stiff-necks, who stare down at them from their super-race perch. But for my money, their woodenness is mostly a screen to hide behind when the stiff-necks show up. They don't think a bit more of such tinhorn foreigners, who starved them into a trap corral, than anybody else would. When you think of the medicine they had to swallow, losing their country and whole way of life to a bunch of barbarian invaders, you couldn't blame them for their standoffishness. The kind of a dose that was forced onto them would freeze the glad-hand off of anybody. Anyhow, while they finally gave in to save what hide they had left, they managed to hang onto a dignity and prideful background that never melted down. As they couldn't do much of anything active about it, boxed in like they were, they just took to buttoning themselves up behind their stone faces when any of the claim-jumpers came nosing in. Otherwise, among themselves, they loosened up to be as fine a bunch of people as you'd find anywhere. Being on the inside with Tom was a help to me. He was always playing me up as something worth having around, until I was made to feel like I'd been elected top hand of the outfit.

This was particularly true when I was around his dad and mother. They were a pair to tie to. The mixture of Sioux, Crow, broken English, and sign language they used, kind of threw me at first, but I got onto it in a few days. Anyhow, it was the way they said things that counted; that open friendliness would have stood up without any real words.

Old Yellow Bear carried himself with all the hard-rock stiffness you'd expect to find in a top chief, but that was just on the outside. He could be more fun than a Chinaman in the middle of a dogfight, when he took the notion. He was a tall, square-built jasper, middling dark in color and with a long, hooked nose that would have done to hang himself on a limb. He had a grin like an open horse collar, when anything funny came up, and a way of cracking his knuckles that sounded like he was playing a tune. Every time his eyes lit up a certain way, I knew he was about to tell some comical story or spring a joke on somebody.

His wife, Willow Leaf, wasn't far behind him. She was a short, chunky woman, with the twinkliest eyes I ever saw. She must have been a looker when she was young; it hadn't all wore off, either. I liked her on sight. She seemed to take to me, too. She was always fishing special pieces of meat and what not out of the pot for me at meal times. When Tom told her about my being a stray that missed the home bedground, she went all out in making things extra pleasant for me. Never was she too busy to tell me about her people or ask about my back trail. And she even topped Yellow Bear at framing up jokes about whatever was going on around the place.

Some of their jokes and stories would have probably struck most properly brought-up white ears as being about as tangy as some of Willow Leaf's stews tasted, but it was all in fun and without any dirty underside. Most of their talk was the same; they didn't call a bull a gentleman cow nor try to pretend babies came out of a cabbage patch. Yet it all stood up as clean as anybody's language, if you didn't try to twist it around to fit some of your own maggoty thinking. I got straightened out on a lot of warped ideas about Indians that spring.

The weather stayed fine all the while, new grass was unrolling green blankets on the hillsides and wild flowers were painting great splotches of color on the sunny slopes. Yellow Bear came in from inspecting buds on the cottonwoods, one morning, and said it was time to move out into the tepee.

They had been living in a log cabin the agent had talked them into building. It was more comfortable in cold weather. Most of the tribe had some sort of houses to winter in, but the bulk of them usually moved out into the fresh air as soon as spring showed up. When Willow Leaf got the tepee set up and everything put to rights, I could see why. It was snug and warm on bad days, even more so than a drafty house. Sunshine sifting through the canvas walls made plenty of light, while it could be aired out anytime by simply rolling up the walls. With the kettle bubbling over the little fire in the middle and the smoke-hole drawing good, I'd prop myself up against a bedroll and listen by the hour to the yarns and old-time legends few white men ever get to hear. At such times, I'd not have swapped my place for the best stiff-backed chair in any house west of Omaha.

Tom had made a great to-do about the way I'd played square with their old belief in the black ram of Splitrock Canyon, and won us both a clean escape from the Long Shadow as a reward. He really spread it on. I guess he told everybody on the Reservation about it, making me out to be the high mogul of the Big Mystery. His folks acted like they were as proud of me as though I'd counted coup on half the U. S. Army. The only thing that kept me down to size was the solemn-like way they seemed to feel about the whole deal. It was kind of like white folks do when they tell Bible stories or talk about the dear departed. Meanwhile, Yellow Bear kept wishing his other son would show up in time to meet me and hear my story.

This boy, they called Red Horn, was Tom's half-brother. He was a few years older, the son of Yellow Bear's first wife, a fur trader's half-breed Piegan daughter who died when he was born. Horn, they said, had gone over in the Miles City territory with a couple of friends, who claimed to have some sort of a job lined up. Along toward the last of our visit, Tom left me to enjoy his folks and the tepee fire while he spent several evenings scouting around among the neighbors for any news of Horn being back on the Reservation. He seemed dead set on getting connected up with his half-brother, if possible, before we went home. Though that was kind of a natural thing among Indian families, I began to have sort of a sneaking suspicion he was dumping me off on the old folks so he could go have a time for himself, without having to drag me along. It left me looking through the wrong end of the spyglass.

Then, the next to last day of our stay, he said he was going to make one more try at finding Horn. He was already saddling his horse when I came outside right after breakfast.

"Go see Lame Eagle," he said, when he saw me coming. He swung one hand in sort of a catch-all circle off to the west. "Him Horn's friend. Horn mebbyso there long time, nobody know."

"Hope you guessed right," I lied, heading back into the tepee. "Be too bad to waste all that ridin'."

The way he seemed to be hurrying off, before having to cook up some excuse for not asking me to go along, ruffled my feathers all the more. It looked like I'd maybe worn my welcome too thin. That, or he was just fed up on having a dumb white man on his neck when he wanted to do something interesting. All I could think of was maybe Tom had set me up on a limb just so he could cut the limb off under me. The best side of my mind told me that didn't nowise add up, but I couldn't help fanning a little fire under the sore side. The whole thing dumped me into a blue fog.

I flopped down under a cottonwood, wrangling the idea of heading back to the ranch, come daylight, just to show him how much I cared about what he done. I guess it was thought of Ben that snubbed my thinking up short. Anyhow, something joggled my wits back to the fact that I was there for a special purpose, a thing I had more or less lost sight of under the enjoyment of a good vacation. My mind slowly pulled itself back into the stock-detective groove and began looking for any off-center signs I might have missed. The first thing I knew, I found myself asking why Tom had been doing so much riding off by himself the last few days. I couldn't figure him being mixed up in any crooked work, yet I couldn't get around the fact that he had seemed glad enough to herd me around where there was nothing to see, then suddenly started acting like he was up to something that I wasn't supposed to know about. The more I thought about it, the more my blue fog smelled like it was hiding something that had been dead too long.

I was still fighting my head over this new angle when Yellow Bear wandered over and sat down alongside me. He talked for quite a spell about this and that, mentioning several times about how he hoped Tom would bring Red Horn in this time. I wasn't paying too much attention to his ramblings, until he started unwinding about a starving winter when he was young. By the time he got done telling how his dad had saved their whole outfit by killing a white buffalo and giving it to the sun, the shadows were beginning to slant off toward the east and Willow Leaf was making uncharitable remarks about people who would rather empty their heads than fill their stomachs.

The afternoon was half gone by the time we got down toward the bottom of her kettle. Tom rode in just in time to help us finish it.

He seemed happy as a mating grouse. The fact that he hadn't found out anything about Horn didn't seem to be bearing down on him very heavy. The way he acted, kind of twittery and plumb pleased with himself, set my thinking off at a new angle. Something in his eyes suddenly called to mind a half-remembered crack old Yellow Bear had made about young mens' wits going to decorate the girls' coup sticks. Maybe that was it! all his brother-hunting talk being just a cover-up for some girl he'd been trying to get his loop on. The idea shot up like a toadstool after a spring rain.

My spirits lifted to match it. Discovering what looked to be a clean out for Tom was like a gush of moonlight on a dark night. I was grinning all over inside myself. My first urge was to rib him about it; old wooden-faced Tom going soft on a girl! That was one for the book! However, I knew it wouldn't be company manners to jump the gun in front of his folks. I wasn't sure how any of them would take it. I, accordingly, backed up, caching the idea away to use on him in private, while we rode home.

That kind of thinking was what let me in for a jolt when I found I was the cause of it all.

CHAPTER 13

The whole thing started a little before sundown that day. All at once, people began drifting in by groups, families, couples and lone riders. Every bunch that came along turned their horses out and started building camp. Inside two hours, we had enough tepees circled around Yellow Bear's little meadow to make it look like Sitting Bull's outfit waiting for Custer, over on the Little Big Horn.

I'd noticed Willow Leaf doing what looked like a lot of cooking for four people the last couple days. I never gave it much of any thought. Indians are always doing things that don't make sense to anybody else, unless they have it mapped out for them.

Now she began dragging roasts and doughgods and five-gallon-oilcans, full of stews and a bunch of guess-whats, out from under a pile of robes and camp gear in the back of the tepee. Somebody had built a big fire in the middle of the camp circle. Others were busy emptying their wagons, buckboards, pack panniers, and parfleches. Grub, clothes, blankets and the fancy rigging Indians often tote around with them was soon scattered all about the place. The women were mostly herded around Willow Leaf, over by the fire, chattering like a bunch of magpies while they worked hot coals out of the fire to cook or heat up whatever they had brought to eat. The older men squatted on the grass in little groups, smoking and visiting, seeming to have cut themselves off from everything else in camp, yet never missing a move with their beady black eyes. Kids ran everywhere, while the older boys and girls horsed around like older boys and girls do everywhere.

I wandered around for a while, like a flea on a dog's tail, wondering what to do with myself. Nobody seemed to mind my being there, but I couldn't see that they aimed to encourage it too much. Most of them spoke to me, friendly like, when we met, then went on with what they were doing. Nobody bothered to tell me what the shindig was all about or where I was supposed to fit in. Even Tom's folks were too busy visiting around to pay me any attention. Tom himself had disappeared somewhere shortly after the crowd began to gather. About all I could do was divide my time between sniffing the flavor of cooking meat and feeling like a stray horse in somebody's flower bed.

It was coming on dusk when I noticed different ones begin to slip off to their tepees. Most of them came back in a short while, all rigged out in their fancy Indian outfits. It looked like some sort of a celebration shaping up, but there was no hint of what it was all about. All I could do was sit back and let my curiosity push against my hatband. I'd made up my mind if they wanted to keep it bottled up, I wasn't going to horn in and pull any corks.

Full dark had settled down to blot out everything beyond the circle of firelight, when I dropped down with my back against a wagon wheel to watch a couple of young bucks rigging up a hide drum. I was trying to keep track of what they were doing, without losing sight of whatever might be happening around the camp, when Tom stepped out of nowhere to tap me on the shoulder.

"You come!" he said.

"Where?" I wanted to know. "What for?"

He just bobbed his head, like a turkey about to swallow a worm, and pulled me along. I noticed he was all rigged out in beaded buckskins that packed a lot of hair tassels and fancy ornaments. He had paint on his face and a couple of eagle quills laced into his hair with a silver cord. He looked like something Charley Russell had painted, outlined as he was between me and the fire. A minute later, he was lifting the flap of his dad's tepee and motioning me to go on in.

I ducked inside. My jumpy mind was scouting back over the last week for anything that might have exposed my hand to the Indians. I'd heard they could be real tail twisters toward prowling strangers caught overstepping on their territory. But I couldn't think of any place where I'd left myself open to suspicion. And Tom still acted friendly enough. Maybe that crowd, painting themselves up out in the meadow, was just bunched up for one of their ordinary wingdings, after all. I began to feel a little easier.

Tom was standing over across the fire when I got myself straightened up. The first thing I noticed was some buckskin pants and a beaded shirt he was pulling out of a warbag. He tossed them across to me, along with some moccasins and a concho belt.

"You wear!" he said.

"For why?" I growled, piling myself down on a pile of robes. "What's coming off around here, anyhow?"

"Your clo'es." And I noticed his eyes begin to pucker up at the corners, the way his dad's always did when he was about to spring a whizzer. "I help," he added.

But I hung onto my seat. A quick vision of the squaws riding Baldy Peters with a cactus whip, after they stripped him naked, flashed through my mind. I wasn't shedding my pants in this crowd —not until I first saw the rest of the cards.

Tom's grin spread out till his ears started dodging. I guess he knew what had spooked me, from hearing us rag Baldy about losing his pants. Anyhow, he dropped down on the robes and laid his hand on my knee.

"It you s'prise, Curly," he said, as soon as he could get his mouth shut again. "My father an' other old ones say you mus' have honors. I leave you to ride ever'where an' see ever'body by myself, that you not know till time come. When the great honor is planned for give to a someone, that one mus' not know till all is ready. W'at you call the s'prise, eh? It is the way of my people."

"But what am I supposed to be honored about?" I was getting bogged deeper every minute. "I never done anything."

"HOU! HOU! You do the great t'ing; you haff the open ears for belief in spirit ram. No shoot. No make fun. All time save my life by use good medicine of my people. Ever'body mos' proud. Welcome you as Indian brother. Have big feast. Big talk. Show you b'long as strong warrior."

That was the most words I'd ever heard Tom Little Bear come up with at one sitting. It had me riding without bridle or stirrups. All I could do was hang and rattle, hoping somebody would pick me up before I landed headfirst on something hard. Letting him rig me out in that ornamental outfit, he claimed was a necessary part of the affair, didn't help a great lot.

Then, when we were about ready to go outside, he threw the clincher at me.

I was hunkered down by the fire, trying to get some idea of what I looked like in his little trade mirror, when he suddenly squatted down beside me. He backed and filled for a little while, like he wanted to borrow my next month's wages or something, and didn't quite know how to tackle the question. Then he caught his wind and started unloading in a rush.

It seemed his dad not only hung a lot of importance on the way I'd sided Tom in the canyon affair, as well as out at the ranch, but had also taken quite a shine to me on his own hook. Now he wanted to round out the proposition by adopting me into the outfit as his almost-son.

Well, from what that mirror showed me, I couldn't see how joining the family would do any more hurt. Anyhow, he had been pretty nice to me, and there was no sense in spoiling the party. Also, from the looks of things, the whole shebang was shaping up into something I'd like to be in on the rest of the way out.

Tom's face lit up like a full horse tank at sunset when I told him I'd string along.

"That make you my almost-brother, for sure," he said. "Or—" and sort of a half-bashful look slid over his eyes, "or mebbyso blood-brother, if you like, eh? That, we could make with other ceremony. You think good?" His question hung in the air like the calling of a curlew lost in the fog.

He had me still fighting my way up into the air, but I told him to go ahead and we'd let the tail go with the hide. I didn't want to hurt anybody's feelings, now that the thing was wound up to go. Besides, it was beginning to look interesting, now that I knew I wasn't about to be herded off into some other world, with a ghost sheep for company.

Tom was happy as a bobcat in a henhouse. He hightailed off to tell Yellow Bear that everything was set for a finish ride. I thought for a minute he was going to kiss me, the way he threw an arm around my shoulders and squeezed my hand till it hurt clean up to my elbow. And I'll have to admit I felt a little cocky myself. This having somebody act like they really wanted me around, and throwing a blowout to prove it, was pretty heady stuff for a stray of my caliber.

The rest of the night, though, was kind of like a moving picture run off by a green hand, who hadn't learned how fast to crank the machine. We took on a big feed, with everybody eyeing Tom and me, like they expected to see something. Old Yellow Bear made a long speech that outdistanced me the first lap. Then some more of the old men reeled off a bunch of stuff that was just as far out of my reach. This was followed by some kind of a ceremonial dance, that Tom and I got shoved into. I couldn't understand most of the

Indian talk, and their dance was pretty much of a blind trail to me, but I followed Tom's lead the best I could. None of it was anything to build up pride in myself. I just strung along through some more speeches—those old boys sure loved to talk—which wound up with a white-haired old-timer making some sort of an offering to the gods and a couple others singsonging what I took to be some kind of a prayer. Between not being able to see a lot of it in the milling crowd and having scant savvy of what I did see, the bulk of it went over my head. But according to the way Tom outlined the high points, later on, the whole deal seemed to wrap the two of us up as top hands with the Great Spirit.

One thing I remember the best was the surprised look on Tom's face when he discovered they were throwing the works at him, too. I guess he had been so busy setting things up for me that he forgot about how he saved me from ruining both of us. However, the old men had seemingly figured it out to suit themselves. The upshot was that they rigged it to surprise him with the same honors he'd been working so hard to see me get. I was glad they squared things up that way; it left me feeling less like crawling into a hole, when I had time to think how he'd been the mainspring of the whole works.

My adoption into the tribe, as Yellow Bear's almost-son and Tom's blood-brother, was quite a performance. I've wished a lot of times since that I'd had wits enough to soak up more of the details of what went on. About all that stands out clear is the ring of half-wild faces backed up against the darkness, the jumping firelight seeming to make them look like one of these pictures the sky pilots use to show what becomes of cowboys and wicked gamblers. Some of the young men were stripped down to their G-strings and copper hardware. A lot of the old ones sat bundled up in their robes, setting time back a hundred years. Most of the others were rigged out in beaded buckskins, their faces painted, and their moccasins beating time to the pounding of hide drums. Over it all, rose and fell one of their high-pitched chants, beating against the night in a way that took you back to before any white man ever discovered the world wasn't flat.

I lost all track of time, but it must have been around midnight when Yellow Bear got up and walked over to the fire. He stood there for a minute, while the racket choked off into a dead silence. There wasn't a sound to be heard all the while he was making another long speech. Then old white-hair sent up some more prayers, after blowing smoke to the sky, earth and four winds. The next thing I knew, somebody prodded me to my feet and hauled me into the center of the ring, showering me with a lot of words I couldn't understand. He seemed to want an answer, though, so I nodded and signed that it was all right with me, whatever it was. I guess I had it figured about right, for Yellow Bear came over a minute later and wrapped his robe around me while he pronounced my new name and claimed me as his almost-son.

The whole thing ran on for quite a spell. It seemed he was giving me the full treatment, his hand on my heart and mine on his, our arms locked together in a funny over-under sort of way, and a lot of solemn talk while white-hair was making some kind of medicine over by the fire. And all the while there was all that wild singing, that woke the coyotes up out there in the night, and the barbaric beat pounded out of the hide drums in a way that pulled the blood all the way up from my toes. I can still remember how it made me feel like I'd slipped back to when that country was first made. Hearing everybody calling me by my new name, Man Who Walks Up the Mountain, didn't do anything toward hauling me back into the world of clocks and calendars.

And it was as Man Who Walks Up the Mountain that I stood up with Tom Little Bear and watched the old medicine man nick our wrists so the blood could run together, and seal the ties of blood-brotherhood in the time-honored fashion. I never did know how much like a white man it made Tom feel to see our mixed blood dribbling down over his hand; but if somebody had touched off an army musket out there in the dark, about then, I'll bet I'd have been one of the first to grab a skull-buster and start a-thirstin' for walk-a-heap scalps.

CHAPTER 14

Ben's face brightened up a half when I told him about not finding any sign of horse stealing among the Indians. Ben always had a weakness for favoring the underdogs. He had it figured out that the Indians had been rolled in the dirt a-plenty.

He finished hearing what I had to tell, then said, "Good job, Curly! If there'd been any evidence, you'd surely have seen it, being half Indian yourself—now-w-w."

I caught his grin and ducked out with a satisfied, "Thanks, Ben!" I knew he wasn't trying to really rib me about my new family; that good-natured little "Now-w-w!" was just his way of showing a lot of savvy. And I don't think he passed on anything I told him about how I had joined the wild bunch, either. Ben wasn't the kind to run off at the mouth, just to hear his brains rattle, especially about other folks' affairs.

Everybody knew where I'd been, though. They naturally had to unload a bunch of cracks about me going to see my folks, and how soon could I start drawing rations instead of having to work. They had to have their fun.

" 'S one way of gittin' that fine ranch yo're allus a-moonin' about," Baldy remarked solemnly across the breakfast table one morning, and I caught his eyelid drooping toward Blondy Evans. "Too bad, though, it's allus the old, fat squaws't have the good land allotments."

"That's why I settled for a pair of young ones," I bounced back at him. "Yep, a pair of young good-lookers who had just inherited the old man's place to go along with their own."

"Aye! an' so the loddy's a'ready a beegomist," Bobby joined in, shoving his Scotch-terrier mug around the kitchen doorframe. "I fear-r-red a' this goddin' aboot in fur-rin' par-rts micht lead tae excosses o' some kind."

"Humph! excess of the imagination is what he's got," Baldy

snorted. "And it would need only one squaw tangled in that kinky hair o' his t' cut that down to size."

"Yeah, that's why your dome's looked like an ostrich egg ever since the army salvaged you out of old White Owl's camp in '74," I yelped, ducking out the door a second before his plate of hotcakes splattered against the wall above my head.

Baldy's three weeks with White Owl's band, after that little run-in with the Sioux cost him his horse, saddle, clothes, liberty, pride and pursuit of happiness, had left him with kind of a sunburnt memory that was still somewhat tender in spots. I knew he'd simmer down to normal in an hour or so. He always did. But in the meantime, I figured it would be just as well if I kept on going to where my horse stood waiting.

I was lined out to finish checking up on what stock we had running back in the Thunderbolt Hills, that morning. I hankered to get that job off my hands as quick as possible, so had saddled up before breakfast, to save a little time. Now I was extra glad I had. I made it onto my horse while Baldy was still waving his fists a dozen yards behind me. The hills looked like a good place to be until he cooled off.

The Thunderbolts was a tangle of broken ridges and blind canyons that stretched north from Rope Creek almost to the Reservation. The canyons were narrow and rocky. Most of them led nowhere, even if you could get through without breaking your neck. The hills were worse. In most cases, they stood almost straight up and down, with rock walls and pinnacled backbones. There were a few trails here and there through the lower canyons, where they ran down toward Warbonnet Mountain; but if anybody had ever been loco enough to pick a way back into the main range, he must still be there. At least, I never knew of him showing up to brag about it. The south slopes, where a fair amount of feed grew, was part of the Broken Arrow range. A scattering of our stock always hung out there. Now, with all this outburst of horse stealing crowding in on us, we had to keep tab on the hills, along with all the rest.

I cut a circle around back of Warbonnet that morning, but found no sign of any two-legged coyotes prowling the neighborhood. I'd covered everything from there on west the day before. The rest of the morning saw me giving the network of canyons to the east a pretty good going over. I was feeling right good about not finding anything out of line in any of it, as I swung up over a ridge to head for the ranch with my good news.

I squinted up at the sun. It stood at around one o'clock. That meant I'd better go home the long way around, if I didn't want to find myself rung in on some other job for the rest of the day. As easy going as Ben was, he usually had a stack of odd jobs lined up for any jasper with spare time on his hands.

My thoughts were balancing the prospects of getting roped into a couple hours with a posthole digger or the long end of a pitchfork, against the chance of talking Bobby out of a midafternoon chunk of that huckleberry pie he'd been building with his breakfast fire, as I worked up through the scattered junipers toward the ridgetop. The higher I climbed, the more the pie seemed to get the edge on the argument. Bobby's juicy treat began looming bigger and bigger until, just as I was about to poke my head over the rim, I suddenly found something besides Bobby's pies to claim my attention.

That flicker of movement could only be a rider carefully threading a patch of brush down in the canyon. It was only the ghost of a stir among the bushes, caught with the corner of my eye between two breaths, but it was enough to jar my wits back into line. Though there was no more sign of disturbance, I knew, without telling, that there was somebody down there.

I promptly jerked my head down off the skyline. The way things stood just then, all of us had developed sort of a hankering for a first look at any strange jaspers out on the range. We figured whoever was helping himself to the valley horses was probably as tough as such characters are supposed to be. Bumping into one of them unexpected could be plenty bad medicine for an ordinary cowhand whose mama had neglected to include a pair of hair-triggers in his teething outfit. I didn't waste much time backing my horse down below the rim and sliding out of the saddle.

But it seemed I was doing all right. Whoever it was in the canyon, must not have noticed me; he was still coming. There was no mistaking that occasional click of hoof on rock. I was beginning to feel my pride swell up under my hatband as I got my Winchester out of the scabbard and crawled up behind a big boulder. I knew, of course, that the fellow might turn out to be any of the local boys. Everybody was hunting horse thief sign. But that didn't douse my satisfaction. I'd won the right to do the first recognizing.

I edged a little rock up against the boulder and focused my eyes through the slit between them. The man was still coming, showing little glimpses of his shadowy figure moving through the thick brush. Every little while, he would twist in the saddle for a look-see on both sides and behind. He sure acted like he didn't want to be seen. I pulled the rock around to better advantage and screwed myself tighter against the ground. A man didn't ordinarily go coyoting through the hills like that unless he was on the dodge.

Then imagine my let-down, a moment later, when I saw Tom Little Bear ride out into an opening shortly below me. I let my wind out with a little squeak of relief as I hunched one shoulder to push myself upright. Then, with my head half-raised, I dropped back down. Something pulled the corners of my mouth down tight as I remembered he was supposed to be over in Wagonwheel Basin that day. I'd heard Ben give him his orders just before breakfast that morning. And riding Wagonwheel was a big day's work. Yet here he was, a dozen miles in the opposite direction, and the sun only an hour past noon. It just didn't add up!

Nothing added up. I was hunting for a herd of answers as the Indian rode around a bend, on up the canyon. He was still acting like a road agent working clear of a sheriffs' convention. Why all the secrecy? Where was he heading for? Why had he short-cut his job to sneak into this snarl of hideouts that everything but coyotes, snakes and lost souls stayed clear of?

The horse thief trouble was already riding the front end of my mind, like it did everybody's at that time. In fact, the biggest part of our work was watching for anything unusual that might give us a lead toward locating the outlaws. Here was something unusual enough to start anybody's head working.

But to think of Tom being a link in any such setup was like hanging an outlaw tag on a good cowhorse. It was beyond sense or logic, any way you looked at it. On the other hand, what else could have brought him into the hills when he was supposed to be someplace else? Or make him act so sneaky? My mind suddenly backfired to recall all those long rides he'd made while we were over on the Reservation. Yes, he'd come up with a good explanation of that. Too, everything else seemed to fit in with his story. Still, how did I know what had really gone on behind my back, or just how much hocus-pocus had been framed up to keep my eyes on the rainbow without seeing the clouds? The brains weren't all in the white camp, when it came to pulling smooth tricks. The country was full of yarns about

Indians who had cut the limb out from under smart palefaces. Mostly, it was just for the fun of thumbing their noses at the Great White Father's idea of liberty and how to corral the proper amount of happiness. Even the steadier ones were apt to jump through the collar every now and then.

But Tom, I growled at myself, just wasn't that kind. He was on the square from the ground up. Otherwise, he wouldn't be trying so hard to build himself a place in the white man's world. There had to be some other answer. I thought some of trailing him up and forcing a showdown, but shoved the idea aside. Maybe I was just scared of what I might find out. I'm still not very clear about that, not being much good at reading my own mind. However, I wound up by making myself believe a blood-brother deserved the benefit of the doubt, until he really showed his hand. Ten minutes later, I was easing my horse on around the hill toward the ranch trail.

I was still fighting my head over the proposition when I forded the creek below the corrals. Then, before I finished unsaddling, another complication came fogging into the yard. This was Dave Norcliff and Shorty Riggins of the Open A Four. One look at their faces and sweaty horses was enough to remind me that troubles were as bad as hound pups at coming in bunches. I promptly kicked the gate shut on my horse and started packing my big ears over to where the two had stopped beside Ben at the blacksmith shop. Ben looked up from shrinking a tire on the chuckwagon to assay his visitors. I guess he smelled something owly, too.

"Howdy, boys," he said casually.

" 'Lo, Ben." Norcliff stepped down from his roan to lean against the wagon. "We're on sort of an unpleasant errand."

"Yeah? Let's hear it." Ben straightened his big body a trifle. He always met tough spots that way, straight up and smiling. His fingers fished the tobacco pouch out of his vest pocket and started loading his pipe. His eyes lifted in invitation for details.

"It's this surge of horse stealing." Norcliff's words fell like little icy hailstones on a tin roof. "And that Injun of yours. We've about decided they're tangled up in the same rope."

"That's pretty strong talk." Ben's mouth tightened as he dragged a match across the wagon tire. "You got things to back it up?"

"We figure so."

Ben sucked in a gulp of smoke, and I noticed the way his fingers were worrying the match stick into tiny bits. You could tell the words

88

had got under his hide somewhat. Yet his voice held level as he demanded, "Let's have it!"

Norcliff boosted one foot up on the wheel hub, absently pushing his spur rowel around with the flat of his thumb. I could almost see his mind sorting over the best way to begin. It was plain he was bidding for help instead of hostilities.

"These rustlers," he said at last, "are right clever jaspers. You know how they take only stray bunches of stock from odd corners of the range, when everybody is busy somewhere else. Nobody has ever got a glimpse of them or seen any definite signs of how they are working it; the horses just disappear. They finally hit us. Took nine head. Time we discovered it, any sign there might have been was tramped out by the rest of the bunch. We combed that whole end of the range without finding a thing. Then, just this morning, I happened to drop down into a little basin up on the head of Piñon Creek. There are some sandy spots in there, which showed where a few shod horses had crossed ahead of at least two barefooted ones. The trail played out after they left the basin, but it sure stacked up as what we were looking for. Finding those barefooted tracks on top of the shod ones, and knowin' Injuns are about the only ones to ride unshod stuff, it all adds up as some of the Reservation boys driving valley horses out of the country."

He put his foot down slow-like and straightened his back against the wheel. "I'm a reasonable man, Ben; you know that. And there's no question but what most of the agency Injuns are square enough. But there are always a few unreconstructed characters among them, same as we find among us white folks. These few, whether white or red, are the ones to cause trouble, when they start ridin' their imaginations. It happens about every so often. And it's got to be stopped, like it always has before."

He shoved his hat back and squared around with his jaw stuck out. "Now, concludin' it is Injuns, it's hard to figure they could work so smooth unless they had a spotter here in the valley. And who would be spottin' for 'em but another Injun? That Little Bear kid of yours has worked himself in pretty solid around here the last six, eight months, especially with you. That might be pointed out as having to do with the fact that yours is the only outfit that hasn't been raided."

"I'm afraid you're barkin' up the wrong tree," Ben's tied-down voice broke in. "I had Curly, here, over on the Reservation for more than a week, still-hunting for any evidence along that line. He never found a thing. And it'd take more than guesswork to make me believe there's a crooked hair in Tom's head."

"All right, then, tell me this: Where was the redskin s'posed to be ridin' day before yesterday?"

I saw Ben's eyes pinch down to blue slits as he knocked the ashes out of his pipe and tramped them into the dust among the match pieces. I reckon he could feel some hidden trap starting to snap shut. His voice, however, was steady as a rock in a windstorm when he said, "That would be Tuesday. I had the kid moving a bunch of two-year-olds up on Coyote Bench that day. All day!"

"Then how come Shorty saw him sneakin' into the Thunderbolts along about noon? Coyote Bench is a long stretch west of there."

We all swung around to line our sights on Shorty. He was one of these little bantam-rooster jaspers, who figure a lot of loud crowing and high-power strutting is going to fool somebody. Now his loose-hung mouth seemed to feel it was sunning itself under the load of knowledge about to shine through the pale little eyes, that crowded down like dirty-brown shoe-buttons astraddle of his pudgy nose. What Norcliff had said about his discovery seemed to work on him like a kid blowing up a pig's bladder.

"You sure it was Tom?" Ben snapped.

"Absolutely!" Shorty cracked back, squeezing his chicken-breasted front out another inch. "No chance of mistake. Besides, he was ridin' that Shosoni outlaw of yourn."

I felt my breath catch hard. I remembered Tom riding Shoshoni that day. We had saddled together. And nobody could mistake that big chestnut.

"Did you trail him up?" Ben's voice hit my eardrums again.

"Somewhat. Kept on his trail round a half hour; then he slipped me in some branchin' canyons. He prob'ly winded me. Them hills are a plumb jigsaw puzzle. Nobody could folla nothin' in there, once they got sidetracked."

Shorty braced back in the saddle, with his head cocked up like waiting for us to start clapping. He was pretty proud of his job.

It made me sore for a minute. The idea of him trying to build a deadfall for Tom, that way! Then what I'd seen only a few hours before suddenly rose up to slap me back on my heels. I promptly changed my mind about wanting to talk.

"Anything else?" Ben asked. He sounded like his mouth was full of ground glass.

90

"Well-l-l"—Norcliff shifted his hat to the other side of his head—"Pinchpenny Schwenn lost eleven head off Cayuse Flat the night after Shorty saw your Injun hightail into the hills, where you say he'd no call to be. That was the second bunch Schwenn had lifted; they took four the week before. That should spell out something—"

"Yeah, you gotta admit yore Injun'd never overlook a chance to help raid old Pinchpenny," Shorty broke in eagerly. "He's been threatenin' a-plenty ever since that deal he got last fall."

I couldn't argue about the runty puncher's having a point there. Tom had said a lot of things about getting even with Schwenn. And everybody knew the length of an Indian's memory.

"So that's how she stacks up," Norcliff went on thoughtfully. "We savvy your interest in the kid, but he's forced our hands. Now we're asking you to turn him over. If he can clear himself, I'll be as glad as anybody. But we'll have to have a showdown. You can see that."

"Yes-s, I can see how the figurin' shapes up," Ben said slowly, carefully sorting his thoughts. "Horse stealing can't be excused. Not even among friends. But I still believe you've read your sign wrong. The pattern just won't fit Tom."

"Injun cussedness never does, till yo' get a choke-rope on it," Shorty horned in again, licking his lips like a hungry wolf. "A necktie party's the only way—"

"That'll do, fella!" Ben's whiplash voice eased the soggy lump that had suddenly flopped into the pit of my stomach. "If you came over here to—"

"We didn't!" Norcliff cut in bluntly. "Shorty's plumb off his orbit. But we do insist on some action."

"You'll have it!" Ben nodded. "But not in any half-cocked fashion. And without any more of this necktie hogwash."

Shorty took that and said nothing. He got pretty red, though.

"It looks," Ben continued, "like we'd all best keep a tight lip on hairtrigger suspicions. Jumping the gun, would be apt to either scare the thieves off or saddle us with mistakes we'd be mighty sorry about afterward. Now, the tracks you found is a prime lead; it's worth a strong bet. Crooks usually stick pretty close to what worked the time before. My idea is that you should set up your outfit to double-guard that particular neighborhood for a while. In the meantime, I'll have my boys checking on every move the Indian makes. Should you snag the raiders, it will let my boy off the hook. On the other hand, if it turns out that Tom's playing the way you think, I'll bring him in myself, pronto. What do you say?"

"Fair enough, Ben." Norcliff stood up and shoved out his hand. "We'll be glad to string along with you, and keep our suspicions under cover till something develops."

It made me feel better to see that handshake. Hard as he was, I knew Dave Norcliff was square, while Ben was about the whitest thing that ever stood on two legs. Between them, Tom wouldn't be railroaded on suspicion.

But was it only suspicion? That question kept hammering at the base of my brain as I watched the two Open A Four men ride away. Shorty's story matched my own experience too well for any restful thinking.

I was glad to make it into the bunkhouse before Ben's gimlet eyes started probing my shrinking soul. I was in no shape to meet his mind-reading ability. Maybe I had the wrong angle on things, but I couldn't figure where shooting off my mouth would help anything. I'd have staked my last dollar on the Indian. You can't partner with a man all winter without finding out something about how he's built inside. Still, the lineup of appearances had too many possibilities that couldn't be overlooked. I flopped down on a bunk and wrapped my head in a cold, soggy blanket of pure midnight gloom.

Nor did a couple hours of fence straddling do anything to brighten up what I could see of the affair. I was still piled up in the bunkhouse when Charley Norris and the Indian came in, just after sundown. They acted as happy as two pigs in a swill bucket. I rolled over and sat up, trying to decide whether to be more disgusted with them or myself.

"Where you yahoos been hidin' out today?" I grunted, cocking an eye for anything that might show on Tom's face.

"Not bedded down in the corner, like you," Charley said through a grin. "We're workin' men."

"Lotsa ride all day," Tom chimed in. "Me all over Wagonwheel, an' Charley finish horse hunt in river brakes. No like bunkhouse puncher, eh, Charley?"

"Bunkhouse puncher's right," Charley agreed. "Allus find 'em inside, outa the weather, when work's a-doin'."

I quit. I knew when I was whipped. And I hadn't found out a thing.

Nor did I discover anything more that evening. I couldn't ask direct questions without exposing my hand, and Tom's face was blank as a Chinaman's when I did auger him around to talk about his day in Wagonwheel Basin. I went to sleep, trying to sidestep thoughts of what might turn up before too long.

I reckon that was what made me so restless that night. I kept rousing up every little while, without being able to figure any reason for it. I woke up the last time around midnight. That time, I stayed awake.

I judged it was about twelve. A slice of moon had just crawled up the ridge behind Squaw Butte. My ears caught the merest whisper of sound as I snapped wide awake in the darkness. For a moment, I lay there trying to figure what had disturbed me. Then another faint rustle pulled my eyes around toward the bunkhouse door. I held my breath. It was moving silently as a cougar on a limb. The next instant, I could make out the slim body outlined against the moonlight. Then the door swung shut as soundlessly as it had opened.

Tom Little Bear! There could be no mistaking that panther-like figure. I half rose in bed, mouth open to call out, then as quickly sagged back down, slow and careful, so as to not set any hounds baying.

My tired brain started going back around the same old dreary circle. I was beginning to savvy what they meant by a little knowledge being a bad thing to pack around.

Conscience and common sense told me to go to Ben with what I knew. The Indian was certainly up to something. The moonlight glimpse showed he was dressed and packing his boots. Yet I just couldn't pry myself out of bed. I'd once watched the finish of a pair of horse thieves. It hadn't been pretty. And for me to help shove the only real side-kicker I'd ever had into that same picture—well, it was just too much for me.

Anyhow, I reasoned into my pillow, if Tom was pulling something crooked, Ben would find it out soon enough; if he wasn't, my raising a ruckus would only make a bad matter worse. I decided to sit tight. We'd see how things stacked up after the Indian got back.

CHAPTER 15

Yes, I was probably what you would call sort of a moral coward that night. I won't argue the question with anybody. All I can say is I was just an ordinary human stray with a cold lump in his stomach. The fact that I really wanted to do the best I could for everybody concerned, without rightly knowing how to go about it, didn't win me any sleep. I was still fighting my head over the deal when, an hour or so before daylight, I heard a horse pound into the yard. It slid to a stop up at the ranchhouse and somebody started hammering on the door.

I had my head out the window in two quick moves, but it was still too dark to see much. It was a long hundred yards across to the house. All I could make out was the shadowy blotch of a horse, its head sagged low from hard riding, beside the porch. Then I heard the squeal of an opening door, followed by the mumble of voices.

Bad news? It must be! Nothing else would cause a man to run his horse to a whisper that time of night. And from my knothole, I could feature the bad news as only something connected with Tom Little Bear.

My legs suddenly felt as clammy as a drowned corpse below the hem of my shirttail. In fact, I was kind of chattering all over as I crawled back into bed and bogged my head in the pillow. It looked like the pay-off for sure.

Minutes later, I heard the visitor disturbing the horses in the corral; changing mounts, I knew by the sounds. My ears could have tracked a ghost through a cotton patch about that time. The corral gate creaked shut a moment later. Then came the whisper of quick-stepping hoofs crossing the yard, soon blending into the swift drumming that drifted back through the darkness from down the creek trail.

I lay there cold as a harpooned frog. Even my blood felt like something dripping off an ice wagon, as I thought about what was coming. There seemed to be only one answer to the whole affair. And, try as I would, I could figure no way to dodge it. Worse yet, I had no time to dodge. My bumble-footed thoughts were still running up blind canyons when the door slammed open and Ben's bellow rattled the window panes.

"Everybody out, pronto!" he yelled. "Rustlers hit our horses in Badger Basin. We're on their trail. Bring your guns an' get goin'!"

Then he was gone, his feet pounding toward the corral, as the bunkhouse exploded like a popcorn popper over a hot fire. Baldy finally got the lamp lighted and rescued his pants from the water bucket, as Jed struck the floor on his head, both feet tangled in his blankets. "What—where—how—?" Nobody had an answer. And nobody waited for answers as they grabbed for clothes and weapons.

Blondy was first out, diving through the door with his gun belt in one hand and Charley's boot on his left foot.

Charley made one try at the left-over, Number Six boot before heaving it into the woodbox with some rancid opinions of locoed feather-heads, as he hopped around on a bare, Number Ten foot. He must have found something to take its place, though, for he was there to haul me up for air when Jed caromed dizzily off the side of a bunk to knock me windless with his bullet head.

Ben had his own horse saddled, and was busy roping out mounts for the rest of us, as we came stringing out. There was no time for explanations. That suited me. I wasn't nowise anxious to hear who or what had set the dogs on Tom Little Bear. When we surged away from the ranch in a cloud of dust, just short of daylight, I was happy to stay back in the tail end of the bunch. I was afraid somebody might start wondering why Tom wasn't with us, and what I knew about it. My main thought was the hope they would get it all figured out without my help.

This spookiness kept me off by myself as we loped through the growing daylight. I could see a dodging horse thief in every scraggly juniper or odd-shaped boulder. All of them looked like Tom.

We were halfway around Agate Butte when the red rim of a new sun popped out from behind Warbonnet Mountain. The Thunderbolts were only a few miles ahead. I couldn't help wondering if we were to meet boys from the other ranches, or what. That early morning caller must have given Ben some definite shapeup. Who had it been? And what kind of a showdown were we heading into? Yesterday's discovery of the Indian, where he had no business being, and his sneaking out of the bunkhouse at midnight, loomed bigger and blacker every minute. My tongue dripped with questions whose answers had me scared pea-green. My thoughts jumped from a friend I would have bet on to Ben's opinion of a jasper weak minded enough to hold out information on a back-stabber; from hoping we would corral the thieves to dreading what we would find in the process. It was a good thing for my fingernails that I was wearing stout buckskin gloves.

Finally, I couldn't stand it any longer. My nagging curiosity started edging me over toward Jed Hart. I felt I just had to know what I was riding into. The rest of the outfit was bunched around Ben, as we fogged down a long grassy slope into the edge of the Thunderbolts. Jed was kind of out to one side. I spurred up, angling over toward him. I knew he would tell everything he knew without stopping to ask questions, something that struck me as a right good habit about then.

Jed, however, missed a golden opportunity to make a talk. I was almost up to him when Ben's yell swung me around.

"There he is. This way, boys!" he called, at the same time throwing up one hand in a circling wave as he cut sharply left down the hill.

I reined around with a jerk, trying to locate what he had spotted. Then I saw. One glance was enough to jam the breath back down my throat. A lone rider was sitting his horse on a little pinnacle across the bottom. And there could be no mistaking that big Shoshoni horse nor the figure outlined against the rising sun on top of him. There was no other such pair as Tom Little Bear and Shoshoni in the country.

But why was he camped there? With the start he'd had, he should have been halfway across the Reservation by this time. Did he want to be caught? Surely he wasn't trying to hang onto the innocent gag, after all that had happened. He wouldn't have a chance! He must be loco!

A moment later, he started moving down the slope toward us. I knew it was all off then. He was a gone Injun!

I sneaked a glance around at the other boys, trying to figure an out for myself. I could feel my guilty covering up for the Indian stand out like a fresh brand on a rustled steer.

It was then that I got another jolt. Nobody was acting hostile toward Tom. Instead, they were all packing friendly grins and acting like he belonged there. It sure had me puzzled. And Ben's first words only made it more so.

"Hello, Tom," he said. "Had any luck?"

"Some good," the Indian answered, swinging the chestnut in close. "They go Oxbow Canyon way. Got long start. One hour, mebbyso two."

"Think we can catch 'em?"

"Not by chase. Take cut-off, mebbyso can do."

"What do you mean—cut-off?"

Tom stepped down from his horse and squatted on his boot-heels. One hand reached for a dried goldenrod stalk while the other one smoothed out a little spot on the bare ground. "See?" He drew a long wavery line in the dust, looping it around in a half-circle curve. "This Oxbow Canyon, where thieves go."

The rest of us were all down, bunched around him like a flock of crows. We knew how Oxbow Canyon swung off west to circle the end of the Thunderbolts, its north end opening out onto the Reservation. So far as any of us knew, it was the only passable route through that upended territory.

"Go this way." Tom shoved his stick across the neck of the loop he'd drawn. "Save ten, twelve mile. Get plenty ahead."

"But that's the worst part of the Thunderbolts!" Ben objected. "I never heard of anybody making it through that mess."

"Plenty bad," Tom agreed. He stood up, his hands going into a string of sign talk that pictured a lot of dead-end canyons, sheer rock bluffs, sliderock slopes and a snarl of gulches running every which way. "White man mebbyso never find way. My uncle cross there one time. He tell me of it. I go like he say. Think it be a'right."

"Hm-m-m?" Ben shoved his hat over one eye and scratched the back of his head. "Secondhand information from years back is a pretty poor bet for such a pl—"

"Aw, le's gamble on the kid," Baldy broke in. "The whole idee's crazier'n a hoot owl, but these Injuns do savvy things us whites'll never find out. Anyhow, them horse lifters've got too much lead fer a tail chase."

"Only chance we've got," Charley added.

Ben shoved his hat back in place and swung into the saddle. "As good a shot as any," he said, motioning Tom to lead out. "We'll give it a try."

The rest of us swung into line. It did look like a paying chance—if it worked. And if the Indian wasn't leading us into a dead end while his friends made a clean getaway.

This last possibility really had me rimrocked. As much as I was hoping to see him come out in the clear, the damning things on the other side of the ledger kept me bogged in uncertainty. Was this ride on the square, or was he just playing us for a bunch of suckers? Should I unload my guilty conscience on Ben or string along with the Indian, for friendship's sake, till I saw how his scheme worked out? I knew I owed Ben a lot, but Tom was the first real side-kicker I ever had. And we'd been through a lot together. My thoughts nagged at the idea that he might be up to the very thing half-broke Indians are usually accused of, while my eyes watched him ride on the posse end of the chase with all the seriousness of a born lawman. There seemed no way to make the two halves of the picture fit.

It was almost an hour later that I screwed up enough gumption to work myself over beside Ben and ask for details. Where did Tom actually stand in this showdown? How come he was on the job in such a big way? Who and what had popped the lid on the whole setup?

Ben's face lit up with a grin at my puzzlement. I guess he got a kick out of seeing me all snarled up in something he knew the straight of from the beginning. At the same time, he tried to smooth my feathers by explaining how he and the Indian had been in cahoots all the while, and had left me out of a few things that didn't rightly fit in with a closed hand.

"Tom's been shooting square all the way," he wound up. "This last play is his own idea. He mapped out most of it when he routed me out this morning."

"Was that him?" I blurted out before I thought.

Ben nodded, stopping suddenly to study my face with a funny expression. I reckon he saw plenty of color there, from the way I felt. However, he only grinned kind of knowing-like and said, "I might have known!"—whatever that meant.

Then he settled back in the saddle as he went on to tell me that, while we were over on the Reservation, Tom had discovered the thieves were some renegade members of his own tribe. To his way of thinking, even though the outlaws were bad actors, they were still his people. He couldn't bring himself to expose them to the white foreigners so long as they didn't tangle him in any of their deviltry.

He made his play to work it fair on both sides of the board by keeping still while he tried to locate the thieves and auger them into laying off of our valley. Call it Indian reasoning, if you want to, but it was the best he could figure to save Ben from getting hurt without throwing the hooks into his own outfit.

"Then all his ridin' around alone wasn't hinged on makin' me an Injun!" I growled, kind of nettled over the memory. "I was some suspicious at the time. But—"

"My fault," Ben broke in. "I set him up to play a lone hand whenever he figured it might be best. That's why you weren't in on a few things that happened later." He flashed me another "I know you'll understand" grin and went on with his story.

It seemed Tom couldn't get much of a promise out of the renegades. That left him dangling between the hawk and the raven all the way through. He finally set out to ask for a showdown by visiting their camp. That happened to be the day Shorty Wiggins trailed him. I guess he read them a sermon, but didn't get too much satisfaction out of it. My glimpse of him, the day before, must have been when he was on his way to see if his advice had made any impression. It hadn't. Instead, they were planning another raid. They wouldn't tell him just what they had on their minds, but something gave him a hunch that they were aiming at the bunch of horses Ben had been running in Badger Basin.

This put him out on a limb for sure. Ben was his friend—an almost-father—the one man who had given him a chance to walk in white moccasins. I guess he had made a lot of promises to his spirit medicine about backing Ben to the limit in everything he did, like Indians have a way of doing with sworn friends. This development put him smack up against the fork in the trail: he couldn't tell Ben about it without practically handing his tribesmen over to the sheriff; and he couldn't just sit back and let Ben be raided by the Indians. It was a tough proposition, any way you looked at it. He finally decided to ride herd on the horses himself, and say nothing. He thought he might be able to scare the thieves off without their knowing who he was, if they did make a try for the herd. On the other hand, if they decided to take his advice about leaving Ben's stock alone, nobody would ever be any the wiser. It was a long shot, either way, but he hoped to put it over without anybody on either side getting hurt.

Unfortunately, he was up against too many odds. His scheme to guard the herd fell flat on its face the first thing. The Indians had the horses already on the move before he reached the basin. Right there, he dumped his blood-ties overboard and hightailed to the ranch for help. He knew the outlaws would have to swing clear around Warbonnet Mountain in order to hide their trail and stay clear of the ranch. That, he figured, would give him time enough to rouse our outfit and get on top of them before they made it into Oxbow Canyon.

In spite of the fact that the thieves had moved faster than he figured, leaving us with a tail chase, this information took the clouds out of the sky for me in a way you'd be hard put to imagine. I felt like a million as I slid down a gravel slope after Ben. Later, picking my way across a tricky hillside, I wished I could get up next to Tom and tell him how good I felt. However, he was well out ahead of the rest of us, and I had my hands full in trying to keep my horse from sliding over into the canyon just then.

As a matter of fact, everybody had about all they could do to keep themselves right side up. It was about the raggedest tangle of broken gorges and jumbled hills that ever lay outdoors. Where the hills weren't sliced off by sheer, bare cliffs, they were studded with bald rimrock ledges; each rock-walled gorge was worse than the last, and all were interlaced by a snarled mess of gulches that had no more head nor tail than a wad of store-twine in a kid's pocket. The bare gulches and blind canyons, running in any and all directions, looked like they might have been clawed out by the Devil having a fit while the earth was still hot.

Nor did any of it get better. To describe that ride would make a story in itself. Leading our horses over narrow ledges that were mighty thin lines in still thinner space. Crawling over smooth rock slopes that were nearly as bad. Picking our way up and down through bare rimrocks overhanging boulder-studded gorges an eagle's flight below. Sliding down slippery pitches on our horses' tails and then inching back up over murderously shifting sliderock. Time after time, it looked like we'd reached the end of the trail for sure. Yet Tom always found the spot he was looking for, usually the only passable way out of whatever jackpot we were in.

How anybody could remember four-year-old directions through such a conglomeration of busted-up nature is beyond me. It didn't seem to bother Tom, though. He dangled along without batting an eye, even when it looked like we were riding plumb off the end of the world. If I hadn't decided to stack all my chips on him, I could easily have switched back to thinking he was pulling a whizzer on us to help his Indian friends. I guess some of the other boys were beginning to figure the same way, before we finally tobogganed down that last cutbank hill into Oxbow Canyon.

And we were in time. His scheme brought us through to find the canyon floor as trackless as an unpinned Sunday shirt. Baldy slapped the Indian on the back, yelping his own brand of sulphur-frosted compliments. The rest of us were just as happy over the way he had led us across the Thunderbolts, without anybody getting his neck broke, even if we did make less noise about it.

Tom himself was the only one who didn't seem to find any great joy in the deal. Instead, he had been glooming up more and more like a rainy afternoon the last few miles. Now he rode off like Old Man Misery in person, when Ben began scattering us into the brush on both sides of the canyon.

Blondy and I both remarked about his cross-grained actions, as we picked out a hiding place. The job he'd managed should have puffed anybody's head up to strain his hatband. All we could figure was that this trip, on top of his all-night ride, had most likely drained him down to the roots.

However, we didn't actually give it too much thought. Dumpy spells can move in on the best of us occasionally, without any good reason. Anyhow, we had plenty of other things to keep our minds busy about then. Ben's rush to get us all under cover, and his ambush set up to suit him, before the thieves showed, had everybody hopping. His idea was to let the Indians ride into our arms, making everything easy as possible in hopes that nobody would get hurt.

He had it figured. There was practically nothing to it. The three Indians, hazing our herd of stolen horses, walked straight into the middle of our outfit twenty minutes later. I sort of regretted that at the time, halfway hoping for a little skirmish of some kind. I'd been all steamed up to get me a sure-enough scalp. But the reds weren't about to risk their hides against the odds we had set up. They came into camp without a holler, when they saw we had them treed.

Tom stayed out of that part of it. He hung back when we rounded them up, then moved over into the brush while we collected a few guns and lined them up with their feet on the ground. I guess nobody was paying much attention to him during the excitement.

The first move he made, that I noticed, was just before we started loading up the bad boys and tying them in a string for easy handling.

101

I just happened to look around when he suddenly came out in the open and walked over to where one of the crooks stood kind of off by himself. His face looked like it had come out of a thundercloud. The rustler—a half- or three-quarter-breed, by his looks—turned to face him with a hard-eyed sneer. Tom's face was just as hard. His voice was even harder, as he cut loose with a batch of Indian lingo that sounded like a witch doctor's curse. Whatever it was, it sure made that breed act like a whipped dog. I never saw such a sudden letdown in anybody.

"Looks like Tom was gettin' in his 'I told you sos.'" Charley grinned, reaching for his saddle horn. "Musta been describin' a horse-lifter's future life."

I don't know whether Tom heard him or not, but he spun around on one heel and walked over to his horse, like a man with two wooden legs. And he was anything but happy; you could see that. The sharp, pinched look that had settled down around his nose made you think of a beat-out old man. It started me wondering if that lecture hadn't maybe packed more powder than anybody guessed.

I was still wondering an hour later. We were drifting back up the canyon behind our recaptured horses and the three candidates for the state pen, when my curiosity finally pulled the pin on me. I eased my horse over toward Tom while I rolled a smoke; then asked him for a match, after faking a hunt through a couple of my pockets.

I got my cigarette going and hooked one knee over the saddle horn, easing along for a little careless palaver while we let our broncs catch up some of the slack after their tough trip. I tried to make it light and cheerful. The way I tossed out compliments on the way he had found the trail through the Thunderbolts, and how happy he had made Ben by getting his stock back, I thought I'd done pretty good. Yet I soon saw it was me that was doing all the talking. I wasn't even getting any answers. Still, I rambled along for quite a spell, like I didn't notice his clamming up.

This one-sided stuff, though, began to wear kind of thin after so long a time. I stood it as long as I could. Then, all at once, I leaned over and came out with it:

"It looked like you gave that jasper quite a going-over, Tom. You must know him pretty well?" I tried to bear down on it as a straight question.

And I guess he took it that way. Anyhow, his answer was a whole lot more than I'd expected. It pulled my mouth the rest of the way open and just about cured me of horning in on personal things.

"Yeah, him I know," he said, after a stiff-lipped wait that was long as a piece of rope. He was staring straight ahead over the big chestnut's ears. The corner of my eye saw that pinched look draw down tighter around his nose and mouth, while his face faded into the blankness of a lead dollar. "Know him plenty. He"—and his voice faded out almost completely—"he Red Horn, my half-brother."

CHAPTER 16

With our collection of horse thieves roped to their saddles and Ben's herd headed in the right direction, we made good time getting back to the ranch. The whoop-it-up outlaws had melted down to where they looked more like a gang of egg-sucking dogs humped up in the corner with their tails between their legs. I felt kind of sorry for them, they seemed so washed out to nothing. All I could think of was some salty, bunch-quitting broncs whose orneriness had got them rim-rocked on a badlands cliff, with no way to get down to feed and water and the company of the home remuda.

Still, I knew it was no more than what a man deserves for buying in on such a deal. They had it coming. Tom got most of the story out of them the next day, bracing them in their own lingo with what sounded to me like a bunch of war-talk if they didn't come clean. He made them see they had their tails in a crack, bearing down till he had the details all mapped out for Ben.

It seemed they had taken all their other stolen stock out over the Flint Creek Hogback, where it was too rocky to trail anything. It was a long, hard drive that way, swinging away west of the Thunderbolts and coming onto the Reservation through a snarl of lonesome canyons. But like most crooks, success went to their heads. They dreamed up the idea that nobody could catch them, anyhow, so decided to make this last haul the easy way through Oxbow Canyon. We felt pretty lucky that Tom had drawn cards on our side, as once in their hideout, there was little chance that anybody would have caught up with them before they pushed the stock on out of the country.

It was a pretty slick program. The way Tom explained it, the three Indians had hooked themselves up with a sundowner over northeast of Billings. This jasper, operating as owner of a horse outfit and re-spectable dealer, took whatever the Indians brought in without any questions asked. Of course, he didn't pay much, but it was quick cash, what there was of it. The stock went into a hideout pasture, where it was later rebranded and moved to scattered points under cover of darkness and assorted connections here and there. It worked plumb smooth, so long as nobody pulled the pin on the combination.

Now that we'd pulled the pin, Ben figured the rest of the job belonged to Sheriff Ringer over at Buffalo Springs. Turning in our catch, along with the lineup of their operations, should make it easy for Ringer to build a loop with the Montana officers. Between them, they could probably salvage what horses were still penned up in that blind canyon over on the Reservation. And, with any luck, they might be able to catch the sundowner with his fences down enough to make an all-round cleanup.

"At any rate," Ben told us, "we've cinched things so we can go back to sleeping nights. And that," he went on, "should call for a little celebration." He slanted a long, thoughtful glance at the sky. "You've all been working overtime on this horse stealing job. As some of us will have to lay off to take these two-bit lobos in to Buffalo Springs, we might as well all go. I don't reckon the world will fall down if we hold off pulling the wagon out for calf roundup till we're all ready for business."

That was the best news any of us had heard all spring. Still, it was about what we might have expected. Ben was always leaning over backward to give us a break whenever he could. And nobody could beat him at shaping things up to fit in natural-like with whatever we might be doing, without any backhanded bid for cheers from the sidelines.

I wasn't thinking about that at the time, though. All my brain had room for was the idea of a couple days in town. I guess the others felt the same way. Blondy was already digging his checkered town shirt out of his warbag, his oh-be-joyful yelps almost drowned out by Baldy hollering for me to come trim the tag-locks over his ears. Even Charley Norris cracked his shell enough to be caught singing part of "After the Ball" while he was putting his horse in the corral.

Buffalo Springs was our county seat and the chief town in that territory. Some forty miles up the river from Neka, where we did our regular trading and shipping, it was kind of scattered over a little flat above some old Indian springs at the foot of the mountain. There wasn't anything particularly handsome about its collection of frame and log buildings, but its bigger size and wider variety of business places always held out more interesting things to take the weight

105

off a man's pocketbook. Too, its being the end of the stage line from the railroad, up in Montana, there was always a chance to see some boiled-shirt dude make a try at dodging us savages on his way across to the hotel. Altogether, it was a choice place to head for, when we got to itching for a real good time. Ben's proposition was just the thing to make us forget all the hard riding and lost sleep of the past month.

"I'll send Charley over to Sid Andrews's first thing in the morning," he said, turning back to stick his head in the bunkhouse door. "Jed can swing around by the Seven Up and Keyhole A at the same time. They'll spread the news around so the rest of the neighbors can settle back to normal. Also, if it suits 'em, they might want to back up the sheriff in recovering what horses are left this side of somewhere. We can all meet at Norcliff's and go on to the Springs from there."

Nobody had any objections to that, so we went back to getting everything ready for an early-morning start.

"A couple nights in Buffalo Springs will sure be a gift to the underprivileged." Blondy's voice was kind of dreamy-like as he finished smoothing out his store-pants under his mattress. He was staring up at nothing along the bunkhouse ridgepole. "F'r instance, take Jeddy, here—just think how much heartburn he'll be able to work off on that hefty Swede biscuit-shooter, over at the Elkhorn Restaurant, in that time. With her not expectin' him till after calf roundup, and him figurin' on only the moon an' some bawlin' dogies to soothe his emotions the rest of the spring, it'll be almost like a wedding or a lover come home from the wars."

"Aw, g'wan!" Jed croaked, popping his eyes out like a stepped-on frog. "I ain't got no such girl, liken you mean. That biscuit-shooter's just a—"

"She's just a what?" Blondy broke in. "After you workin' all evening to get your rope on her that last time we was over there, and she finally having to hold you up while you got the loop over her head? Why-y, Jeddie, that's the kind of talk can get you hung up for breach of promise and alienation of affections, not to mention the crime of heartbreak and tamperin' with human souls. Could even lose you a happy home, too. That's why this visit'll mean so much: Instead of all the doubts and misunderstandings that might lead you astray between now and end of calf roundup, this surprise trip will

106

like as not reveal two hearts all set to ride double and live as cheap as one."

"Aw, g'wa-an!" Jed's tongue tripped over itself as the light of a full sunset on the Red Desert painted his round face. "'Tain't no such th-thing. I prob'ly won't even eat there this time. The China-man's place is—"

"Is where you ain't a-goin'!" Baldy snapped, jerking his head around and nigh getting an ear cut off. "Feller't sinks his spurs liken you did, last time, is already crazier'n a hoot owl. And nothin' can change him, short o' sudden death."

Baldy was right. We'd no more than delivered our horselifters to the sheriff when Jed suddenly disappeared. The next we saw of him was when Tom and I wandered uptown with Blondy an hour or so later. There he was inside the Elkhorn, big as life and twice as natural. Looking at him through the window, we could see his moon face shining up at the big Swede girl like a grease fire in a Dutch oven. She had him lined up in front of enough grub to founder a horse, and was hovering over him like the Statue of Liberty mothering a cotton-wood stump.

We left him to his fate and headed on down toward the China-man's. Blondy figured there'd probably be more grub for the rest of the customers at the other place. Anyhow, we didn't want to stampede Jed into some kind of a rattle-and-jerk fit that might shake the ro-mance out of his trip to town.

Buffalo Springs was sort of a string town, tied down by a ring of tin cans decorating the sagebrush along the bluff overlooking the river. Most of the business was bunched up on Main Street's three blocks between the Buffalo Head Hotel and Haygood's Blacksmith Shop. The Chinaman's restaurant was around the corner on Shoshoni Street, a block off of Main and across from the O. K. Livery Barn. Shoshoni Street was mostly a string of vacant lots, where freighters parked their wagons and Indians pitched their tepees when they drifted into town. This more or less empty street was a good place for Saturday-night fights, Sunday horse races and midnight walks for couples assaying the weight of double harness.

We figured the Chinaman's window might give us some details on Jed's hopes and ambitions, if we stuck around there till Big Olga came off shift over at the Elkhorn.

Chance, however, beat us out of seeing if Jed made it to Shoshoni Street. Our scheme misfired when we got tangled up in a game of rotation pool with one of the Forked P boys we met coming out of the Buffalo Trading Company store. This puncher, a redhead by the name of Dotson, was an old side-kicker of Blondy's. Nothing would do but we go down to the Gold Nugget with him for a few games and a beefsteak lunch, while they caught up a year's slack in what they wanted to tell each other. Tom and I went along as a matter of course, to make it four-handed.

It ran into quite an evening. The wall-clock was banging out its bedground call for all honest people, when Red happened to mention the big rodeo Buffalo Springs was shaping up for the Fourth of July. He called it the Northern Wyoming Roundup.

"That's a new one on me," Blondy said questioningly, while Tom and I leaned on our cues with our ears flapping. "Just what is this roundup deal? We're green boys from out in the country, where we don't keep up much with all these town goings-on."

"I can believe that," Red's face split in a big grin, "if you failed to hear about our coming big cowboy contest for the championship of this territory. I thought everybody that wasn't dead and buried knew about it by this time."

"Humph, we're workin' men down our way. We don't have time to sit around and listen to all the gossip. But what's it all about, anyhow? I'm not working right now."

"Well-l-l," Red twisted up a smoke and dragged a match across the seat of his pants, "it's to be something like what they've been having late years at Cheyenne, Billings, Miles City, and a few other places. Bill Moffit, the cowboy dude that runs the newspaper here, seems to be ramrodding it. He sees some sort of a future for the country as a dude playground, attracting outside visitors with cash to spend and such like. He has been makin' medicine for this roundup all spring. Claims it will be a prime way to get this section into the headlines and give the country a boost as a vacation spot. He got Jimmy Swayze, over at the Trading Company, sold on the idea—you know how old Jimmy is always a pushover for anything in the sport or community-booster line. Between them, they stirred up most of the businessmen to back the deal. With Bill being top-hand on the paper, and having a lot of connections all over the country, they figure to pull in a big crowd and have a real blowout. Everybody's countin' heavy that way, anyhow."

"You mean," I let loose with a surge of questions, "they're aimin' at real contests to pick the country's top hands at ropin', bronc an' steer ridin', besides the regular races? And maybe special events for Indians and cowgirls an' all that Wild West spread, like Cheyenne puts on?"

"That's the idea. It likely won't come up to Cheyenne and Miles; not this first year, anyhow. Yet it will be a sure-'nough go-round for everybody, with special judges an' all. If it works out the way Bill and Jimmy are prophesying, it should put this burg on the map within a few years."

"Hm-m-m!" Blondy poked idly at a spittoon with the butt of his cue. "That means we'll have to figure on some reps from our outfit, if we aim to keep the Broken Arrow up in a respectable position."

"Naturally!" Red agreed. "The idea is for everybody to ante whatever they can. The more, the merrier. You've got some good hands down your way. Spread the news around about the cash prizes and chances to rate with the top hands, and most of 'em will be as interested as the folks out in our end. The boys up on Twin Forks, over on White Bull and as far away as Medicine Lodge are all rarin' to go. Your outfit would be loco to miss out. We're sure going to have a time for ourselves, win, lose or draw.

Red was steamed up like a four-bit teakettle.

"You got me persuaded!" Blondy straightened up to look around. "It sounds like a hand to draw to. And I reckon we could make as good a showin' as anybody. Charley's in a class by himself, when it comes to plain an' fancy roping. I'm not too bad myself, specially on calves; and next month's branding roundup should hone off what barnacles I've picked up over winter."

"That's the spirit!" Red thumped him on the back. "We've got as good a set of hands as any man's territory. All we need is a little competition to show 'em off."

Blondy was lost in his own thoughts as he shoved his hat over on the other side of his head and sighted down his cue at the spittoon. One foot dangled down from where he sat on the edge of the pool table. I noticed his boot was going around in tight little circles.

All at once, he slanted a glance in my direction. "You're right salty at toppin' off steers, Curly; leastwise round the ranch. I'd say you could hold your own in pretty stiff company. Bobby'd make out good enough if they have a chuckwagon race. And from the way Tom took the kinks out of that Shoshoni stud, I'd put my money on him in any bronc-peelin' free-for-all."

The way his enthusiasm was climbing the high spots, you'd think our outfit had already good as captured most of the roundup. I knew he and Charley were both top-hand ropers, while what he said about my steer riding stretched me up another six inches.

Tom was the only one to take a dim view of the proposition. "No good!" he said shortly, driving the six-ball into a corner pocket.

"That five hundred cartwheels they're hangin' up for top prize in bronc ridin' sounds plenty good to me," Red tossed out invitingly. "Three hundred for second and a hundred for third makes me wish I'd been brought up to fan the rough ones without getting shook loose every third try."

He fished a chunk of newspaper out of his pocket and smoothed it out on the pool table. It had suffered a week's wear, but still mapped out what was lined up for the three-day celebration. Blondy read off the list of prize moneys, his voice climbing another notch with each event. It sure sounded like somebody stood to make a slug of wampum out of the affair.

"That ridin', now," he looked up, scratching his head, "stacks up like a ten strike for anybody with the right kind of talent. Five hundred bucks would be a real stake to start buildin' something on." He was aiming every word at the back of Tom's head.

I just stood staring at a herd of silver dollars stampeding up over the horizon. My wits were bouncing back and forth between that Someday Ranch, we had been dreaming about, and the big prize money. A year's wages in one lump! And there was no reason why Tom couldn't win it, not after the way he had combed the whiskers of that chestnut outlaw. And supposing I pulled down the hundred offered for steer riding, along with maybe a good purse in the relay race? Man, oh, man! That surge of silver dollars all but washed me under the pool table.

It was Tom that kicked the chocks back under my wheels and brought me up standing. He wasn't having anything to do with it. All he would say was, "Not good! Me stay away from ride!" And he said that with his eyes looking at something else, while his back stayed stiff as a gun barrel.

The more I tried to auger some sense into him, the more bull-headed he acted. We had been back at the ranch for a week before I got the drift of what was really crimping him.

Tom Little Bear had begun to feel like a full-size man down in our part of the country. What with pulling Ben out of that barn fire and riding Shoshoni for the doctor, along with his part in the horse-lifting deal, he stood as high as anybody in the neighborhood. At the same time, he savvied how most of the whites in the country looked at Indians. The Roundup would be strictly a white man's show. Practically all the contestants would be strangers looking down their long, Thoroughbred noses at a Reservation stray. Tom had had plenty of that shoved down his throat when he first rode into the enemy camp. He wasn't about to lay himself open for more of the same; at least, not in the middle of a holiday crowd. He rated pride several notches above the money he'd like to have.

"Your people not like ride 'gainst dirty Injun." His voice had fined down to almost a whisper, while his eyes were as bleak as old Warbonnet's craggy north face in a January blizzard. "They mebbyso make shame talk in crowd. Judges mebbyso have bad eye for Indian ride, so give win to white man for please mos' people. All time no good for Tom Little Bear."

"But we're all behind you. And Ben's voice packs a wallop in this territory. We'll see you get a square deal. A win would make them all take off their hats to you, besides giving you the stake you want. It would be a big thing for Ben, too, having a champ representing the Broken Arrow. Come on, be reasonable!"

But it was wind wasted in the willows. I had to go off with his "Not good!" still battering my eardrums.

I could sort of savvy his angle. I'd had my own face pushed in enough to know how the settled herd started tossing its horns when a stray maverick makes a try for the feedrack. Still, this was some different. Tom had the ability to change folks' opinion about at least one Indian. Nobody could deny his quality when it came to topping off a rough one. Even if he were cheated in the judging, there wouldn't be any cheating in what the crowd saw. Win, lose, or draw, he stood to come out ahead in the point he was aiming for. I couldn't see it any other way.

I fought my head over the thing for several days, always winding up in the fog where I'd started. It began to look pretty hopeless, Tom was all wooden Indian whenever I said anything along that line, or even looked like I might. I finally put it up to Ben, thinking maybe he'd be able to make the Indian see what a fine chance it was for him to get his feet into the white moccasins he'd been hankering for all the time.

"I see your point," Ben said, thoughtfully stuffing his pipe. "A

111

thing like that could stir up a heap of respect. I'm glad you mentioned it."

Looking back, I've a hunch his thinking had been three jumps ahead of me all along, but it was like him to make out like it all came from me. Anyhow, he promised to work on it the first time he caught the Indian in the proper mood.

Maybe it was finding that proper mood, or maybe it was the kind of medicine he used, or the way he used it, I'll never know. Figuring how Ben played his best hands was always beyond me. All I can tell you is that I got the answer I'd been angling for the afternoon we pulled the wagon in from calf roundup. We had dropped down into Rope Creek, a couple miles from home, when Tom pulled his horse up beside mine in kind of an offhand way. One hand played with his bridle reins while he inspected a fleecy cloud off in the west.

"My almost-brother," he said softly, without turning around, "I think mebbyso I change the mind to do w'at you ask. Ben say we all go to Roundup. Ever'body take part for Broken Arrow. Tom decide for make the bronc ride. You think that good?"

"Good?" I yelped. "That's the best thing I've heard in a month of Sundays." I slapped him on the back, jarring the old grin out of his wooden mask. "We'll show 'em what a real twister's like!"

The other boys made the coyotes ashamed of their pindling voices when I broke the good news. You'd have thought our Indian was some sort of a Crown Prince just back from exile, the way they ringed around to pound him on the back and yell about backing him with money, marbles, or chalk. They were all as much in the dark as I was about his change of mind, but that didn't matter. The fact that he was going to ride was all that counted. Why bother with silly questions? The bunkhouse celebration we had that night washed out all the back trails in a way to make even a spooky Indian feel like he'd been elected to the lodge.

Even old Bobby's croaking that "the best laid plons o' mice an' men gang oft' aglee" failed to dampen anything but his own head, when Blondy threw a wet shirt at him.

I was jumpy as a green bronc the rest of the week. In spite of practicing every evening on the three brush popping steers, Ben had the boys corral for me, I couldn't help wondering what it would feel like to show off in front of the grandstand—or if some contest steer might make me feel worse. Yet I kind of enjoyed the feel of a few goose bumps. Even if I didn't win, I told myself, there would be plenty of satisfaction in being counted among the boys qualified to appear in the arena.

I reckon the others felt more or less the same, the way their voices sounded when they made their brags or tried to pretend they didn't think too much of their chances in company as fast as we'd be going up against. Tom was the only one who didn't have much to say. Though his new-found pride stuck out all over him, he went through the whole thing like he was getting ready for a medicine ceremony that would decide the future of the Crow Nation.

All that, however, was water down the creek, when we piled our beds into Bobby's wagon and saddled our best horses for the trip to Buffalo Springs the morning before the Fourth. The jittery spell was over, the sun was bright and the Roundup was only a day's ride away. Everything was set for the three-day wingding. That was something to boost the spirits of anybody who ever knew the scarcity of rangeland blowouts in those days. We were all so busy snorting into the wind and pawing at the top rail that any doubtful questions had been shoved into the discard.

Buffalo Springs was strutting itself high, wide, and handsome. Flags and colored bunting waved from everything that stuck up more than ten feet above ground; happy yells rose in tune to the six-guns popping off here and there; milling crowds jammed the sidewalks, while what looked like all the cowboys between Wind River and the Yellowstone filled the streets. With Ben riding point, and the rest of us flanking Bobby's high-rolling wagon, we raced the dropping sun to a camping spot at the fairgrounds. What extra commotion we kicked up was to sort of tell the world the Broken Arrow was out to leave its share of sign on the Roundup warpost.

What we didn't know was just how right Tom had been in his first judgment. And how near the cross-pull of events was going to come to leaving us with a dead Indian on our hands.

CHAPTER 17

I had just finished getting my three horses ready for the relay race. It was the last afternoon of the Roundup, my last chance to maybe win second in that race. I looked up to see Tom sitting on the infield fence, watching the wild burro riding, an opener they had for each afternoon's performance. He was all alone. It reminded me of a lone eagle perched on a limb. It was hard to tell whether he was watching the burros or just sitting there. His poker-faced thoughts might be aimed at anything or nothing.

"What kind of medicine are you cookin' up, over here all by your lone self?" I asked, coming up behind him. I threw a leg over the rail and nudged him in the ribs. "A day like this should have you pounding out happy-heart songs with both feet."

He just grunted something about "Medicine no good!"

His glumness kind of fogged the milling rainbow of gay-colored shirts, fancy chaps, carved saddle leather, decorated bridles, jingling silver bits and spurs, and the tossing heads of enough prize horseflesh to make a five-mile parade. Flags rippled in the breeze over the grand-stand. Little dust spirals floated up from under horse hoofs to fan out in gauzy streamers against the hot July sun. The foot-high letters of the *NORTHERN WYOMING ROUNDUP* banner stretched themselves across the racetrack in a high arch. Everybody not on horseback was jammed into the grandstand, yelling themselves hoarse as the catty little burros slid out from under rider after rider. It was a day to make a man feel like he owned the world.

I tried to offset Tom's sulky actions as just another sample of that Indian contrariness no white man ever really understands. My voice sounded a whole lot happier than I felt, when I screwed up my sights enough to tell him he had nothing to worry about.

"Spec Ryan and Lance Vincent are the only ones crowdin' you for points," I went on. "The rest are 'way behind. A good ride today will lay it in your lap."

His "Mebbyso!" kind of punctured the pink cloud I was trying to float. I noticed his eyes didn't change from their odd mixture of pride, hurt, and anger. It was plain that somebody had been rubbing him raw.

A lot of people had been putting themselves out to do that very thing all through the first two days of the Roundup. In spite of Ben's solid backing and the rest of us siding him all the way, Tom's entering in an all-white contest bred a batch of backfiring among the ones who didn't know him. Indians at that time, remember, were about as popular in white society as a Chinaman in a California gold camp. Tom had been lucky enough to draw extra-rough horses the first two days, giving him a couple of rides nobody could overlook. This didn't set so well with some of the boys who had to make out with poorer buckers. Along with this, at least two of the judges were sort of on edge because they couldn't vote down our boy's kind of riding without being plain crooked, while to give the decision to an Indian would be sure to upset the applecart among friends and neighbors. Too, a lot of the crowd acted like the Indian should be herded off with his own breed, instead of being allowed to swing his hat in open competition. Every once in a while, somebody like old Mel Classen, who never missed a chance to spew out his hate for anything Indian, would pass out some dirty remark where Tom couldn't help hearing it. Others just looked past him like he was something the cat dragged in, shifting their noses a notch higher to dodge whatever was stinking up the bushes. Our bunch naturally went all out to ease the pressure. Several of the top contestants had also been pretty decent about welcoming him into camp. Still, the overall going was plenty rough for a man who had taken it on the chin as much as he had. I was beginning to feel half sorry I had ever baited him into taking the big gamble.

Now my wits opened up enough to let in the fact that he was playing for the biggest stakes in the catalogue—the chance to walk into a new world with his head up. That was some different from the happy-go-lucky holiday, with maybe a few wins to crow about, that the rest of us had our sights on.

And it looked like fun was all most of us were going to get. True, Charley Norris still held the shade of a lead in roping against a hungry-loop boy from the Forked P. The relay races had me looking at my hole card, while a snaky three-year-old had poured me off on my face in front of the grandstand to wreck any ideas about cashing in on steer riding. Bobby's upset in the chuckwagon race pretty well matched the dogie calf that went through Blondy's loop, like an eel. Altogether, about all we had to look forward to was Tom's bid for waving his coup stick in the white man's war dance.

That being the case, it was no time for his confidence to go lame. I could see that. I did the best I could at pumping him up, slapping him on the back and telling him to come alive. This was his day to climb the mountain—and get paid for doing it.

"Look!" I said. "You've won top scores and respect a-plenty, the way you've showed up the last two days. Another first-class ride today puts you up in the big money, if not plumb on top. That means the strongest boost you've had yet toward wearin' the fancy white moccasins you're hankering for. And we are all with you!"

"Not good!" Tom grunted. "Jus' hate more."

"Aw, you're crazy! You can't—"

"Hi, Curly!" A pair of stiff thumbs raked the length of my ribs to spoil whatever I was going to say.

I spun around to see Spec Ryan's freckled mug facing me. Baldy Peters was right behind him. They had been good friends ever since Baldy broke Spec in as a kid horse wrangler, over on the Hump-backed 7. They both seemed to be feeling their oats about something or other.

Spec poked my ribs again. "You two look to be plottin' something. Serious as you are, it must be plumb wicked."

"Not what you could rightly call wicked," I hedged; "just brewin' a little medicine potent enough to fade you an' Vincent."

"Well-l-l," Spec squinted through the dust from a pair of trick riders, "I sure hope it works on Vincent, and maybe backfires a mite on Tom, here. They're both dark clouds buildin' up to blot out my ambitions this afternoon."

"Vincent!" I snorted. "He's mor'n a cloud. He'd cut your throat for that championship, or some grandstand cheering."

"Oh, I dunno. He might not be so bad, get to know him. And he is a ridin' fool."

"Sure, he can ride. But that's no excuse for tryin' to hog the show."

"Could be other than that." Spec shoved one foot up on the fence rail, thoughtfully spinning a spur rowel with one finger. "I'd say it's more like he's grandstandin' as a cover-up for some plain old-

116

fashioned bashfulness. He's from 'way over around Picture Rock, with nobody along to back him up. That is, he's plumb alone except for that weasel-faced Tip Hall, who seems to have climbed onto the boy's coattails all of a sudden. We know that Hall is more of a parasite than anything to lean on, so that leaves Vincent still pretty much alone. He ain't much, if any, older'n you boys. Could be that he is tryin' to hide the fact that this is his first time out in fast company. Tie that in with his being a plumb stranger up here, feeling more or less lost, and half scared somebody or something might cut the limb out from under him, and you can see how he might build up sort of a false front in self-defense. It's the same thing backwards to the way some yeller-gizzard yahoos turn into big-mouthed braggers."

I couldn't auger against Spec's big Irish heart. It was stone blind to anything bad about anybody. But he still hadn't convinced me that Vincent was anything but a glory-hunter out for all he could get. Though he had turned in top-hand rides both days, the way he went about it was hard for me to take. I guess Baldy felt the same way.

"Dang my hide!" he broke in, "iffen you boys let that star-spangled clo'espin git first money, I'll hire yo' both out fer sheepherders."

"Why you sinful old reprobate!" Spec reached across to yank the old man's hat down over his eyes, exposing an egglike half moon of shiny skull. "The idea of classin' us in with sheep! Just for that, I've a mind to demand a ride on that Julius Caesar horse for your personal crack-brained benefit."

"Humph!" Baldy croaked, clawing his hat back into place. "Yo're crazier'n a hoot owl. Fork that cayuse an' sumpin' plumb sorrerful's due to file a claim on yore carcass."

"Well-l-l, maybe we're both safe," Spec said, turning half around to nod toward the corral. "That big roan seems to have everybody jinxed out of riding him. It's kinda spooky the way things go haywire for everybody that draws his number. First, it was Jude Oaks. He got himself disqualified before making his ride. Yesterday, Steve Tiller cracked up in that chuckwagon race an hour before the saddle bronc event started. Then, today, right after drawing him, Spike Nevins gets that telegram to come a-runnin', on account of his mother having a stroke. The whole thing's plumb screwy."

"Sure screwed us outa seein' if the old devil's as tough as he's supposed to be," I added. "Do you reckon he is?"

"It's anybody's guess. I can't dig up any real dope on him. He's wearing a Diamond H brand and is said to've come from down around

Poison Spider. Talk all is that he's a bear cat, but nobody has any details."

"Well, if he's as snaky as he looks—that Roman nose an' pig eyes—"

"Heads up, fellas!" Baldy's cracked voice broke in with a tinny squeak. "Time to s'lute. Here comes th' royalty."

We all looked around to see Lance Vincent coming across the track from the entrance gate, his nose in the air and eyes over everybody's heads. In fact, it was hard not to see him. The pearl-gray Stetson, purple silk shirt and white angora chaps looked like a Bill Hart movie poster against the silver-mounted saddle and coal-black horse. He was a handsome jasper, I had to admit, tall and well-built and with a face that would give most girls the jumping whim-whams.

I found my eyes wandering down over Tom's sorry batwing chaps, that Jed Hart had discarded the winter before. They were a good match for the weather-warped boots, with spur holes worn in both counters. I didn't need to look at his shirt sleeves patched with pants denim to figure how he must seem to grandstand eyes. The comparison between him and Vincent was something to write home about. Though Tom had all the smooth grace of a rawhide rope in his wiry frame, and all the pride of a Thoroughbred in his face, he still looked like a ragweed strayed into a rose garden down there in the arena. It was plain as the nose on your face that he had to ride his way clean up through and over everything that hinged on appearances or was reaching for his scalp. And there could be no dodging, no tricks, no short cuts in a game of this kind. He had to play it according to the book and beat the whole shebang on its own ground. I squirmed under my shirt. Something in that hole down under my wishbone was asking how I'd feel facing the same setup. My boot toe was still trying to dig a hole in the ground when Shorty Lee came across the infield, packing his saddle.

The pint-sized rider from Temasee Basin had a grin half as big as he was. He turned it all on Tom as he hollered, "Better get you war paint on, Chief. They're about ready to turn us heroes loose on the wild bunch."

"Hunh? Oh, sure!" Something like surprise lit up the Indian's set face as he turned around to see who was making fun of him, now.

But Shorty wasn't making fun of anybody, especially Tom Little Bear. He had spread the welcome mat out in front of the Indian from the start. Now his grin was cheerful as a new sunrise as he slapped Tom on the back and hung his saddle on my hip bone.

"I'm bettin' the rest of my marbles on you, Chief," he said. "Now that I've been whittled down to fourth place, or worse, I've got to make my feed bill on somebody. You're the best shot I see in this crowd to win it for me."

The Indian's face brightened a few more degrees as he twisted sidewise to watch the first of the relay riders come through the entrance gate.

"Bet on Ryan more sure," he said over his shoulder. "He got best horse t'day."

"And best horse may lose him up in the clouds," Shorty countered, pulling his saddle off my leg and stepping down from the fence. "My foresight, honor, an' judgment is still backin' you."

Most of the tightness had melted out of Tom's face as the little rider's words sank in. I saw his head was higher than it had been all afternoon. He even showed a trace of a smile as he watched Shorty drift over to where Rex Chillon was buckling into his chaps. Shorty's ten-dollar grin had to make its way around to everybody he knew.

As we turned away from the fence, my wandering gaze happened to pick up Vincent drifting slowly around the corrals. He seemed to be looking over the bucking stock, something that any of the boys were apt to do at any time. I never gave it a thought. What did catch my interest, though, was to see his runty side-kicker come around the fence corner behind him. Tip Hall was strutting along like a banty rooster trailing an eagle. It griped me just to see them go by.

It would strain your imagination to figure such contrasts as running mates. Tip was pure broom-tail alongside Vincent's clean handsomeness. He was runty and slack mouthed, with little snaky eyes that squeezed the bridge of his nose like a couple of dirty white beans hung straddle of a bacon rind. He talked out over a soggy cigarette that always hung in one corner of his mouth, the whole works seeming to sneer at everything he saw. I watched the two of them fade into the crowd, wondering how such a pair ever got teamed up.

Tom hadn't missed any of it, either, but he went on without saying anything. My big voice pried only a few grunts out of him, as I picked up my relay string and headed across the track to where the other race entries were getting lined up.

My spot was midway of the five entrants. We each had three horses, having to shift saddles to fresh horses every round of the track. My hopes topped my expectations by quite a stretch as we waited for the starter to give us the flag.

I had the good luck to get away to a first-class start. That seemed to encourage my Keno horse. He gave me the fun of making the first saddle change. That set my imagination sky-rocketing halfway around the track. I was seeing all sorts of fine visions till Buzz Davis over-hauled me on the home stretch, sliding past me like I was a poor relation. He had already pulled his saddle when I hit the ground. My few quick moves at changing mounts was not enough. I had to eat his dust clean around the track, coming in a scant length ahead of Red Tyler's bald-faced bay.

Yet I couldn't rightly count myself a plumb loss. Half a loaf was nothing to cry about. I quick-stepped my horses back into the in-field to watch Charley Norris edge out the Forked P boy by a few seconds in the steer roping. That made me feel pretty good. With one championship cinched for the Broken Arrow already, and Tom's chance to double it still open, our outfit stood to go home with its head in the air. Even my second spot in the relays would add a little to the family score.

It was the announcer's megaphone that brought me out of my cloud climbing a few minutes later. "Ladies and gentlemen," he was bawling, "the next event will be the finals in the saddle-bronc riding for the Northern Wyoming Championship. These are all good boys, the cream of the territory. If you don't get your money's worth, watching this contest, it's your own fault. The first rider to come out will be Rex Chillon on Skyline."

CHAPTER 18

The heavy drone of voices in the grandstand pinched down to a whisper, the way the wind sometimes blows itself out all of a sudden as the sun drops. The wall of faces pushed forward like so many starved cows headed for a haystack, as the helpers jerked Skyline's blindfold and jumped back. A split second later, Rex was shooting across the infield in the middle of his half ton of dynamite.

The ewe-necked buckskin was living up to his name. He was showing blue sky under his belly most of the time, as Rex raked him left and right from shoulders to flanks. Then, at the top of a high, twisting jump, the horse swapped ends to come down in a loose-jointed, sidewise swoop. It was a wicked move. Only a tricky switch as he struck the ground let him catch his footing.

It was the play that cost Chillon his chance. Expecting a dirty fall, Rex had loosened himself to unload as they came down. He saw his mistake too late. He caught the stirrup he'd kicked free and squared himself back in the saddle midway of the next jump, but not before a three-cornered chunk of blue sky showed under the seat of his pants.

"Too dang bad!" Baldy grunted. "That'd been a money ride iffen Skyline hadn't outfoxed him."

The pickup men were bringing Rex back to the corral. He didn't seem to be feeling too bad about his luck, so I turned back to watch the helpers bring out another horse. This was long before anybody ever heard of bucking chutes. We did it all range style. The horses were roped out of the corral and snubbed to somebody's saddle horn, or maybe thrown and stretched out, while the critter was eared down and blindfolded long enough to get a saddle cinched on and a man on top. With a corral full of kinky horses and a dozen or so cowboys helping to get the right ones caught and saddled as each rider came up, the process was often as showy as the rides themselves. Sometimes even more so.

Now Happy Tinnen was hanging on the ears of a gangling bay ridgerunner. He had both knees drawn up to dodge the striking hoofs as the horse tried to bust his halter rope and climb into the saddle with the snubber. It took three tries and a skinned elbow for Buck Thompson to get the blindfold on. Meanwhile, Joe Breen was circling around, watching for a chance to get his hull screwed onto the fighting bay.

"Next, is Breen of the Box Four on Widow Maker," blatted the megaphone. "This South Fork boy has been piling up some important points. He'll do to watch."

I saw the blindfold drop into place at last. A minute later, Joe tossed his rig across the bay's back and yanked the cinch tight, all the while doing a little Irish jig to keep from being tramped by both the outlaw and snubbing horse. They made half a dozen complete circles in the process, fighting the whole time.

Then the Box Four rider was up and the bronc cut loose. They were on their own. Joe was fanning with his hat as Widow Maker unwound like a prairie twister crossing the infield. Joe wasn't a showy rider, but his performance pulled a long roll of applause from the grandstand.

"Any special place you want your remains planted?" Shorty Lee asked with a wicked grin, as Spec Ryan tested the cinch on the famous Tar Bucket.

"I'll be plantin' 'em around that first prize d'rectly," Spec grinned back, easing himself into the saddle. "You watch!"

As if trying to call his rider's windy, Tar Bucket came out like a cougar with its tail in a trap. Ryan's grin changed to a hard, set line across his face as the four-legged bundle of unhinged hellishness hogged, sunfished, and swapped ends like an unanchored pinwheel on a spot no bigger than a barn floor.

Spec's freckles stood out like smears of brown war paint on a gray blanket, when the pickup man let him down beside the corral. His dry statement that "This here championship race ain't bein' run over no bed of posies," brought a quick glance from Tom, busy cinching his rig on the struggling Rocket.

Rocket was a snake-headed, long-legged brown with one white eye. He didn't have a decent thought in his whole rangy body. He had come down out of Montana with an outlaw reputation spiny as a roll of barb-wire. Plenty of his would-be riders had been poured off in the dust. As the tougher the horse, the better the chance of a winning ride, Tom had been patting himself on the back for having drawn such a specimen for the finals. I'd been guessing the old heathen would wake the crowd up to the fact that skin color and old clothes didn't always stand in the way of doing a man's job.

"Don't let the old cuss euchre you with that fake pinwheel, when he starts fence rowing," Pink Wilson said, coming up from behind as Tom screwed himself into the saddle. "It's his pet brave-killer. Generally works, too, if you're not hep. I had to learn the hard way." He stepped back with a short wave of his hand. "And good luck, Chief!"

It was something more than surprise that chased itself across Tom's face. I saw his eyes light up like a pair of full moons. It was plain to see that Pink had been elected as an all-time friend. His thanks for the warning exposed more white teeth than I'd seen for two days. It was just the medicine he needed. You could almost see new life run through his body as his helper jerked away the blindfold and Rocket suddenly broke in two.

I felt something swell up against my wishbone as the brown outlaw windmilled into a series of spine twisters that carried him halfway to the judges' stand. The Indian was foreguessing every move of the horse. His timing was perfect. No judge would be able to downgrade this performance! I almost knocked Baldy over as I swung my hat in a circle.

"E-e yow-ee, Powder River!" I howled. "Come on, you—!"

Somebody's surprised yelp, mingled with a woman's scream from the grandstand, plugged the words in my throat as both Tom and his saddle shot skyward. For a moment, he seemed to hang on the rim of that dust cloud; then, the dust let go, skidding him off sidewise, where he suddenly pitched down headfirst against the infield fence.

You could almost hear the crowd suck in its breath. Even the dudes could tell it was a bad spill. That first few seconds seemed like half an hour. Then a ragged cheer drifted down out of the grandstand, as the dusty huddle stirred slowly to life and tried to pry itself up with one hand.

"Hurt any?" Baldy yelled, sidewheeling along on his gimpy leg as the rest of us loped across toward the Indian. "An' what busted?"

"No hurt bad," Tom grunted, trying to make it sound like he had his wind back. He had got himself sitting up. His right hand moved to wipe the bloody smear off the side of his face, but it didn't get very far. His eyes told that he was hurting plenty bad when he tried to move that side. "Guess mebbyso latigo bust," he added through tight lips.

"Hunh! That's dang funny!" Baldy stepped across to the tumbled saddle. "Never knowed you t' overlook weak riggin'."

His voice broke off short as his pawing hands hauled the broken latigo out of the dirt. Then he suddenly grabbed for the other end of the strap, backed-up excitement sending him to one knee.

"Why, cuss my hide!" he exploded, almost tipping over backward in his hurry to show the latigo to everybody. "This ain't no break, not in any man's language! It's been whacked 'most off with a knife. Looke here, fellas, on the under side, up next the ring! Somebody's done fouled our man a-purpose!"

We all moved in for a closer look. The others saw something was out of joint, crowding up like wolves around a crippled cow.

"Mebbyso mistake," Tom cut in shortly. "Nobody'd cut—"

"Wouldn't, eh? Yo're crazier'n a hoot owl. Git that dirt outa yore eyes so's yo' can read sign halfway. Iffen that ain't cut, I'm the King o' Rooshy out on a spree."

"Baldy's right!" A grizzled old Rafter L puncher finished running a finger across the leather. "That's knife work, if I ever saw any."

"Dang tootin', I'm right!" Baldy glared around like a brush wolf laying claim to a dead calf. "Ever'body look fer themselves!"

Tom had pulled himself up against the fence with his good hand. He rubbed the dirt out of his eyes and stepped over to examine the strap. A dozen of us did the same. We all saw the same thing. Aside from one ragged edge, broken by the fighting horse, the latigo showed only the smooth mark of a sharp knife.

It had me rimrocked. While I knew a lot of the boys were proddy about having to ride against an Indian, I couldn't feature any of them being scummy enough to pull this kind of a deal. Real riding men simply aren't that kind of a breed. It didn't make sense.

"—was done d'liberate!" Baldy's hostile voice pulled my thoughts back into line. "An' there's fellers so crazy for glory they'd pull 'most anything to 'liminate a dangerous opponent."

Everybody followed his dead-level gaze as it swung around to where Lance Vincent stood. The Picture Rock rider saw the play as quick as anybody. His face lost part of its color as he took half a step forward.

"Meaning me?" he asked. "You think I—?"

"What's going on here?" The arena boss slid his horse to a stop, looking down like an avenging angel sent to iron out all the dents in the world. "Can't you see you're holding up the show?"

"Yeah!" Baldy bellowed. "An' I'm here to tell yo' she's gonna be held up till we find the miscreant that tried to bust Tom's neck. Of all the dirty, low-down, cutthroat—"

What would probably have been the ripest part of the blowoff was cut off when the manager swung around to shoot some questions at the bunched riders. He got plenty of answers. Somebody pushed the slashed latigo up into his face. Baldy's verdict had him pretty well treed.

"Does that mean the kid gets another horse?" Spec Ryan said, leveling a finger at the man. "I'm not ridin' against any crooked holdup like that."

"Same goes here," Shorty Lee chimed in. "This is a man's game. What little there is of me aims to represent my share."

"You boys figure to let that stinkin' Injun's razzle-dazzle suck you in?" We looked around to see old Mel Classen's beefy face in the fringe of the crowd. "He prob'ly done it himself, on purpose, to pull sympathy. Just like any cussed redskin!"

Mel had always hated Indians worse than the Devil does Holy Water. It was sort of a disease with him. He never missed a chance to sound off on the subject, using his big pull with a lot of the valley ranchers to help him get away with it. Now he glared at the arena boss as if daring him to back Tom's claim.

"Injuns," he snarled, "got no business here, in the first place. This is a white man's—"

"That'll do, fella!" Pink Wilson broke in, his voice rasping like a rusty saw on a tin roof. "This boy is whiter'n you'll ever be, if your hide's anything like your big mouth. And he's got the guts to ride where jaspers like you wouldn't even dare drag a halter. I say he gets the chance he deserves, or we'll blow your little old stampede all to hell. And you with it!"

Pink had been a stranger to all of us. He was from somewhere up on the Yellowstone. Now, Baldy wrapped his arms around him with an "old pardner" beller, dragging him over to where our outfit was lined up with Spec, Shorty and a dozen or so other boys. Trouble had started waving its red flag as a few of the riders edged across toward Mel and some of his friends. Mel was spouting war talk between squirts of tobacco juice. Most of his backers were more or less agreeing with him, in sort of an uneasy way, as they sized up the odds against them on our side.

The arena manager just sat there, sniffing the battle smell and shooting worried glances at first one bunch and then the other. He looked to be wondering if he could get in the clear before somebody opened the ball. He had his mouth half open, fishing for words, when Ben came elbowing through the crowd.

Ben was breathing kind of hard, like he had been really hightailing it from somewhere. His chin was stuck out in that hard-rock way of his, when he had a cat to skin.

"Hold it!" he barked. "I'm handling this." He swung on the arena manager. "This boy of mine was fouled, plain and simple. He is representing the Broken Arrow. I demand another ride for him, if he feels up to it. And we'll have no more of that lousy gab about Indians being out of place in this affair. Get that, all of you?"

The man rode off with kind of a surly twist to his mouth, as though the Indian was to blame for everything. I guess he was glad to get shut of the argument before somebody pulled the pin. Anyhow, he shook himself together, allowing as how he'd be back with the rest of the numbers for Tom to draw from.

Tom had been taking it all in. He had pulled himself up like a general on parade. From the way his eyes settled on all the boys who had backed his hand, you could see that nothing short of riding a buzz saw could stop him now.

Ben watched Mel and his bunch drift off, then walked over to where Tom sat propped up against his saddle. His face wore a hard scowl as he ran a hand gently over the bloody bruise on the Indian's head. He also poked around at the hurt arm and side. Tom tried to make out that everything was all right, but there was no mistaking the way his nose pinched down when Ben's fingers got a shade rough.

I didn't think too much about it, at the time. The Indian ought to know as much about how he felt, as anybody else. And Ben didn't say anything. About all I could see was to sit down and keep the boy company, after Ben hurried off to look after his own affairs.

While Kiowa tried to unscrew Pink Wilson out of the saddle and a whooping rider from Pyramid Butte rocketed across the field on a raw-boned sorrel, trying to build a reputation for sunfishing, I talked over the crooked accident possibilities with Tom. That is, I talked. He didn't say much. Still, I could see his mind was working, like a trail-wise scout cutting for sign. There was a lead to that cut latigo, if we could just find it. For my part, it narrowed down to the way Vincent had been hanging around the corral while everybody had their heads pointed toward the relay race. Tom's saddle had been stacked with several others back of the fence, out of sight. And it had been undamaged when he left it there an hour earlier. It all added up.

I was still trying to break down Tom's "Mebbyso wrong guess," when Ben showed up again. Doc Thornhill was with him. They were headed our way. Doc's feet were kind of skipping along to keep up with Ben's long legs. His breath let go with a big "Whoosh!" as he set his little black bag down in front of us. He leveled a finger at Tom, and Ben nodded.

It didn't take long. One look at the head still oozing blood and a pass at Tom's right side brought out his clipped verdict that "This boy is in no shape to ride. Be a crime to think of it!"

"Can you make him believe it?" Ben had both hands buried in his pockets and his face screwed into a question mark.

"Nothing else to do. Doctor's orders!"

Tom had caught the drift of things. "Me ride!" he said stiffly, getting his feet under him. "No hurt."

"But you can't. I won't allow it!"

Tom turned his back. "Talk no good." He started to move away. "You not boss."

Thornhill batted his eyes twice. Then he jumped over to grab the Indian's good arm.

"All right!" he grunted. "Make a stubborn jackass of yourself, if you must. Never knew a cowhand to have the sense he was born with, anyhow. Have to kill him and bury his head to keep him out of worse trouble than he already had."

He reached down for his satchel, still hanging onto Tom's arm. "Two broken ribs. Shoulder, bad contusion. Head wound sure to reopen at first hard jolt." He looked up. "Get that shirt off! Do what I can to let you commit suicide."

Two more of the boys found they had bit off more bronc than they could chew, while I helped Tom peel his shirt and watched Doc go to work. There wasn't much damage you could see on the brown hide. I'd seen worse things than that buggered shoulder get well without any trouble. But Doc's four-dollar words sounded like a vote for the undertaker, as he cinched the Indian's ribs down under a couple layers of bandage and tied a bandage over the big plaster covering the ripped scalp.

"Maybe that will last till you get bucked off again," he groused. "Have to do it all over again, anyhow, time that next horse gets through with you."

"Feel fine!" Tom slid back into his shirt. "Make good ride now. No trouble."

Doc just snorted. He bent over to gather up his bag of tricks. "All damned foolishness!" he grunted. But I noticed one hand sneak over to pat the Indian on the shoulder. "Good luck, boy. Make believers out of 'em!" he finished.

It sounded like something Ben might have said.

The whole thing made me feel better. I squatted down to lace the sound end of Tom's latigo back into place, then made sure nobody had worked any other shenanigans on the rig. I didn't even bother to look up when Bad Whisky unloaded Izzy Fursome the fourth jump. Izzy wasn't much of a threat to the championship, anyhow.

When I did finally straighten up, I saw Tom getting a drink of water out of the barrel back of the judges' stand. I figured he needed it. Then, on the way back, he stopped to talk with Sheriff Ringer for a minute. At least, they seemed to be talking; Ringer kept hauling at his goatee with quick little jerks, the way he always did when he was up against something interesting. Anyhow, it wasn't but a minute or so. Tom was almost back to where I was when the arena manager rode up with a dozen slips of paper in his hat.

"Here's your drawing, Sitting Bull," the fellow said, trying to raise a laugh for himself. "Your chance at any horse left. Come an' get it!"

He swiveled his green-apple sneer around in a bid for applause, only to find his own face resembling a tomato from his shirt collar on up. Shorty and Spec both had their arms over the Indian's shoulders, horsing him forward like he was one of the family.

"Yessir, Mister General George Armstrong Custer, sir," grinned Shorty. "We're a-comin', all of us, to see our ridin' pardner off on an honest ride."

He reached for the hat and held it out to the Indian.

Tom pulled out one of the folded slips, his eyes on Shorty with a look that would have done you good to see. "T'anks for extra ride," he said shortly.

Everything quieted down as still as a church, as the boys all edged up to hear Tom read his luck.

It seemed like it took him an hour to get the paper unfolded. Baldy shoved through the crowd, like a bull buffalo, to help him out. He got there just in time to meet the opened slip face to face. An instant later, his bugged-out eyes swung around, making him look more like a bull buffalo than ever.

"Julius Caesar!" His yell echoed like the howl of a mating wolf. "Read 'er an' weep fellas! Our boy's done put the big spoke in yore wheel."

CHAPTER 19

Julius Caesar! The name buzzed through the crowd like a rifle bullet in a brush patch. Regardless of how they felt about the Indian, everybody was up in the air over this last-shot chance to see the Diamond H roan in action.

Nor would they have to wait long to see it. Vincent was already saddling for his ride, the last one on the ticket. Tom's reride would follow, making it a sort of neck and neck race between the two top contestants. Whoever cut that latigo had sure enough set the stage for a whizzer of a windup. Things like that seldom team up for a red-hot finish.

Still, a lot depended on the horses. Vincent had drawn Bald Eagle, one of the top outlaws. The Diamond H roan, on the other hand, was still a question mark. True, he was claimed to be bad, but how much foundation was under the claims remained to be seen. Different people have a lot of different opinions about meanness in horses.

I eased over to the corral for another gander at the big outlaw the boys had just roped out of the rough string. Away from the other horses, he stood up saltier than ever. It was hard to mistake that long lower jaw and the little flat ears set too close together on the big, ugly head. I soon shed any doubts about him being all he was supposed to be.

"Lance Vincent on Bald Eagle, comin' out!"

I heeled myself around to see the announcer leaning half-out of the judges' stand, his megaphone dangling from one hand. I swung my eyes in the direction of his gaze as the helpers jumped clear of the twisting red avalanche erupting into the open. Before the bald-faced gelding made a dozen jumps, the crowd had hunched forward like a desert-gaunted herd smelling water somewhere. It almost looked like the whole grandstand had started to tip over onto the racetrack. Nobody was aiming to miss a move of this battle.

You couldn't blame them. Vincent was making a ride to go down in the book. He seemed part of the animal itself. What a picture! That glossy red horse, rippling white chaps and purple silk shirt, topped by the mop of wavy black hair, tossed and spun against the sky like a rainbow riding the churning spray of Old Faithful Geyser. And he was keeping perfect time, playing it like a fiddle. That big gray hat fanned the critter at every jump. His spurs moved like clockwork in their shoulder to hemline raking. With never an off note, he swayed, spun and twisted to every crooked move in a way that only a natural-born bronc rider can ever do. Even a plumb jaundiced eye couldn't spot anything second-rate about that kind of a job. The bull-like roar from the grandstand told what the crowd thought about it.

"Class!" Pink Wilson said above the noise, as we watched the pickup men gather him off the horse. "Plumb class! And style. Spec had as good a horse, but he lacked whatever it is that makes Vincent stand out like a Thoroughbred in a broomtail herd. The rest of us don't have it, either; nobody but real headliners."

Even Baldy forgot himself enough to "allow he done better'n a body'd ever think for a dang swell-head cinch-cutter."

"Next is Tom Little Bear on Julius Caesar. A second ride for the contestant fouled earlier this afternoon."

The announcer's voice pulled the plug on a flood of buzzing interest in the grandstand. The Indian had snagged everybody's notice. His accident and the big powwow that followed it had started curiosity itching all over the place. Most of them didn't really know what it was all about; but whatever it was, they wanted to see more of it. This looked like the payoff on something or other, as well as the unexpected chance to find out how much heft was actually wrapped up in the poison spider outlaw's reputation. Nobody aimed to miss anything.

It was about as bad down in the infield. Most of the boys had already staked themselves to seats on top of the corral. Opinions about the untried horse had been thick as flies around a buffalo kill for the last three days. Betting for or against the Indian's chance of topping Vincent's picture-book performance had run into just as much cross-fire. It was all anybody's guess. We were sitting on half-cock to see who had guessed right.

But right or wrong, none of us were disappointed. We knew we were in for a treat the minute one of the helpers jerked the blindfold off the roan's eyes. The horse flattened himself for a moment, belly halfway to the ground, like a cat about to tackle a gopher. You could actually see his muscles tense like bunched springs. It didn't take much savvy to realize we were looking at an artist in the bucking game. A quick glance at Tom told me this was where two artists meet. In the same instant, I saw the pair of them explode into the air, as if shot from a gun. Bawling like a pitchforked bull at every jump, his head bogged between his knees and back bowed like a steel hoop, the roan sunfished across the field like a singed bobcat headed through a cactus patch.

The last jump broke off in the middle as he went up on his hind legs, his front feet climbing the air. I thought he was a goner. Then I saw Tom's fist flatten his ears before he could topple backward. The roan shook its head with a squeal of rage. You could hear the breath whistling in his nose clear across the arena. The Indian's head bandage was flopping around his ear like a loose scalp. His body was whipsawing to that crazy sort of a double-action neck-snapper the roan pulled every time he scraped the clouds. I never saw anything quite like it, before or since. The horse must have invented it himself. It was the same with the way his spurt of bucking unwound into the air, like a clock spring turned loose, swapping ends and coming down with all four feet on a spot you could cover with a Carlsbad Stetson. Then, suddenly, changing the pattern, as though shoving all his chips in against the hated man-thing on his back, the horse shot out to one side in a high, snaky twist, shaking its body like a wet dog. The next instant, it ducked its head around the off front leg to come down back first in a soggy, boneless heap.

A killer! This was no ordinary outlaw work. Only an educated man-killer would ever set itself up for deliberate murder. I guess I wasn't the only one to fold his stomach back down in place at seeing Tom again back in the saddle, as the critter heaved itself back up out of the fog of dust. Even after having watched him do something similar once before, I had to scour out my eyes to believe it. That he could have got clear in that upside-down fall, and then made it back into the saddle before the horse floundered to its feet, was one of these things that win a liar's reputation for honest story tellers.

But believe it or not, there he was. And both spurs were raking the sweaty roan ribs as, with a wheezing bawl of injured dignity, the would-be killer made a blown-out try at showing he had a bundle of toughness left.

It was a ride to mark time by, in any man's country. Old cowmen, worn gray by experience, tossed away their hats and yelled like Comanches, while they stomped unnoticed on one another's feet. Even the people who didn't know too much about such things, got caught in the stampede and woke up to find themselves seeing history in the making. The grandstand rocked with their roar. Total strangers pounded one another on the back. As a solid body, the whole crowd rose to its feet for a better view of what was to become cow-camp legend from Wind River to the Musselshell.

Nobody will ever know how Tom Little Bear's thoughts were running about that time. Or maybe he was past thinking. That kind of pounding could do things to a man's head, especially when he already had a split scalp and a few busted ribs. I'd had my insides horse-churned enough times to realize he was making a ride like few men ever sit through. I guess it takes somebody with the pride and ambition of a long line of fighting chiefs to take the punishment that sort of a job calls for.

A good many people seemed to feel the same, the way the time-keeper shot himself in the foot with a blank cartridge, and Judge Robinson stood tromping on the megaphone while he yelled through his hands: "That's enough! Pick 'im up, you hazers! He wins by a mile!"

"For a bronc-fightin' fool, Chief, you sure take the biscuits!" Spec Ryan's grin was bright as the open door of a bunkhouse stove. He shoved out his hand as the Indian slid down from behind the pickup. "Boy, I'm proud to lose to you!"

"I knowed it!" croaked Baldy for the dozenth time. "I told yo, all our champeen needed was a real hoss."

"I'll second that." Shorty Lee jumped off the fence to slap an arm across Tom's limply sagged shoulders. "A real rider on a real horse! You're plumb genuine!"

A surge of me-too grins came crowding in from all corners. They all seemed to have forgotten Tom was ever a different breed. And there was no doubt about his having made the grade as a full-scale top hand. It wasn't till Sheriff Ringer bulled his way through the crowd that the three-deep pack of glad-handers, milling around Tom, finally split apart.

"We located the cinch cutter," Ringer held up his hand to announce flatly.

"Who was it?" The question seemed to come from everywhere.

"Tip Hall!"

"Hall?" Shorty echoed in the same breath. "What sicced you onto him?"

"A few deductions by a man who is as much a champion at brain work as he is at riding." Ringer laid his hand on Tom's arm. One hand twiddled his goatee as he glanced around the circle. "The two usually go together," he added thoughtfully.

"But how come you had deductions about that scissor-bill?" Spec asked, turning to the Indian. "Him being nothin' but an alley rat?"

"Jus' think about rats." A half-smile drifted across Tom's face. "Only rat do rat tricks. Vincent not rat. All you not rats. Not much lef' to figger."

"But a little intelligent figuring got a lot of answer," Ringer broke in. "We picked up the pair of tinhorns Hall was working with. They caved in and spilled the works when they saw we had 'em cold. It was a deal to clean up on some big bets. They'd staked their pile on Vincent, then tried to cinch it by hiring Hall to do the dirty work. His part was to put some kind of a kibosh on Vincent's two most dangerous opponents. He managed to cut this boy's latigo, but fortunately slipped up on whatever he had in mind to try on Ryan. It took our friend, here, to spot the seam in the blanket."

Tom had kind of edged back from the sheriff's words. His natural bashfulness was having a hard time trying to hide the shine in his eyes, as he pulled the flopping bandage off his head.

"Hey, gimme that!" Spec stepped over and lifted the bloody rags out of his hand. "I want to frame it, along with that championship picture I'm aimin' to get."

Tom looked blank as a poleaxed steer for a minute. Then his face dissolved into a mixture of wonder, unbelief, pride, surprise, and the shine of a new sun bursting suddenly out of a fog bank. "You want—? You think—?" Tom stammered.

"I want!" Spec stuffed the bandage into his pocket. "Things like that only happen once in a green moon. Can't afford to pass it up. We'll drift over to Hitchen's shop for the picture this evening."

Tom was still trying to make his head believe what his ears had heard, when a voice back in the crowd wanted to know what happened to Hall.

"Holed up somewhere," Ringer answered. "But we'll get him. He can't hide out indefinitely. And there will be nobody to cover for him from here on out."

Half a hundred eyes swung slowly around toward Vincent. I guess he could read the same question in all of them. It was a tight moment. His color had kind of faded out, but his backbone was still all in one piece. He took a couple steps forward and braced himself.

"Go ahead and say it!" he snapped. "You've been wanting to for three days: birds of a feather, and all that, or he wouldn't have been with me."

"Now take it easy!" Ringer interrupted. "Nobody's accusing you of anything. In fact, there's nothing to accuse you of, except being the second best bronc peeler in the country. I got it all from that pair of tinhorns over at the jail. They were just coppering their bets on you by suckering Hall in to give them the odds. He simply hung himself on your tail, under pretended friendship for a lone stranger, as a dodge to use your company for an excuse to sneak around the corral to get at the saddles. Knowing Tip Hall, it all fits him like a new shirt."

I caught the shadow of a nod as Vincent straightened up another inch. His face had brightened a lot, and most of the stiffness had run out of his body. Yet there was a hard set to his mouth.

My first thought was that he might still be a little on the prod over the way he had been treated. Then I heard kind of a wordless growl run through the crowd. I heeled around to see the same sort of cold tightness pinched down on everybody's face. It wasn't till a snarly voice back in the crowd suggested a necktie party for would-be murderers that I tumbled to where the hostility was pointed. Sheriff Ringer had just opened his mouth to speak his piece, when Tom's voice broke the tension.

"Guess medicine work for me," he broke in, his white teeth flashing in the first real grin I'd seen all week. He moved out in the open, where he could face everybody, his body kind of twisted sidewise to favor the cracked ribs. "Mebbyso Hall kick Vincent more worse than strike me."

"Huh?" Vincent leaned forward, as if half-expecting another barb. "Meaning what?"

Tom's grin spread a mite wider. "Mean he cause me draw big roan. Only horse can give ride to beat you."

Somebody laughed. It was a full-bellied hee-haw. The idea of such a backfire seemed to hit everybody in the funny bone at the same time. That picture of the smart jaspers outslickering themselves, to the tune of lost bets and a stretch in the hoosegow, washed out Tom's little crackup in one spurt.

135

"Just like the pup that thought the porcupine was some new kind of a cat!" howled Shorty, sagging over against Pink till he caught his breath. "Man, oh, man, how them quills is gonna smart!" He was off again.

An unbelieving sort of a look had slid across Vincent's face. Then his mouth suddenly began to tip up at the corners. At the same time, I saw his back straighten up, as though he had slipped a full shoulder-pack. It seemed he was better looking than ever.

"Could be, Chief," he said, turning his wide-open grin on Tom. "But my personal idea is that you are the only one geared to make a winning ride on that horse. Something tells me I'd never—"

"Hey, there he goes!" Joe Breen swung an arm toward the lower racetrack gate.

"Who? What?" yelled half a dozen voices. Everybody jerked around like a bunch of toy balloons on a string. Then we spotted the hunched-down rider on a buckskin cayuse drifting out from behind the horse barn, trying to act like he belonged there. But it was a losing play. Even without that spotted calfskin vest and big Mexican spurs, and his face twisted down out of sight, anybody could tell it was Tip Hall.

"It's him, all right!" Spec was already loping toward his horse. "Let's get 'im!"

The sheriff was right behind Spec. "This is my job!" he yelped. "We can't have a mob."

If anybody heard him, they didn't show it.

"Well," he shook his head, gathering up his reins, "I reckon it's all right, long as you just trail along to see how things come out."

The sheriff was a pretty practical man.

"We'll dang well make something come outa that lousy little varmint!" Baldy promised, making a grab for the nearest saddle, which happened to be Blondy's. "Crooks liken him—"

"Prob'ly'd even swipe another man's horse," Blondy finished the sentence, as a flying jump landed him behind the old puncher. "I reckon I'd best go along to see you an' him don't team up to steal everything in sight."

"Aw, shaddup an' hang on! Can't yo' see this is a chase an' time's a-wastin'? Anyhow, you know I jest mistook yore sorrel for my blue, him bein' closest."

The rest of the argument was drowned in the pound of running hoofs, as Vincent and Tom pulled up beside me. A dozen or so of

136

us were trailing Spec and the sheriff out the gate at a long lope. We saw Tip just going out of sight behind a row of houses, between us and the corner, as we came out in the clear behind the grandstand. Some of the boys swung off to the left, figuring to cut him off should he try for a getaway out through Main Street. Ringer bored straight ahead for the corner. Most of us stuck with him, betting on his judgment. He was right. When we rounded the string of houses, we saw Tip's dust still curling up over the little flat rimming the river.

There was only one way he could go in that direction. It was all bald bluff under the flat along that side of town. The one way down to the river was by the old stage road grade, which led on to the bridge and across to the railroad depot. Beyond the depot was all open country. We had him on a one-way track, where there was no dodging.

Baldy whooped like a scalp-hungry Sioux when we broke over the bluff to see our man fogging it across the bridge. I caught one glimpse of a scared face twisted back over his shoulder, as we jumped our horses down the grade in a cloud of dust. Tip was working his quirt and riding like the Devil sued for murder. But even he must have seen he was running on a short rope, by that time. We were gaining every rod. As he started up the slope toward the depot, Vincent and Tom plowed past me to swing into the lead beside the sheriff.

I could hear Shorty cussing the slowness of his horse from somewhere behind, as we topped out on the flat south of the depot. Then the sheriff let out a cloud of blue steam up ahead. I looked up to see what was cramping him; I figured we'd been doing right well.

The next breath, however, I wasn't so proud of us. My eyes had swung around enough to locate what had uncorked the sheriff. A long freight, loaded with sheep, was just rattling out over the switch points. Off to the right, where Tip had cut away from the road, the buckskin cayuse stood sucking in some of the wind that had been run out of him. Then I spotted what had sunk the prod into Ringer. The little cinch-cutter was halfway up the side of a sheep car, and still climbing. We started a run for the rocking cars, but a long, wailing whistle told us we had started too late. The hunched body on the third cartop ahead of the caboose was melting out of sight by the minute.

I heard Spec damning the luck of gutter rats and two-legged coyotes. He was even sorer than the sheriff, who looked like he'd had his nose rubbed in something not nice to talk about.

"I'll wire ahead," he snapped, turning toward the depot. "Somebody'll pick him up down the line and—"

"It looks to me," Rex Chillon broke in, cocking one eyebrow up toward the brim of his hat, "like he's already gone down the line— plumb to the end. Even a spell in your little old jailhouse couldn't put a man in a sorrier fix than being forced to skip the country on a sheep train."

Spec looked kind of buffaloed for a second. Then his eyes started to light up like a pair of carriage lamps popping out of a tunnel. "A skunk having to refugee himself under a sheep's belly!" His grin broke open to unload a belly laugh that boomed like a war drum across the flat. "Nothing left him but adopt a mama woolly for protection."

"And he grabbed it like he'd come home to stay," Blondy added, trying to make himself heard through the chorus of whoops boiling up like an unplugged geyser.

"He'd just as well stay, permanent," Shorty declared, "once this story gets around."

"And she'll shore enjoy gittin' around," Baldy promised. "Plumb an' complete, stink an' all. He'll never git back up in the air this side o' Mexico."

Tom pretty well wrapped up what counted most, when he swung his horse over alongside Vincent. "I t'ink," he said, slowly sorting out his words, "sheriff take stink animal off you, stink animal take 'no-good Injun' off me, sheep take stink animal off for all-time brother. Now, you'n me make for good ride. Nobody smell anything. All fine medicine, mebbyso, eh?"

I guess Vincent figured that kind of medicine was all right. At any rate, as Baldy put it some time later, "The way them two wound up shakin' hands, you'd 'a' thought Tip'd contrived the hull thing, jest to make champeens outa both of 'em."

CHAPTER 20

"Seein's how everybody's short on words," Blondy broke into a long silence, "I'd like to rise an' remark we've sure had ourselves a fine free-runnin' summer this year. All that horse stealing was wiped out, Tom set himself up as a head-high citizen with that bronc-ridin' championship, beef roundup has gone without a wrinkle in the blanket, and Jed has made it almost through to the long nights of winter without his big Swede biscuit-shooter cuttin' his hobbles. That, I claim is—"

"Aw, g'wan! I ain't—ain't—" Jed wiggled out from under the chuckwagon, trying to get a loop of the dangling brake rope off his neck. He looked like a snared woodchuck coming out of its hole. "I—I mean she ain't my—"

"Yeah? Then how come she writ you that letter last month?" Baldy broke in on his sputtering. "Wimmin that ain't don't use red ink on sky-blue paper an' put 'S W A K' outside the env'lope."

"Natural outcome of that midnight sashay down Shoshoni Street the last night of the Roundup," Blondy suggested. "And close-herdin' the gal in the dark shade of that cottonwood the best part of an hour. Such things usually work out to—"

"Aw, g'wan, jughead!" Jed came out through the rope on all fours, his unshaved mug rounding out the woodchuck impression. "I never!" he barked. "Leastwise, no hour. She wouldn't—I didn't—I mean, we—we—Aw, heck, you wan't even there!"

As the rest of us strangled over Blondy's wild guess, Jed's whiskery muzzle tipped up like a pup caught sucking eggs. Then he suddenly flopped back under the wagon, muttering to himself. He sounded like a squirrel working on a pine cone.

"True love must have its way at all costs," Blondy chuckled in the early dark, as the racket tapered off. He eased his back against a bedroll and hitched his legs over closer to the fire. "But I still claim we had a prime summer."

Nobody dragged up any arguments. I guess we all felt about the same. It was our last night on fall beef roundup, and the outfit was busy tasting the finish of a hard job that made the grade without hitting any snags.

Besides, it was one of those once-in-a-hundred early-fall evenings that makes a man feel ten feet tall. The honey-sweet warmth of afternoon had sort of boiled off to let the sharp, winy scent drift up from underneath. A fire wasn't nowise necessary, but it felt good, holding back the velvety dark, while the stars hung down within a couple of arms' reach and the sky draped itself like a big, blue blanket over the spine of the Elkhorns. The hush of drowsy night voices hung in the air like the whisper of some old, old tune faded out to a shadow. Soft stirrings of the contented beef herd floated up from the coulee bedground to melt in with the munching of night horses out beyond the bedwagon. Farther away, where the remuda grazed, the lazy tinkle of the old bay mare's bell kept tune to the spooky love songs of a pair of coyotes away off in the distance. Along with the sweet smells of October's Short Blue Moon drifting down off the high peaks, it was a time to make a man forget everything behind him and quit caring about what was ahead.

I reckon it's maybe just as well that way. Had we been able to see all the things slated to happen the next few months, most of us would have plumb overlooked a couple hours built especially for old men's dreams.

Old Bobby pretty well cased the subject one time, when Ben was fighting his head about a bad-looking tomorrow:

"Blind prophecy," Bobby told him, "is mairly the trioomph o' imagination o'er intollegence."

We weren't having any triumphs of imagination that night. Neither did we see any trouble clouds showing on the horizon as we pulled the wagon in to the ranch next day. That all came later.

Now, there is something kind of odd about how most big events are built up by a string of little stray happenstances. Looking back, you can usually see how the whole deal is like one of Bobby's "what-the-hell" puddings made from two weeks' leftovers. This particular affair took in quite a collection of makings. The main highlights included an outlaw horse, a Thoroughbred woman, a two-bit cow rustler, some smart Indian headwork, a set of heart throbs and the granddaddy of all white lies.

It all started right after we finished loading out our beef at the Neka railroad corrals. We had finished our drive the evening before, without any particular trouble. Neither had there been anything to get excited about during the loading this morning. Everything rolled along, like the doctor ordered, to find our string of beef cars ready to be picked up by the afternoon freight. We watched it rattle out of the yards, with Charley Norris and Jed Hart waving to us from the caboose platform.

The railroad, at that time, issued round-trip passes to beef shippers. This was so they, or some of their hands, could go along to look after the stock. There were often some down cattle to be prodded to their feet at the occasional stops, a job for men with cow savvy. No less important was their help with the unloading and reloading at the lay-over feeding stations.

Charley and Jed had won the free trip this fall. Charley had been saving his wages for a coon's age to try out a pleasure cruise down around the West Indies and Gulf of Mexico. Jed had been nursing a honing of the same size for a good visit with his kinfolks down in the Arkansas Ozarks. Ben had been predicting an easy winter, with little extra work before January, so he said they might as well go and get it out of their system. As soon as the cattle were delivered in Omaha, they would be free to take off on their dream trips for a couple or so months.

With the train whistling for the Badwater Crossing, a few miles up past Squaw Butte, the rest of us hightailed back uptown. Ben had paid us off the night before, and we had an itch to get rid of some of the money dragging our pockets down, before heading back to the ranch.

It must have been crowding two o'clock when I came out of the Neka Trading Company with my investment in blue Levi's and a new pair of Hyer boots under one arm. I was kind of dallying on the store steps, working on the last of my bag of chocolate drops, when my eyes picked up Tom Little Bear just going out of sight around the corner toward the Thunderbird Livery Barn. As I crowded the last two chocolates into my mouth, I noticed Ben was just leaving the postoffice to head in the same direction. I wrapped my arm a little tighter around my treasures and stepped down onto the sidewalk.

We'd left our horses at the barn, so I figured everybody was getting lined up to start home.

By the time I rounded the corner, however, I found something a whole lot different had started. A black-whiskered, bull-built sort of a jasper was out in front of the barn, trying to cut the hide off a big blue-roan gelding with a blacksnake whip. He not only had a running W on the blue's front feet, but had also run the rope up through a heavy spade bit. The horse was down in a heap. His bleeding mouth was dragged in tight to his skinned knees. Every time he moved, the bit gouged deeper. And every time he bawled his tortured misery, the man cut savagely at his foreparts, lifting a chunk of raw hide at every stroke. Meanwhile, a running fire of the dirtiest adjectives west of Kansas City caromed off the barn wall. Hard-shell range kid that I was, the sorry mess was enough to tip my stomach half over.

I was about fifty yards behind Ben. Tom had pulled up beside the disgusted-looking barn man, perhaps half that far farther on. My short glance had no more than collected the outline of the picture, when I saw Tom step up and say something to Black Whiskers. The big bruiser twisted on one heel to snarl a reply. Whatever it was, it brought the Indian's head up with a jerk, his eye flashing war signals and mouth putting it into words. In spite of his half-grown lankiness, he faced up to the big jasper with a sermon on dirty horse-beaters that would make your hair curl.

I guess it was plain surprise that held the fellow up as long as it did. Anyhow, Tom was down to the last chapter before Whiskers suddenly bowed his back to throw the whiplash straight at the Indian's face. Tom got one arm up in time to save his eyes, but the whip ripped a red slit through sleeve and skin halfway to his elbow. Fortunately, the barn wall was there to catch him, as he spun around and stumbled backward.

The next instant, Ben had dealt himself a hand in the play. How he got there in one jump is beyond me. But big as he was, Ben could make some surprising moves in a pinch. Tom hadn't much more than struck the barn, when he landed on Whiskers like a Nebraska tornado, jerking the whip away and spinning the man half around.

"Let's see you hit a *man,* you lousy coyote!" he growled, just above a whisper. "And with your hands! Or don't you use your dirty yella paws on anything but kids and helpless critters?"

The last came as Whiskers stood half crouched and motionless for

142

a moment. His lips skinned back from his teeth as Ben's words took hold. I never saw so much downright hate on the face of anything except a trapped wolf. The next second he charged like a rump-shot grizzly.

I'll never forget that fight if I live to name fourteen grandkids. They were both moose-strong and about the same age, around thirty. Ben's cougar-like speed and action well offset the other's extra weight and killing madness. His driving punch stopped Whiskers' first wild charge to start them in a toe-to-toe slugging match. Whiskers lost on that deal: his fists only landed about a fourth as often as Ben's. Ben was going round him, like a cooper round a barrel, when he suddenly bowed his head in a bull-like lunge. Both hands were clawing for Ben's body. It was plain he wanted to get the other down on the ground for some heavy gouging. But that didn't work so well, either. As Ben pivoted sidewise, his fists came up from underneath with a pair of uppercuts that rocked the horse-beater back on his heels and left his face a bloody smear.

Whiskers bawled like a shot-stung bull—and charged again, just as wickedly. It kept Ben stepping to stay on his feet. Then the jasper suddenly paused in midstride to throw a kick at Ben's groin. Ben managed to catch the heft of that one over on his thigh, but it hurt. I saw his lips go white. In the same breath, he closed in to smash a left hook into Whiskers' one good eye. A long, looping right landed just under the wishbone a moment later. The rest of it was too fast for me to sort out. I never saw a pair of wildcats tangle, but I'll always remember what such a scrap should look like. Both of them were down and up and over and under like a pair of uncoiled watch springs. Ben swapped a split lip for two smashing drives at the other man's belly, then sidestepped as Whiskers tried using his foot again. That play was a sad mistake. Ben caught him off balance, with one foot in the air. You could have heard the solid crash of his fist against that black jaw halfway uptown.

When Whiskers woke enough to sit up, he found Ben asking if he wanted any more. The fellow just pulled up his knees and waggled his head groggily.

"Then set a price on that horse!" Ben continued. "I'm buying him."

Whiskers got one eye partly open. "Like hell!" he lisped through the hole where two teeth had been. "I ain't sellin'."

143

"Think again, fella!" Ben stepped over and picked up the black-snake. "Or do I have to lick it outa you?"

"Not by a damn sight! I got something to settle with that strikin' bas—Ow-w-w!" His voice broke in a shrill yelp as Ben suddenly shot the whip out to rip a ragged chunk of leather from his boot top.

Something told me the whip got more than the boot top, the way Whiskers grabbed his leg. For a long moment the two glared at each other, wordless and murderous. Whiskers broke first. I reckon he saw there was no other out. He was too pooped to run and too weak to fight; Ben had really wrecked him. He finally hunched himself into a knot, like a calf born in a snowdrift, his tongue flicking in and out like a crippled rattlesnake.

"Le's see your hunnert an' fifty then, wise guy," he mouthed.

I caught my breath. That was a plain holdup, considering average horse prices. Besides, everything about this horse shaped up as being a fair stretch below average. Still, Ben was game. He never batted an eye at letting himself be caught out on a limb. Reaching over to tear a chunk of paper off my boot wrappings, he scribbled a bill of sale and tossed it over to Whiskers for signing. Meanwhile, he thumbed through a bundle of bills, sorting out six twenties and three tens, which he swapped for the paper.

"Hope he kills you!" Whiskers muttered under his breath.

"Just so you don't try to beat him to it!" Ben fired back, without any reservations.

"That's just about what he's apt to try," the barn man threw in, watching Whiskers limp away to get himself repaired. "He's a mean character. The way he bought this horse just so's he could kill him, proves that."

"What was the setup?" Blondy asked. He had drifted in with Baldy just in time to see the finish of the scrap. "Somebody selling horses for that purpose around here?"

"Not exactly." The barn man sagged back against the doorjamb and snapped his suspenders. "It was them movers going through to Buff'lo Springs as brought it. They was trailin' it behind their wagon when they stopped here for water. I was helpin' him an' the missus fill their kag, over at the pump, when this black-hearted jasper invites hisself over to look at the horse, maybe figgerin' for a dicker, I dunno. Anyhow, he'd no more'n got alongside the blue, when I heard a squeal an' some prime cussin'. The mover looked around and yelled a warnin', but not 'fore the horse had struck a second time.

144

The feller got clear 'thout a scratch, but he was shore mad. In fact, he was so mad he swapped the movers a plumb sound forty-dollar mare for the critter. Wanted to beat it to death for revenge. Admitted as much to me, later."

"Must be crazier'n a hoot owl," Baldy grunted. "Who is he, anyhow?"

"New man in the country, it seems. Only seen him a couple times, when he put his horse up here at the barn. He don't talk much. Heavy drinker, too, I hear tell. It's said he's got a homestead some'eres over 'round Tepee Springs."

The idea of the fellow being a nester didn't help make us feel any better toward him. Homesteaders weren't much more popular than Indians in Wyoming's open-range cow country at that time. Although the Tepee Springs jasper was off our range, eighteen or twenty miles to the northwest, he was still something we'd be happy to do without. This general dislike, added to what we'd seen on our first introduction, didn't broaden our views to any extent. We spouted off on everything from Baldy's idea of gun-runnin' such a sidewinder out of the country to Ben's gruff, "What's past is best buried," as we rode back to the ranch.

Tom didn't take any part in the argument. He stayed trailing along behind, leading the blue-roan. However, the way his black eyes pointed up every time Whiskers was mentioned, showed he wasn't apt to forget anything.

CHAPTER 21

I reckon his chumminess with that brute of a horse didn't help any with the forgetting. The animal had plainly been spoiled from away back, finally developing into a plumb outlaw. Tom, however, seemed to blame everything on Whiskers. At least, that's the way he acted when I said anything about it. Ben was all for turning the old warrior out on the range, before he hurt somebody, but the Indian had different ideas.

"No good, turn out," he objected. "Horse then not forget meanness. Better he know friends; then good horse you have for big money."

"Forget that money!" Ben snapped. "I got good value. And I don't want you having any accidents with that horse."

He let things ride, though, with kind of a "we'll see" sort of a grunt, when Tom shut the blue-roan up in one of the small corrals and set himself to packing feed and doping the beast's skinned hide.

Personally, I thought the Indian was loco. I couldn't see any future in that raw-boned, gangly legged, Roman-nosed chunk of white-eyed hellishness. Tom had to snub him to a post and tie up a foot every time he tried to play doctor. Even then, it was only luck and catlike dodging that kept him clear of those yellow teeth and striking feet.

"Yo're crazier'n a hoot owl!" Baldy grunted, watching him patch up a freshly torn pantleg one evening. "That cayuse'll git something more'n pants one of these days. And even iffen yo' do escape bein' massacreed, what've yo' got but a jugheaded outlaw the Devil hisself couldn't work?"

"Devil work is trouble," Tom told him shortly. "To make forget, take plenty time."

"Forget, hell!" Baldy stomped off to his bunk. "That old blue twister ain't forgettin' nothin', now or ever."

The rest of us more or less nursed the same notion. There didn't look to be any other answer. And we all picked up the name, Twister, as a prime monicker for the gelding. Along with his twisted mind and crooked actions, his body looked as if it had been twisted together with haywire in the dark. Even if he'd had enough meat to cover his knobby joints, it was hard to imagine him as anything a man would want to be caught riding in public.

Fortunately for the horse, though, Tom seemed blind to all that. In fact, he showed a lot of both liking and admiration for the blue-roan. He was always sing-songing away in some kind of horse talk whenever he was around the corral. In the course of time, we began to notice that Twister was accepting these attentions without going plumb on the warpath. This gradually developed to where the critter would stand motionless under the Indian's quiet hands and nicker after him when he went away.

Even Baldy was forced to backtrack enough to admit, "That dang croonin' gibberish o' his seems to've done something to the crazy old man-stomper."

But whether it was the crooning or simply the general effect of human kindness, I wouldn't know. At any rate, the horse seemed to like it. October ran into November while the two of them continued to use up most of Tom's spare time just fooling around the corral.

It was the Sunday morning after Thanksgiving, as I remember it, that the payoff came.

Tom had drifted outside, without saying anything, leaving the rest of us dawdling over a lazy breakfast. Blondy was sagged halfway around in his chair, augering something with Baldy. All at once, his drifting side glance hung fast on the front window. A second later, he kicked back his chair and made for the door.

"What stung him?" Baldy swung his head around in surprise. Then he suddenly jackknifed out of his chair, his eyes on the window. "Well, cuss my hide!"

He was halfway to the door when the rest of us caught up with him. We all jammed through the door just in time to see Tom riding Twister through the corral gate. And the outlaw was moving steady as a rocking horse. It was hard to believe! We just stood there with our mouths sagging open, like a bunch of baby robins, while he jogged across the yard and down to the creek and back. Both of them seemed right at home.

As if that wasn't surprise enough, all of us were struck by the complete change in the whole horse. It wasn't just his behavior; instead, it was the way his looks and action stood out as something we'd never seen. He was still raw-boned and ungainly as ever, but with his head up and Tom on his back, he caught your eye more like a cactus that had suddenly sprouted a bloom. And the way he stepped out, with that prideful bearing and silk-smooth movements, made you admit you were seeing a lot of horse, in any man's language.

He eventually turned out to be one of the best horses on the ranch. His brains were working all the time, picking up cow savvy almost overnight. And in spite of his animal-cracker looks, we found he could outrun and outlast almost anything in the neighborhood. He had only two things wrong with him. One was the way any sudden loud noise seemed to set him crazy. The other was that he wouldn't put up with anybody but Tom on his back. To everybody else, he was still the same old snake-headed outlaw.

"Which is all right with me," Ben said one afternoon, watching the two of them come down out of the Thunderbolt Hills with an old longhorn bunch-quitter that nobody had been able to bring in the last couple of roundups. "I'll never find a better hand to ride him, anyhow."

"Howsomever, yo're crazier'n a hoot owl to ever trust him," Baldy warned the Indian a few days later. "You maybe figger he's adopted yo', but his mind's jest a-teeterin' on a thin aidge. It's bound to tip over the wrong way one o' these times, when he gits yo' in some jackpot."

Tom just said, "Mebbyso; I guess not," and went right on riding the blue-roan.

Still, it kind of bothered me. I harbored a lot more faith in Baldy's half century of horse savvy than I had in Twister. It didn't seem reasonable that such a hair-trigger disposition could carry two personalities like that, without getting them mixed up sooner or later.

That was why I jumped to the conclusion the horse had backfired on Tom the afternoon I found him piled up, half dead, down in the river brakes.

It was a couple weeks before Christmas. Tom and I were holding down the ranch by ourselves, at the time. Ben had gone over to Bull River, on some horse-buying deal, taking Baldy along with him. With Charley and Jed not expected back for a month or so, and Bobby siding Blondy up at Billings for over the Holidays, things kind of depended on the two of us. Of course, that was no hardship. There wasn't much to do, except shovel hay to a few late-calving cows and see that the ranch didn't run away.

Tom and I pulled out to ride the river brakes for strays this particular day. He left right after sunup, or what would have been sunup on a clear day. Why we hadn't done this job the first thing after Ben left, while the weather was still good, is one of these things that are hard to either explain or find excuses for. Maybe we had just been having too much fun playing ranch managers. Or possibly some sort of a vacation idea had slipped up on our blind side. Anyhow, we let one day pile up on another, until we woke up one morning to find a four-inch white blanket on the ground and everything frozen up tighter than a rawhide casket. We promptly decided we'd better get busy. And getting busy immediately socked us with the fact that our shortcomings had led us head-on into a miserable day. A cold, cutting wind had set in out of the northwest. The washed-out sun was all but lost behind a dirty yellow overcast. It was no trouble at all to smell more storm in the air. Cold reality lost little time in prodding me with the need to hurry, if we didn't aim to get tangled up in something worse.

"Let's split up on this deal," I suggested, when we were halfway down Rope Creek. "Working the brakes from opposite ends will save a lot of time. We can meet at Sheep Canyon to bring our gatherings out on a straight shoot for home."

"Is good!" Tom agreed. "That way finish today." He pulled Twister around to head off cross-country for the south end of the brakes. "See you at Sheep Canyon."

I figured we would come out about even. Sheep Canyon was around two-thirds the way up the river toward where Tom would start my way. We should come together somewhere near the canyon. The prospect of getting the brakes cleaned out in one shot made me almost forget how the cold was clamping down. I sure admired my idea of splitting up to make shorter work of the job.

That good feeling was still warming my frost-puckered face when I shoved my little pickup of strays into the mouth of Sheep Canyon shortly after noon. The canyon, however, was empty as a barfly's pocket. Tom was nowhere in sight. Neither were there any cattle there. As it was too cold to sit around staring at the scenery, I hazed my gather on up the canyon, where they wouldn't scatter, and set out to meet him.

Half an hour later, I was still going. And I still hadn't seen anything of the Indian. I began to get a little worried. My uneasiness built up as I zigzagged back and forth in hopes of cutting his trail. All I found was several of the critters he was supposed to be gathering. None of them seemed to have been disturbed. Something was plainly wrong! Old Man Worry drummed that into my skull while I loped back and forth over the jumbled landscape at a pace that lacked even my usual small amount of common sense.

Then I ran into a little bunch of cows drifting slowly my way. They were all together. It looked like somebody had routed them out. I began to feel a lot better. It shouldn't have been anybody but Tom. I rode on around the next bend. There was no Tom in sight. And no more cattle. My spirits fizzled out like a burnt firecracker.

Something spooky started crawling up my spine. I hurried on. Cattle tracks, yes; the few I had met farther back. But no sign of any horse following them. I forgot all about being cold.

My mind was going around like a treed squirrel, trying to size up possibilities against probabilities. It would take hours to comb out all those gashes and gulches. And time was already eating into the afternoon. I was still fighting my head over the proposition when my Banjo horse suddenly threw up his head with a nicker. I sat staring out between his ears, half holding my breath. Then it came, a sharp whinny from somewhere around back of a rocky point. I wasn't too sure of the sound's location, but old Banjo seemed to know all about it. I let him have his way, as he pulled off to the right through a dry wash. A few minutes later, he brought us smack out to the trouble spot.

Tom was lying at the foot of a little shale-covered slope. He looked as near dead as anything I ever saw. He was all crumpled up motionless in the snow, the blood all over his face and coat to make the picture complete. Twister was right behind him. The old outlaw stood with his ears cocked forward, watching me ride up.

My first thought was Baldy's prophecy. If I'd had a gun, I'd likely have shot the horse right then and there. Instead, I could only promise revenge at the first opportunity. I got down and rolled Tom over. For a moment, I thought my first guess had been right. Then I caught sort of a low, bubbly groan. I began to have hope. But I could see he was in bad shape, unconscious and all over blood that had run down from his split scalp. One arm seemed to be broken, too. I'd have sold him pretty cheap, if there had been any bidders around. Still, there was some life in him, near as I could tell. I bound up his head the best I could with my neck muffler and cinched his arm to his body with my hair hackamore rope.

When I finally got around to look over what had happened, I saw where he'd been chasing a cow around the hillside. Tracks showed where the running horse had hit a slick spot of frozen snow and loose shale, throwing him into a hooligan down the steep pitch. They had both rolled all the way down, probably together most of the way, judging by the looks of Tom and the way Twister's saddle and hip bones were skinned up.

This discovery jarred me awake to another fact: Not only was Twister blameless for the accident, but he had stayed with his hurt rider until help showed up. His tracks proved he hadn't moved a dozen yards from the Indian in all the time they'd been there. That really got me. Any other horse I'd ever known would have at least wandered off to graze.

Nor was that all. Always before, the blue-roan had made it plain that I was full member of the enemy tribe. Now he just walked up quietly, ears tipped inquiringly forward, to look over my shoulder as I boosted Tom up out of the snow. There wasn't a trace of the old man-killer about him. It was plumb peculiar.

I had intended putting the Indian on Banjo, but something suddenly made me change my mind. I can't explain it. Probably it had something to do with Twister's actions; at the time, though, it seemed there was more to it than that. Anyhow, it all at once hit me that the horse wanted to help. And he never turned a hair when I reached for his reins and led him up beside the down Indian. Neither did he make an off move during all the horsing around I did in hauling that dead weight up into the saddle and lashing it down with my lariat. Instead, I distinctly remember how he kind of braced his feet and scrooched down, a couple of times, to give me the edge in hauling Tom's body up into place.

Maybe horses can't reason, like some folks claim. I won't argue. But you can't tell me that old outlaw wasn't using something besides animal instinct, the way he hunched around to help me get the Indian on board. I'll swear he followed my lead in every move I made. Then he traveled all the way home like he was packing eggs—picking his way like a cat through rough going and swaying into a gentle running walk on the trail. Every move he made looked to be as carefully figured out as if I'd told him how to do it. Likewise, at the ranch, he stood like a rock while I unloaded Tom and eased him down on my back for a quick carry into the house.

However, I didn't stop to think much about all that till later. I had other things on my mind right then. Tom roused to sort of a semi-consciousness as I got his clothes peeled off and him into bed. He passed out again while I was getting a fire going. That didn't do my confidence any good. I could see, without half trying, that he needed a lot more than I was able to give him. Doc Crowley seemed to be the only answer.

But to get the doctor? That meant leaving the Indian alone while I rode twenty miles to Neka. Nor was the nearest ranch any closer. In the meantime, he could be dying any minute, smashed up the way he was. On the other hand, if I stayed with him, about all I could do would be help him die. I could see I was pretty well rimrocked.

I batted my brains for some kind of a better out, while I filled some jugs with hot water, banked the fire, and tied down his blankets so he couldn't fall out of bed. I still hadn't found any easy answer. It looked like fish or cut bait. In the end, I shut the door behind me, with what must have stood for a prayer, and headed for the barn. It took only a few minutes to shove Twister and Banjo into the corral and rope out a fresh horse. With a last glance at the yellow spot of light in the kitchen window, I swung into the saddle.

CHAPTER 22

The trail to Neka looked like the longest stretch of real estate in the world, as I loped away from the ranch. The evening was already pinching off into dusk. I knew it would be well into the night before I could get back with Doc Crowley. And in the meantime—well, I tried to not think too much about that part. I guess I was a pretty scared young human.

The farther I went, the lower my spirits sagged. What if Tom woke up in some kind of a delirium, maybe blundering around to set the house afire? What if I was too late getting back with Doc Crowley to do him any good? It was beginning to spit snow again. What if it blew up a blizzard before I got to town? The trail never had looked so long and empty. The cold lump in my empty stomach was dragging down like a slug of bullet lead.

I'm still not ashamed of the way I yelled myself hoarse when, three or four miles down the trail, I saw a rider top out on a small knoll off to my right. The knoll was a couple hundred yards up the Tepee Creek Trail, from where it branched off of our ranch road. The bundled-up rider was jogging along, head turtled down in a big sheepskin collar to face the wind. I thought for a minute that my bawling was just blowing back in my teeth; the rider kept going, paying no heed. Then I heard my last yell slide down into a blown-out squeak of relief as the figure turned to face me, pulling up the horse. I immediately cut out through the sagebrush at a run.

"Hey!" I hollered, charging up the side of the knoll. "I need some help. Tom's maybe dyin'. He's all alone. I can't—"

"And who is Tom?"

The soft voice set me back in the saddle with a thud. I rubbed the frost out of my eyelashes and edged my horse closer. But there was no mistake. It was a woman's face that looked at me from above the sheepskin coat and batwing chaps. She tried to hide a smile as I worked at pulling my mouth shut.

"You were expecting someone else?" she said, sobering down all of a sudden. "I didn't mean to laugh."

"N-no, I wan't expecting nobody. I—I just saw you an' thought to get some help. I—"

"Is something wrong?" The low voice, now all sympathy, pulled the trigger on my whole tale of woe. I was really worked up.

"Of course," she said, without batting an eye, when I finished. "I'll be glad to do what I can. Would it help if I rode over and looked out for your friend while you go for the doctor? I could at least keep the fire going and be a little company for him."

"Sure!" I yelped in dizzy satisfaction. "That'll be great! Just folla my trail back to the house; there's a light in the window. I'll see you there!"

This last was over my shoulder as she headed up the ranch trail and I loped away in the direction of Neka. I was two miles down the line before I came to enough to wonder who she was and what such a handsome woman was doing out there in the middle of nowhere, at that time of day.

I did a lot of thinking from there on. She was a mighty pleasant subject to help keep my mind off the growing snowstorm and half-blotted trail heading off into the thickening dark. I did my best to keep her face hung up in my mind, like a picture on the wall. I could only liken it to a magazine cover I'd seen somewhere—outright beautiful, but kind of clouded over like it might have been nursing some troubled thoughts. She was around twenty-five, I judged, and built on one of those tiny Thoroughbred frames that even a cowhand's winter outfit couldn't hide. The only sticker was, I couldn't figure where she'd dropped from. I'd never seen anybody like that in the Splitrock country.

It wasn't till I got back with Doc Crowley, bucking a blinding snowstorm, sometime after midnight, that I found part of the answers. She gave some of them to Doc, as she passed him tools out of the water boiling in a bread pan, fixed bandages and helped him patch up Tom's cracked skull. I just stood around with a lamp in each hand, like they told me, listening to her replies while thinking how lucky it was that a new homesteader had to go to town for grub that particular day.

"But what's the matter with your man?" Doc blurted out, in his usual explosive way. "Is he sick, letting you make a day's ride for groceries in this kind of weather?"

She was bending over a pan of dressings at the time. I noticed her hands go kind of still for a second, like she'd run against a trip rope. Yet I didn't think much of anything about it at the time. Her voice sounded all right, when she spoke up a second later:

"He is over at Medicine Lodge, on business. I was alone. I simply found myself out of some essentials I'd neglected to get."

"Can happen. Dangerous trick, though, in this country. Now, if you'll steady this arm while I splint it—"

Doc was all business for the next few minutes. Then he turned to me. "When will Ben be back?"

"He figured the last of next week."

"If the weather doesn't hold him up. Hm-m-m. And this is only Wednesday. That means you've got to have some help."

Doc walked over to look at the calendar, chewing at his bristly mustache. He made me think of a Mexican goat working on the herder's straw hat.

All at once he swung on one heel, his finger stabbing out like a school ma'am's pointer. "You said your name is Mrs. Paget?"

"Yes, Betty Paget."

"And your man is to be gone for some time?"

She nodded.

"Then how about lending a hand here? This boy's life depends on some careful nursing for the next week or ten days. Curly, here, isn't qualified for anything he can't do on horseback, it's not safe to move Tom, and I can't stay. If you could take over the job till Ben gets back, it would be the finest thing since anesthetics were invented."

His proposition pulled my breath up short. This Betty Paget was the kind of a woman that bachelor outfits like ours have wild dreams about. And the comfortable cheerfulness of her just being on the job suddenly loomed up like a bonanza strike on a sand flat. I'll swear Doc looked just like Santa Claus when, after a second's pause, she lifted her wide gray eyes from Tom's bed to nod agreement.

"There's no good reason why I can't," she said, with kind of a wire edge to her voice. One hand lifted up to smooth the tangle of black curls back from her face. "Being alone until after New Years, it will be no particular inconvenience, I'm sure. And these boys do need help."

Doc reached over to pat her on the shoulder, his craggy face breaking out in the grin that made everybody forget his barking voice. "Good girl! Now let's have some coffee, so I can get started back to town by daylight. And"—his eyes canted my way for an instant—"you might spike Curly's with some of that whiskey. Otherwise, I'll have to work on him, too."

It was only then that I discovered I'd somehow jackknifed myself backward into the woodbox, without even kicking off my chaps and overshoes.

That next week was something that still warms a flock of memories. The storm had blown itself out enough to let me haze in the bunch of strays we had left in Sheep Canyon. Aside from feeding our winter horses and scattering a little hay to the stock that was making out in good shape in the fenced alfalfa field, I didn't have much to do but watch Betty help Tom get well. She was something to watch —everything a man could ask for to come home to. Too, she was doing a top-hand job with Tom. Doc was out on Sunday. He ran her into a corner, red-faced and waving her hands against his bawling praise for the nursing that had the Indian already in the clear. I'd have chipped in on this part, if I'd known how to handle words like he did. As it was, I just stayed screwed into Ben's rawhide rocker and let my feelings climb the air at their own gait. It sure looked like Lady Luck had moved in for the winter.

I was still straddle of my private pink cloud when Ben showed up the next week. It was Thursday evening, shortly after dark. He made it in just ahead of a real old ring-tailed blizzard that had been chewing at his coattail for the last five miles. It was the day before Christmas.

Tom was able to be propped up in bed, for the first time. Betty had banked him up against a pile of pillows so he could enjoy the little Christmas tree she had wrangled me into rounding up for a table decoration. I had to admit it was worth looking at, right sightly, in fact, the way she had euchred me into helping her rig it up with popcorn strings, homemade candy and some little presents we had concocted for each other. It made a real homey layout, especially with her all prettied up, like for a party, and the fire spilling warmth and cheerfulness all over the place.

I was cutting wood, out in the shed, when Ben rode in. The first I knew he was home was when I let myself in the back way with an armful of wood. He stood just inside the front door. His face still hangs in my mind as the picture of a kid who had suddenly woke up

156

to find himself inside a candy shop. He was still hanging onto the doorknob, and one foot was tipped up like he'd forgotten to put his heel down. I saw his eyes, kind of wonder-big, whip around the shiny lamplighted room. That is, they got halfway around. There, they came to a sliding stop, locking themselves on the tricky little figure standing by the stove. I didn't blame him. He'd never see anything prettier, that dark hair all rumpled up and a dab of cake frosting on one side of her chin.

It struck me that she was seeing things, too. At least, there was something mighty queer in both their faces as their eyes met. They just stood there, staring at each other for a minute, as if they were talking without words. Maybe I was kind of confused, but that's the way it struck me. Anyhow, it only lasted a minute. Both of them wheeled around, sort of startled-like, when I dropped my wood into the box with a crash.

I thought they looked a little mite foolish about it, but maybe that was just some more of my imagination. Everything seemed normal enough when I straightened up from the woodbox.

"It looks like things have been doing around here since I left," he said to me, with kind of a questioning grin on his face. He was starting to unbutton his coat, fingering one button at a time, kind of absent-minded like. "Or am I too froze to know what I'm seeing?"

"They have and you're not." I grinned back at him. "Broken Arrow's really been makin' history lately." I motioned in the general direction of the stove. "This, here, is Betty Paget, Ben. She's to blame for everything good that's happened since a week ago yesterday."

"How do you do, Mr. Duane," she said, kinking a little smile. "I hope I am not intruding. Curly and Dr. Crowley pressed me into service while you were away. My husband and I are new settlers over northwest of here."

"Mighty glad to know you, ma'am!" Ben got his foot down and made it across the room without losing his footing. His grin was spread out like a busted seam in a wagon-sheet as he shook hands. "This is the greatest homecoming I've had since the year it froze all summer."

As they stood there hanging on to each other's hand, like one was scared the other might disappear up the chimney if they let go, a sort of a whisper pulled my head around to see Tom braced up against his pillows. His eyes were lighted up like a pair of new conchos as he watched them. He was mumbling something about "Spirit

Watcher" and "Great One," as his fingers played with the little medicine bag he always wore around his neck.

I walked over to hang up my coat. Something in the air made me wonder if I hadn't better say a few words to my own Great Spirit, too.

I don't know much about such things, but it looked like somebody must have been listening. At any rate, things couldn't have worked out better, if we'd had it made to order.

I'd never had any experience with story-book Christmases, but I guessed I could recognize one when I saw it. This one had everything. The outside work was all up in shape, with the stock in good order. After we'd brought Ben up to date on Tom's accident, and how well he was doing, we all settled down as happy as a bunch of dogies in a clover patch. One look at Betty, busying herself around the stove, while Ben sprawled out in his big rawhide rocker, his pipe going and one foot hooked over the fireplace screen, was enough to trap any stray into wanting to be house broke. There was the decorated tree and table loaded with hot grub. The fire was spreading out warmth and comfort, like a warm blanket. The wind whistling down the chimney and whipping the storm into a white smother outside, seemed like something a whole world apart.

Ben acted about like I felt. I had never seen him loosen up like that before. He had dished out a whole flock of compliments on the way we had handled things while he was gone. Between admiring our Christmas fixings and cracking jokes with Tom, he made out to keep Betty blushing over a string of ten-dollar words about her part in the deal. Baldy, he said, had stayed over at Bull River to spend the Holidays with his niece. That left it to the four of us to celebrate in our own way. All I could think of was the color picture some artist had fixed up for the cover of the *Rocky Mountain Stockman*.

Right after supper, Ben got the notion to pack the tree over to the bed. He claimed it would make the Indian feel more like he was in on the affair, for sure. Judging by Tom's looks, when he set it down, that was only saying half of it. I looked up to see Betty's eyes shining even brighter than the Indian's. Maybe Ben noticed that, too. Anyhow, he shoved her into the rocker and set me to washing dishes, while he stirred up a batch of Tom-and-Jerrys. Altogether, we made a plumb perfect "Home for Christmas" setup, even to the snow piling up on the windowsills.

I guess Tom felt pretty much the same way. It was something

plumb new for him, too. I never saw such a mixture of pleasure and unbelief on anybody's face, as we opened our few packages, munched popcorn and followed Betty through some of the old songs. Every little while, I'd see his fingers go for that little medicine bag.

That medicine bag must have packed a passel of real authority inside its buckskin cover. Tom never would tell me what kind of insides it had; he claimed it would break its charm to talk about it. It's hard to believe there was anything but superstition about the thing. Yet, it, or something else out of the ordinary, seemed to be working in our favor all the way through.

Tom's busted skull and arm were healing up amazingly fast—Doc said it was against all the rules of medical history. Maybe he meant it. It was often hard to tell whether Doc was telling things straight or springing some kind of a joke. Anyhow, it cleared the air for a lot of good feeling.

Maybe the blizzard had something to do with our feelings, making the cosy shutinness seem just like a continued party. The storm didn't blow itself out till Sunday night. And all the while, Ben and Betty were hitting it off like two of a kind. She acted like a kid out of school, taking everybody along with her in whatever fun she might think up. He was never far behind. Tom had improved enough to enjoy it all. He even took part a little bit in his own quiet way. As for me, I wouldn't have swapped places with the governor. Still, it was Ben who was always out in the center, making the biggest splash. He had shed his shell to show a fun-loving streak as wide as a barn door.

That is, he showed it whenever he was around the house. But nights, after we'd gone out to the bunkhouse to bed down, his light-heartedness seemed to hit hard going. I could tell something tough was grinding on him. It had me puzzled, with everything shaping up so fine. I was figuring back over the past weeks, trying to locate any misplays I might have made, when he suddenly set me back in my bunk with a blunt question:

"D'you know who Betty Paget is?"

"Why, no," I stuttered. "I—I guess she's just Betty Paget."

"Exactly! And that means she's Buck Paget's wife."

"Who's Buck Paget? I never—"

"Yes, you have! You watched me knock hell out of him for cutting up Tom and that blue-roan last fall. I hunted up his name on that bill of sale, to make sure."

"What? You mean—?"

"I sure do! And to think he snared a girl like Betty!"

I reckon my popped-out eyes showed all the blankness I felt. Anyhow, he went right on with his explanation:

"Jim Perry told me about this Buck Paget, the last time I was in town. Meant it as kind of a warning, I guess. He'd heard about our ruckus and, living over on lower Tepee Creek, had come to know what sort of an ornery jasper he is. Paget, he said, is a mean character when he's had a few drinks, which is more often than not. Furthermore, he's been making some threats that would warrant me keeping my eyes open. Jim is a good neighbor, and didn't want to see me run into some kind of a deadfall."

"I don't reckon you have anything to be afraid of," I snorted.

"Probably not. But it was neighborly of Jim to tip me off. You can never tell what sort of a turn a warped brain like that might take. And with him filing a homestead on Tepee Springs last fall, he'll be around where it's handy to keep feeding a grudge. Anyway, there he is, and will likely remain. Jim says he is figuring on stocking up in the spring. Meanwhile, he spends most of his time off some place where he can booze and gamble, while his wife holds down the claim. His general cussedness has soured everybody over in that community. They all keep clear of his place, in spite of their sympathy for the woman being alone days and weeks at a time."

"Then that's why she had to ride to town for grub last week," I broke in, the light of discovery exploding in my face like a busted watermelon. "He left her without—"

"Yes, and most likely without any fuel, either. Jim said folks had seen her out rustling wood. The lousy coyote! In midwinter, too. And she's such a plumb Thoroughbred. Oh, Hell!"

I heard him thumping around in his bunk, like a sick calf in the woodbox, when I finally went to sleep. And I was a long time going to sleep that night, too.

I woke up the next morning, saddled with the notion that we ought to deal ourselves in on the affair. The idea of Betty having to put up with a thing like Whiskers was hard on my stomach. But Ben couldn't see it that way. It was plumb off our range, he said, and any interference would only complicate things for her. Moreover, he threatened to lift my scalp if I ever even looked like I knew the Paget history.

That's how things stood when he took Betty home a couple days

160

later. It had cleared off, still and sunny, after the storm. Tom was out of danger, she wasn't needed any more, and a lot more stubborn talk about how she had to be getting back to look after the homestead. She put up another big argument about Ben's idea of going with her, claiming it was absolutely unnecessary, but he was just as stubborn. They rode off shortly after breakfast. I noticed he was packing along half a quarter of beef and some other stuff in a grain sack.

It was away after dark when he got home. He was as proddy as an old longhorn with a new calf. The shreds of juniper bark I found still hanging to his lariat explained some of it. However, I knew it wasn't just the work of snaking in wood and cutting it up for her that griped him. Helping folks was Ben's long suit. But the idea of Betty being left alone in midwinter, without grub or fuel, while Whiskers was off enjoying himself, God knows where, really ground him raw.

He shot off one big burst about "screw-brained women" who let some slick high-grader take 'em into camp, and then went through hell and high water under a nutty idea of wifely loyalty; but mostly, he went around like a sore-head bear shot full of porcupine quills, saying nothing. This showed up most whenever something around the house reminded him of her.

As a matter of fact, there were plenty of reminders for all of us. Betty had sparked a rainbow that stood for a lot of things we hated to let go of. After she left, it seemed like everything we looked at had lost most of its color.

And thinking of her back under the thumb of that chiseling horse-killer didn't help matters any. It was likely a good thing that Tom was still under wraps. The way his hard, black eyes shifted toward where his rifle hung, every time Whiskers was mentioned, reminded me of some of the old-timers' opinions about true Indian nature.

When he was able to get out to Twister's corral again, I could see he was still working on ways and means not favorable to Betty Paget's husband. I don't suppose he actually classed Betty along with the horse; still, it was his weakness for both of them, coupled with their mutual source of trouble, that filled his mind with a double-barreled load of war medicine. Ben had to put up quite a talk to bring him around to accepting white man's reasoning. Even then, I had a hunch this acceptance wasn't anchored any too deep.

That was why I was more or less edgy when we drifted over to call on Betty as soon as Tom was able to ride. I didn't know but what the Indian reasoning might win out if we ran afoul of Whiskers. Consequently, I talked myself hoarse, trying to make him see the heft of Ben's advice about making sure she was alone before showing ourselves. I guess it was my picturing the whole thing as a scheme to keep her clear of more trouble that finally won his promise to play it cagey.

One or both of us rode over there every once in a while, after that. Whiskers was seldom home. What few times we did see him or his horse, from the timber fringe up on the ridge, we cut back around without him knowing it. Betty was always tickled to see us, whenever we showed up. I reckon we were the only callers she ever had; at least, the only ones she could call friends. Tom took off for a visit every chance he got, whether I went along or not. He usually took her some trinket he'd made in sort of appreciation for all she'd done for him. I guess he'd have cut his own throat for her, if there'd been any need.

I don't know how often Ben managed to satisfy himself that Betty was making out all right. It seemed he was off by himself a lot of times that winter and spring. I knew better than to ask questions. Yet the way he grumped around and sat staring out of the west window of an evening made me wonder if he didn't have a little Indian nature in his makeup, too.

All this naturally tapered off somewhat when we got busy with spring work. Then, too, after Whiskers brought in a little bunch of cows, following the March thaw, it was harder to find Betty alone. Along with this, Ben tried to snub down his spookiness with the idea that maybe things might adjust themselves after the jasper got interested in building up his outfit. That was reasonable thinking, but I noticed he made it a point, every so often, to see how the adjusting was coming on.

It was about this time, around the first of May, that we woke up to the fact that we had plenty to think about, without worrying over the Pagets. That was when we first discovered rustlers had moved in on us.

CHAPTER 23

Our new trouble started when Blondy found a dozen Broken Arrow heifers missing off the head of Rope Creek. At first, we naturally thought they'd just drifted away someplace. Then Charley Norris discovered another little bunch had disappeared out of Badger Basin. We all rode for two days without finding a hair of them. Jed Hart even cut a circle clean around Warbonnet Mountain, looking for some sign. He drew just as big a blank.

Jed was headed back home, trying to think of some other possibility worth a look-see, when he met Dave Norcliff over on Piñon Creek. Dave was on the same kind of an errand. The Open A Four, he said, had seventeen head vanish a few days before. Jim Perry had also lost some, along with the Roundtree boys, Sid Andrews and Hank Bonnett. Even Buck Paget's little scissor-bill outfit had been nicked for nine top cows. Everything fit the same pattern: somebody was picking off small bunches in odd corners, where they likely wouldn't be missed until after all sign had been tromped or weathered out. Figuring the losses over so much territory, in such a short time, it almost had to be an organized gang job.

Everybody was up in the air. It was a good deal the same wrinkle the old Ruston gang had worked over in the Burnt Cabin neighborhood a few years before. That was before my time, but I'd heard plenty about how they half crippled some of the ranchers before they won themselves a necktie party. It was plain that Ben had visions of history repeating itself, when we buckled down to a range tally of our losses. It was a lot heavier than we'd first thought. A week later, Baldy failed to locate eleven two-year-olds that had been with a bunch hanging out over back of Pipe Spring. The rustlers were still in business!

Checking our tally against other ranchers showed us to be the hardest hit of any of them. Still, the whole valley was suffering. Baldy came out from town with a load of groceries to tell us the whole country was on the warpath. Sid Andrews and Jim Perry were beginning to talk up a vigilante crowd. All they needed was Norcliff and the Roundtrees to make it a going concern. Even old Whiskers was ready to throw his hat in the ring. Baldy said he was parading the street with a gallon jug of Old Crow and a 30-30, bawling all kinds of uncharitable remarks about a country that would stand by while a struggling newcomer lost a slice out of his two-bit herd.

"Paget was crazier'n a hoot owl, till he fell down an' shot a hole in the sidewalk." Baldy's face lit up with the memory. "That seemed to some'at satisfy him for the time bein'; leastwise, he went right off to sleep a minnit later. Red Sumpter had some o' the boys come bed him down in the livery barn till he got rested up for the balance o' the campaign. Right bloodthirsty, he was, though he might be sorta dang'rous in a posse."

I can't say that Baldy's story worked up any particular sympathy for Whiskers, but I noticed Ben took it sort of solemn-like. Maybe his mind had jumped ahead to figure how this might backfire against Betty. That's just a guess. But he seemed overquick to point out how the loss of part of the man's little herd could easy wreck his chance for the success that might make a decent citizen out of him.

I don't reckon any of us did much worrying about Whiskers' bid for good citizenship. Personally, I'd have been glad to see rustlers, or anything else, freeze him out of the country. But with Ben calling the play, and him looking like he had Betty on his mind, we did a little extra riding to keep an eye on Paget's range. Most of this was left to Tom and me. Our line riding ordinarily covered most of the country from the west fringe of the Thunderbolts to where Whiskers' territory more or less joined ours. By stretching our days somewhat, we could usually take care of everything to the ridge east of Tepee Springs. Times when we had to spend a day or so down toward the river, we'd make it a point to cut for sign over Tepee Springs way the first thing next morning. It all worked out pretty well, in what Ben called a neighborly way, without giving Whiskers cause for accusing us of stepping on his toes.

Unfortunately, none of our riding seemed to pay off. Stock kept on disappearing, a few head here and there, all over the country. We lost fifteen or twenty within the next ten days. According to the moccasin telegraph, the other ranchers were getting the same kind of

164

a deal. The worst trouble was, we were losing twice as many as anybody else.

Things dangled along like that for maybe a couple more weeks. The rustlers seemed to be pushing their luck along at the last. Paget claimed to have lost three head out of a bunch he'd been close-herding near their cabin; right under his nose. Dave Norcliff had one of his prize purebred bulls taken along with seven top-grade cows. We were shy another eleven out of our two-year-old bunch at Pipe Springs. Andrews' vigilantes were all dressed up, with no place to go, while the rest of us were all going without getting anywhere. Everybody was jumpy as a bunch of old maids in a dark alley. I reckon we would have just plain run ourselves ragged, if it hadn't been for Tom Little Bear.

The day the big showdown started was just like any other sunny afternoon. It was on a Thursday. I recall that day in particular, because of Tom riding Twister on Mondays and Thursdays all during that time. We had been up Piñon Creek, over to Pipe Springs, and then swung down through the fringe of the Thunderbolts toward the river.

Shortly after noon, we ran into Charley Norris. He had been riding the juniper ridges that ran up into the Thunderbolts from Rope Creek. As he was working toward the east, we figured to meet up with him again at the river and go on in to the ranch together.

It was one of those hot, sultry afternoons, so common to the high country along the tail end of spring. We were dried out like a couple of cork legs by the time we sighted the river. Our horses showed they felt the same way by swinging off from the easier round-about slope to head directly across a scab-rock flat toward a little cove just above where the river spilled into The Narrows.

I told, back here a ways, something about how Splitrock River snaked its way through the sage flats and foothills on its way to what we called The Narrows, at the foot of the valley. The Narrows was the funnel-like bottle-neck through which the stream surged into the big gorge of Splitrock Canyon. This opening was a steep and crooked slit-like gap, a few yards wide and less than a mile long, which seemed to have been made by some shakeup that split the mountain in two. Time and weather had worn the sheer-walled, gutlike channel into a regular sluiceway, with the normally quarter-mile-wide stream suddenly pinched into its narrow width. Here, the water took on more the look of some prehistoric monster racing hell bent for leather, foam flying from its savagely whipping humped back. Most people were careful to stay out of its reach. The bulk of the fifty-mile canyon below was on the same order. Raw cliffs and craggy walls crowded in on both sides. This kept it pretty well shut off from everybody, except what Baldy called "fellers that swap their brains for a spook sheep," and outlaws on the dodge.

I was still down on my belly, sucking up water, when I heard Tom's voice above the roar of the river. I hitched up on one elbow to twist around in his direction. He was a couple rods away, down on his knees, pointing at the ground where he'd been drinking.

"Come, Curly!" he called, in sort of a tense way. "See this!"

"Whatcha find?" I asked, heaving myself up to waddle over toward him. "Nuggets'r something?"

His answer was a motion with the pointing finger. I bent down to look—and stayed that way. Plain bug-eyed wonderment held me doubled over like a busted whipstock, trying to digest the marks of half a dozen fairly fresh cow tracks heading out into the river.

The little cove we were in was sort of a quiet backwater, caused by the stream piling back on itself as it hit The Narrows. A yard-wide shoreline of sandy wash had settled along the strip between scab-rock and the river. Protected as it was from the sweep of the current, the tracks were easy to see, until they blacked out under the deepening water.

We both straightened up at the same time, staring at each other like two chambermaids at opposite ends of the same keyhole. Neither of us had to tell the other what he was thinking. Free cattle didn't deliberately walk off into the middle of that churning river.

It was a half hour later that we sat down to assay our findings. Or rather, Tom's findings. Only an Indian could have located the bits of sign he discovered scattered along the quarter-mile of riverbank. Aside from the narrow strip of sand, where we had been drinking, a dozen or so yards along, scab-rock ran clear down to the water, and was washed clean. Over this, he ranged back and forth, like a coon-hound on a cold trail, pointing out bits of misplaced rock and hoof scratches that no ordinary jasper would ever have seen. Some, he reckoned to be right new, while others were so weathered out that he balked at guessing their age. But all of them, in his opinion—and mine, too, after he explained the how and why of things—were made by stock moving down to the river. Altogether, it looked like a lot of animals had gone there over a sizable stretch of time. The three dif-

166

ferent marks of horse hoofs, he picked out, said the cattle had been driven.

"Must be the rustlers' trail, all right," I agreed. "But where'd they go from here?"

"Down river," Tom grunted, like explaining things to a mental defective. "Go no place else. Can't cross that." He swung an arm toward the tumbling water.

My eyes slid across the current boiling canyonward as though sucked through a funnel. He was right. Nothing could cross that runaway stream, or get out over the rock ledge on the opposite side. Such a devil-spawned outlaw, crowding its center up into a foamy backboned ridge, sure wouldn't let go of anything it once got hold of. Even I could see that, after he pointed it out.

"But why would anybody throw cows in there?" I puzzled. "Nothing could live to come out the other end."

Tom didn't answer right off. He seemed to be sorting something far back in his mind. I tried studying my mind, too, but all I found was sort of a loose rattle. It didn't improve any as I watched the sun slide down toward the west end of the Thunderbolts.

Then the Indian's voice suddenly broke in on my jumbled wits: "Oven Crick Canyon," he was saying. "There no place else."

He picked up a scrap of rock and began drawing his ideas in the sand, the only way an Indian can ever explain anything. The way he had it figured was that the rustlers were divided into two bunches. One set was coyoting around the valley, picking up stock to shove into the river. Their partners would be hid out somewhere down the canyon, set up to gather in anything that The Narrows spewed out. There were some spots of fairly quiet water around the bends below, where good swimmers could make it out onto the sandbars. Of course, there was bound to be some loss, but whatever did make it through would be clear gain. Anyhow, the way the current sucked everything toward the center would hold most of the critters away from the rock walls of The Narrows. And the beauty of it was, it made a plumb trackless getaway route. But for those few stray hoofprints in the sheltered cove, half the country might have passed that way without spotting anything.

"That much sounds reasonable," I agreed, after a little head scratching. "But how would they get cows out of that canyon?"

"Mebbyso game trails there." He reached for his rock again. "Go

167

down canyon for water. That make way for cows to go up an' cross Elkhorn divide to Montana. Smart thief mebbyso find way."

This Oven Creek Canyon was only a short stretch below The Narrows. It opened into the main gorge on the opposite side of the river from where we were. Heading up across the state line, it meandered down through a nest of busted-up country that only cougars and mountain sheep could appreciate. It meant a couple days' ride, around by the ford, to get over there from our side of the river. As there wasn't anything over there that anybody wanted, not many of the valley ranchers knew much about it. There was a chance, though, that somebody might have figured a way to work stock out through it and over the state line.

I studied Tom's scratchings and dry-combed my head some more. The idea had possibilities. Still—

"Hey, what's the powwow?"

I jumped a foot, even with a seat-of-the-pants start. But it was only Charley. He'd seen our horses and cut across to join us. And he looked as bamboozled as I felt about what we had stumbled onto. He got down to look at the tracks while we filled him in on the way we'd doped the thing out.

"Well, I'll be cross-hobbled and throwed for a fall!" His eyes jumped from the cow tracks to the river, then back to us. "That's one of the slickest plays in the book. You boys sure hit the jackpot."

He turned suddenly toward his horse. "Ben figured on going over to the Bent Triangle for that vigilante meeting this evening. Maybe we can catch him, if we hurry."

I was right behind him. When I swung around to go for my horse, I saw Tom still squatting on his heels. He was threading one of Twister's reins through his fingers.

"Come on!" I called. "It's gettin' late. Ben'll be gone."

But Tom shook his head. "You go for Ben," he said. "I see mebbyso get 'round mountain an' down to river below Narrows. Might find cows there someplace before night."

Charley stopped with one foot in the stirrup, his head swiveling around. "That's an idea, Tom. You might make another strike. And say—" He brought his foot back down, thoughtfully canting an eye skyward. "There is sort of a coyote trail around there. I happened onto it winter before last. Trailed a deer over it a ways. It comes out beside the lightnin'-killed pine you can see just beyond that red-streaked rimrock, up on the east point o' the hill." Our eyes followed his pointing finger aimed at the jutting rimrock. "From there, it twists down through some broken rims to a narrow gulch. The gulch might open out to the river, I dunno. It's hard to tell what goes where, unless you follow it up, and I had no call to do that. But allowin' it does lead to the river, my offhand guess is that it'd be somewhat opposite to Oven Canyon; a game trail to water, maybe."

"Good!" Tom nodded, squinting at the setting sun. "Mebbyso time for look-see 'fore dark. You get Ben!"

"And if we're not here, you'll know where to find us," I added, suddenly switching ideas, to go with the Indian.

"Have luck!" Charley stepped up on his horse. "And leave some trail markers, if you find a way through," he called back over his shoulder.

It wasn't what you'd hardly call a trail; a body could have missed it entirely. Rock slopes and wind-scoured ledges don't hold travel marks very well. And late afternoon shadows made it worse. Without Charley's dead pine to center on, and Tom Little Bear's tracking sense, we'd never have got anywhere. It was his gimlet eyes that first spotted where a rock had been dislodged. After that, we picked out three or four tracks, one at a time, in the few spots of softer ground.

Farther on, there were some other marks, here and there. They all looked pretty meaningless to me. Tom, however, read them as a rider going down and back a few days before. I tried to kid him about the color of the horse and age of the rider, but found myself out on a limb when he bent suddenly sidewise to pick three black horsehairs off a dead mountain mahogany bush.

Twenty minutes later he stopped to point out a blurry skid-mark in the dirt. "Dif'rent horse," he grunted. "Mebbyso two, t'ree week old."

That shut me up for good. I turned the headwork over to him, while I started wondering how we'd ever find our way back out of that place in the dark.

But the trail, if you could call it that, led us on down to the gulch Charley had mentioned. And it kept going, like he had guessed. Deer and elk had both used it, their tracks occasionally blotted by horse-hoof marks.

But I soon found the place wasn't rigged out for any picnic. It was narrow as a sod-buster's mind and crookeder than a money-lender's pet schemes. Time and weather had gouged the high walls into a one-way alley, half blocked with tumbled boulders, rock outcrops and scraggly brush. It seemed like we were forever corkscrewing our way over, around and through the obstacle course nature had set up. I was beginning to think we had walked into the Devil's own trap, for sure, by the time we at last squeezed out through a slit-like crack in the lower canyon wall.

This opening was offset enough that nobody would ever have noticed it as an actual break in the canyon wall. Yet, coming at it from the gulch, it furnished a direct outlet to the river shortly below The Narrows. And there was still light enough to see the darker mouth of Oven Canyon across the river, almost dead ahead of us. Moreover, this particular spot in the river was fairly quiet water. I guess some kind of an uptilt in the channel bed sort of held it back until it broke over into the next rapids.

I pounded my compliments into Tom's back. Here was the third straight trick he had taken. I knew he'd go through hell and high water to locate Ben's stock, but I'd never guessed he'd do the job by brain power.

"No cows here," he fired back, hamstringing my big blowoff. "Mebbyso bring Ben on no good chase."

"Horse feathers!" I snapped. "You didn't expect to find any cows hangin' up on these canyon walls, did you? Just wait till we get over on Oven Crick. My money says we'll find plenty there."

And that wasn't half of it, as we were to discover later.

The offset opening into the canyon made a good hiding place. Hunkered up behind some rocks, we could see up and down the river and quite a stretch up Oven Creek. There was nothing in sight anywhere we looked. Still, if there were some of the rustlers over there, holding the cattle, the chances were all in favor of a lookout hid out somewhere to ward off any surprises. We augered the possibilities for quite a spell, but finally decided we'd better wait till dark before making any move, providing Ben and the boys didn't show up before then.

As a matter of fact, it was hard to figure anything definite about Ben. Everything depended on whether Charley made it to the ranch in time to catch him before he got away for the Bent Triangle meeting. A fifty-mile chase would eat up a lot of time. Also, night travel, and maybe some trouble spotting our trail markers, could louse things up further.

Meanwhile, the rustlers might be squared away to shove their gatherings out of the country, if not already on the way. It looked like a poor time to sit on our hands. The best bet we could see would be to work our way up Oven Canyon, as soon as it got dark, and try to locate the herd. Then, by coyoting around to get above them, we'd have a chance to set up an ambush that would hold up any getaway before help moved in from the other end. The way things stood, it looked like the only sensible thing to do. That's why the shut-down of dark found us tying our clothes on top of our saddles and swimming across the slack current, hanging onto our horses' tails.

We pulled out on a little bar shortly below Oven Creek. Night and a clear sky carried a lot of chill with it. We humped ourselves around, shivering into our clothes and draining the water out of our rifles. There wasn't too much time to waste, if we aimed to get ourselves lined up before the moon rose.

However, just as we started up the shoreline toward the canyon mouth, Tom suddenly pulled his horse back with a sharp hiss. I almost bumped into him. Then I saw what had stopped him. I had to pinch myself to make sure my eyes weren't seeing spooks. That little light bobbing out from around the last bend in The Narrows was plumb unsettling. I felt my breath stop for a full minute, watching it ride the crest of the current midway of the stream. It was almost abreast of us before I finally made it out to be a weighted can or bottle plugged with a kerosine wick. We just sat there, watching it float past us to disappear down the gorge.

"Now what?" I half-whispered, still too jumpy to speak out loud.

"Sign talk," Tom whispered back.

We both knew the roar of the water would drown out any ordinary noise we made, but that didn't loosen our tongues.

"Sign good for us, too," Tom went on, after a minute's study. "Tell us mebbyso better hide."

He was already leading Twister back toward a wall-like bulge of the cliff that looked big enough to keep both horses out of sight.

CHAPTER 24

Our hideout was a hundred or so yards below the mouth of the creek. Here, the canyon wall elbowed out almost to the river. Behind it, was a three-cornered pocket that held the horses and left us room to watch whatever went on. Our medicine was still working strong.

I was still shaking hands with luck, when we heard a faint yell from up the creek. Maybe ten minutes later, we caught the uneasy bawling of cattle. I craned my neck around the rock to see a rider coming out of the canyon, heading our way. Looking farther, I could make out the shadowy shapes of a couple more jaspers, who were crowding a few head of cows down toward the water. The first man had dropped down the riverbank almost to where we were holed up.

We'd no more than got this all digested before Tom nudged me and pointed upstream. I pulled my eyes around to follow his finger. Though his figuring had taught me what to expect, I had to bat my eyes a second time and pry my mouth shut to actually believe it. The thin string of dark backs and tossing heads, coming down the river out of The Narrows, looked like a warped imagination come to life. I had to shake myself back to reality. There must have been thirty or forty head, outlined against the water by the starlight. One red-and-white carcass was tumbling along, head down and splayed feet showing in the air, as it turned over every little bit.

As they set in toward the east bank, in the quieter water, the handful of decoys took over like trained performers. Their hoarse bawling pulled the newcomers in to the bank without a bobble. The riders didn't have to even wet their horses in getting the swimmers headed up the canyon. Inside twenty minutes, the whole bunch had moved on up the creek, out of sight, the pickup men with them. If I hadn't watched it all with my own eyes, I'd have been hard put to believe it.

We sat there in the dark for quite a spell of time, just going over the way we'd hit the jackpot. All the pieces were falling into place like the parts of a jigsaw puzzle. All we had to do was play it out for the big win. Such a run of luck just couldn't come unhinged at the last minute.

"We make scout in mebbyso one hour," Tom finally summed up our joint ideas of the next move. "Other cows there. All wait for these ones. They bedded down good pretty soon."

"Unh-huh! Nothing to it." I wrapped up in my slicker against the chill I'd forgot about during the excitement. "This waiting's slow business, but we've got to give 'em time to settle down."

And it was a good thing we did. I hadn't been hunched up against the soft side of a boulder more than half of Tom's hour, when I saw him jerk his head up suddenly to look across the river. I heard it myself a moment later. Something was coming down the rocky gulch.

"Ben!" I muttered under my breath.

"Mebbyso other rustlers," Tom warned. "We see."

We saw, all right. The two riders who came out of the gulch a little later struck right across the river, like a pair of homing pigeons. It was easy to tell they weren't strangers to the place. They came ashore shortly above us. There was light enough to see that they were none of our outfit, though the bulky jasper on the blazed-face horse seemed kind of familiar.

A moment later, I recognized him for sure. His horse stumbled over a rock, as they turned upstream toward Oven Creek. It wasn't much of a stumble, but the high-powered damning the animal got could have come from nobody but our old aggravation, Whiskers Paget.

"Him!" The word whistled between Tom's teeth as his face swung toward me. His eyes glinted like a pair of hot coals in the dark.

I just plain sagged back against the rock while my brain caught up with events. This meant that all of Paget's bawling around about losing cows was simply part of the coverup. The picture slowly took shape in my mind. All his wild-eyed riding over the country, to holler for vigilante action, had been a plumb fake, a dodge to let him locate unwatched stock without rousing suspicion. And his particular hostility toward Ben accounted for our extra-heavy loss. It all matched up like the seams of a shirt.

We watched these two jaspers ride on up the creek while we digested this new angle. The best we could figure was that the gang had made its last raid and were now bunched up for their drive out of the country. That fit in with our earlier guess that the rest of the stolen stuff was somewhere up the canyon. Morning would probably see them on their way. Should Ben be held up long enough for them to move out ahead of him, he'd be screwed down to a tail chase. That would really be a losing proposition for our side. As narrow and crooked as the canyon was, any kind of a rear guard could hold up the strongest posse in the world until they got the stock clear.

On the other hand, if a rear guard could hogtie pursuit, a pair of bright boys, up ahead, could just as easy stop the outlaws from going anywhere. That brought us right back to our original idea of sneaking around to block the upper canyon.

"Ben's bunch ought to be here 'fore sunup," I reasoned. "Charley'll know we're somewheres ahead, so they'll just keep comin'. Then, when they bump into Whiskers' outfit, and the rustlers try for a getaway, we'll be forted up in the canyon to bottle 'em up. It will be just like trappin' skunks in a holla log."

Tom nodded slowly. "Better than all on one side." He got up and shed his slicker. "Go now! Moon come plenty quick."

We inched around bend after bend, in the blackness of the canyon, for upward of a mile before finding anything. Then we found it all at once. Tom's stop was so sudden it almost set Twister back into my saddle. We were facing a long, oval basin, where the crack of a canyon opened out after making a sharp right-angle turn around a shoulder of the wall. The five outlaws were directly ahead of us, all hunched around a fire and drinking coffee. They didn't seem to be worried about anybody discovering them, which was easy to understand. Up beyond the fire, their saddle horses grazed among the blotched outlines of scattered cattle. More cattle were farther up the basin, the outer ones fading off into the blacker shadows under the canyon walls.

It was the men, though, that claimed most of our attention. We studied them the best we could in the firelight. Two were plumb strangers, while we couldn't make out anything of the one with his back to us. But there was no mistaking the slab-sided puncher holding up a Texas hat and wearing shotgun chaps. He was the new hand the Keyhole A had taken on early that spring. And we had no trouble picking out Whiskers; he loomed up big as life and twice as natural, when he reached across the fire for the coffeepot.

I turned at a wordless growl from Tom. He was bent half forward, his eyes locked on Paget's bulky shape. I'd read about animal blood-lust in a human face, but that's the first time I ever put much stock in such a thing. It wasn't pretty. All the hate stewed up over the blue-roan's abuse, Betty's rotten deal, and the cattle stolen from the man Tom called his second father, seemed rolled into one skinful of pure poison.

It must have been a full breathless minute later that I saw his arm snake toward his rifle. His lips were making low guttural noises that I recognized as Indian death talk.

"No!" I hissed, grabbing his hand. "You'll spoil it! We gotta block the canyon first." I knew I had to talk fast. "Time to shoot him when they run."

Fortunately, he wasn't too far gone to get my point. Or maybe he decided revenge would be just as sweet if he tasted it a while first. It could have been either. What mattered right then was that he did back up and listen to me.

A few minutes later, he grunted agreement to my hoarse whispers and helped get our horses tied back in some brush off the trail. We could see there wasn't enough cover to risk riding around the herd. Our only show was to sneak along the base of the cliff on foot, where fallen rocks and a scattering of buck brush faded into the darker shadows.

We sat there for a little spell, waiting for them to get sleepy and us to absorb a few more details. The fact that Tex had come in with Whiskers made it look for sure like they planned to all go out with the herd. They'd made a good cleanup and, but for us, stood to make a clean getaway. I could see where they might figure to cash in and then move on to some other range while the heat died down around our territory. Or they might be planning on bringing some Montana stock back through Oven Canyon for a payoff on our side. The thing had a lot of possibilities.

I breathed some of my speculations into Tom's ear as we sat watching things through our brush screen. Whiskers and Tex had gone out and changed their saddles to a couple of fresh horses the other boys had picketed out. Then they had another round of coffee before starting to roll up in their blankets. Tom agreed with me that they were a little spooky, even safe as they figured they were. There was no doubt they were ready to ride at the drop of a hat, if necessary; or maybe sooner, should the moon light things up enough for travel.

It must have been crowding midnight when things finally quieted down. A hint of lightness in the eastern sky warned that the moon was on its way. Tom had climbed to his feet for a last look-see at the rustler camp. When I caught his nod, I inched myself up and wiggled the stiffness out of my knees.

"You go lef' side; I go other," he whispered, making a couple half-circle sweeps with one hand. "Make less noise."

I nodded and pulled off to the left. He didn't need to add that if one of us got caught, the other would still have a chance. Neither did he mention any doubts about my ability to get over those rocks on the enemy flank without attracting attention.

I don't know that he had any such doubts, but he was pretty well acquainted with me; and his sudden idea of splitting us up did sort of look more like headwork than happenstance. At any rate, it was lucky for both of us that he was across the canyon when that rock twisted under my foot. High bootheels are unhandy in some places. This was one of them. I staggered ten feet, whanging my rifle barrel on a rock, before I finally turned a hooligan and landed under a greasewood.

I was just a little above the half-dead campfire at the time. The racket I made sounded like a jackass in a tin barn. Rustlers started popping out of their blankets like fleas off a singed dog. One gun threw a chunk of lead into the rocks behind me. Another spoke to me from right overhead. Then they were all running for their horses.

Cra-a-ck! Whan-ng! It was Tom's rifle echoing from the opposite wall.

"Ben, move up!" he squalled, firing again from farther up. "Sid, Dave, head 'em." Another shot kicked up dust between Tex and the buck-jumping jasper ahead of him. "Charley, Jim, on your side!"

Things were going like a sheriff's raid on Buzz Cassidy's back-room during an election campaign. I got my head up where I could see, turning my Winchester loose as I rose. It helped snarl up the stampede. My first shot, a mite too far left, sent Tex diving behind a boulder. A few more helped start the horses bucking against their picket pins. The rustlers were dodging and shooting like a bunch of old-time Mexicans having a revolution. They were sure rattled. Yet you couldn't really blame them. The way I was working the lever of my rifle, along with Tom's crazy yelling and shooting from a different spot every time, must have made it look like a real surround to them. A whole posse couldn't have kicked up more racket. I doubt, though, if our wild bombardment in the dark hit anything.

It was the outlaws themselves who worked the most damage. I

176

saw most of that play. It looked like a regular Bill Hart movie. Horses were plunging all over the place. Long, orange lances of gun-lightning stabbed every which way through the dark. Everybody was yelling and stumbling over themselves. And, back along the trail, I could hear Twister going wild over all the noise.

One horse yanked his reins loose just as Tex got to him, sprinting from his boulder shelter. As the animal dodged out of sight in the shadows of the upper canyon, Tex spun on his heel to grab the buck-skin Whiskers had saddled a short time before. Whiskers was headed for the same horse, about thirty feet behind. As Tex hit the saddle, the big jasper let out a cussing yell to stop. But Tex wasn't interested; he was already bent over the buckskin's neck and on his way. I saw Whiskers' gun flash twice, but I guess the Texan was out of line. Or maybe the buckskin lifted in a jump just as Paget fired. Anyhow, the horse got the bullet. As it rolled in a kicking heap, Tex picked himself up to dodge under the cover of some cattle.

The rest of the horses had pulled their pins and left with the three other men. I could hear them pounding off up the canyon, swapping shots with Tom, somewhere up ahead. I guess Tex was on their trail. Anyhow, Whiskers was all that was left in sight. He stopped to watch the last horse disappear, cussing like a hamstrung pirate. I tried to get a bead on him, but missed him a mile.

I was lining up for another try, when he suddenly dropped his empty gun and raced back toward the mouth of the canyon. A sharp snort jerked my eyes around to see Twister just coming into the open. The length of sarviceberry limb dangling from his reins was proof that the excitement had been too much for him.

By the time I got my rifle around, Whiskers was dead in line with the horse. I didn't dare pull the trigger. The next instant, he dived under the animal's neck, yanking at the knot in the tied reins. I tumbled downhill, yelling at Tom, but I knew it was a lost cause. Neither of us had a chance to shoot without killing the horse.

I threw my hat on the ground, almost blubbering at the fix I was in—too far off to grab him and not daring to shoot. It's a wonder I didn't bite myself, when I saw the big crook jerk the blue's head around and screw himself into the saddle.

I heard Tom coming, screeching like a cougar at every jump. The moon's rim lifted above the canyon rim to pick him out under the south wall. But he was too far away. Whiskers had just time to unroll a string of damning adjectives in our direction before Twister took over.

I reckon that voice must have brought back a few old memories to the horse. Anyhow, the savage bellow hadn't much more than smeared the atmosphere before Twister suddenly tied himself into a knot and quit the ground. Whiskers' voice pinched out in sort of a wheeze as he grabbed a handful of saddlehorn the second jump.

I'll always feel sorry it wasn't daylight the next few minutes. That was the kind of a performance a man sees only once in a blue moon. Rotten as he was otherwise, you had to admit he was a top-hand rider. And, this time, he knew he was riding for a showdown. The blue-roan was hell and destruction in a horsehide. In a spot, no bigger than a barn floor, he uncorked the dizziest collection of devil-dyed gut-twisters that ever humped a saddle. His long, ugly head whipped like a snake at the top of each jump. His feet resembled four pile drivers, all centered on the same post, when he hit the ground. Corkscrewing, sunfishing, pinwheeling and bawling at every turn, he whipsawed through the churned-up dust like a powder keg exploding through sixteen bungholes.

Whiskers was doing a job, but he was in trouble from the first. It was plain he was using both hands and riding his spurs. Twice, I saw starlight under his pants. Then his body began to flop like a wet sack in the middle of the more crooked jumps. It must have been the desperation of a damned soul that kept him on top, fighting for balance.

Then, almost within the bat of an eyelash, I saw Twister suddenly fold up, like he was trying to swallow his tail, at the top of a bone-shaking jump. All four feet shot out to one side as he half rolled in the air. He landed flat on his back, with a soggy-like, jarring thud.

When we got to him, he was still squealing his hate as his bloody front feet hammered at what was left of Whiskers. We finally had to rope the quivering horse and drag him bodily away from his victim. Even then, it took Tom the best part of an hour to quiet him.

Meanwhile, I took a little scout around the basin. There wasn't much left of the camp except the mussed-up bedrolls and a pair of pack panniers partly full of grub. Upward of three hundred cattle were scattered on up the creek, most of them bedded back down after the big hoorah. I only found one horse, his picket rope tangled in some brush. Tex had evidently got away, trailing his partners afoot.

Thin daylight was starting to crawl down over the rim of the canyon when I got back down where Tom was still fussing over Twister. I was just in time to meet Charley, sneaking up the canyon with half the valley ranchers behind him. He'd had to ride plumb to the Bent Triangle to catch up with Ben. Later, they'd had some trouble finding their way down into the canyon in the dark. They looked kind of funny when they found we'd already done everything but take the cattle home.

"How many rustlers did you get?" Ben asked, looking around.

"Too dark. No shoot good," Tom said flatly. "All hightail up Oven Canyon."

I opened my mouth to speak, but Tom's eyes stabbed me before I could say anything. He was plainly telling me to stay out of it. That puzzled me. I knew that catching his most despised enemy knee-deep in a mess that wouldn't wash was the joy of a lifetime to him. And I'd noticed he seemed to be fighting his head over something just before the boys showed up. Still, I'd never figured his powwowing with himself would cover the idea of hogging the limelight on the payoff. Even though my foozling the works, when I fell down, really put me in the back row, I figured I was still part of the picture.

I was some hurt and a whole lot mad. It wasn't like Tom to try to be the big it. Yet that's about the way it sized up, the way he was going at it. I eased myself down on a rock, letting my empty stomach sour the rest of my disposition. He could be the big, lone hero, if he wanted to. I didn't care!

The next minute, I forgot all about both my disposition and the fit of sulks. My head snapped up to give clearance for both ears. Ben had seen the dead buckskin lying a dozen rods above the pulverized Whiskers.

"I thought you told me the rustlers all got away?" His words were drumming in my ears.

"Un-hunh, go quick." Tom faced him without a flicker.

"Then who's that?"

"Betty's man."

"What? You mean Buck Paget?"

"Yes."

Ben batted his eyes and shoved back his hat. His face was one big question mark.

"Just what is this?" he finally demanded. "Where does Paget fit in?"

"Come with us," Tom lied evenly, never turning a hair. "He chase

rustler, too. We find him on trail to river. All jump thieves together."
He lifted an arm toward the dead buckskin, still wearing Whiskers'
saddle, and the empty gun a few yards to one side. "Shoot much.
One rustler hit him. Mebbyso only a scratch, but knock him off horse.
His foot hang in stirrup. Buckskin kick him dead 'fore I can shoot to
kill horse."

My lower jaw had dropped somewhere down around my belt
buckle as he was talking. Now I pulled my mouth shut by degrees as
it slowly started to dawn on me what he was up to. My thick skull
would never have opened up to light from that direction in a month
of Sundays. But he had seen the whole shebang, as it would work out
in the long run, if the real truth got out.

The way he assayed it—and he was probably right—branding
Whiskers as one of the outlaws would be more than likely to backfire against Betty. A lot of ordinarily nice people have a way of going
off half-cocked over such deals. Some of them would be sure to lump
Betty in with her rustler husband, causing her a heap of grief she
didn't deserve. He was all for Betty, no matter what. So, right or
wrong, he had decided to stave off any chance of her getting a bad
deal by throwing his own personal feelings overboard. The things she
had done for him, while he was cracked up the winter before, just
plumb outweighed any neighborhood applause that might shower
down for his part in snagging the rustler kingpin. It struck me as one
of the finest things I ever met up with. I doubt if many ordinary
men could have picked such a decision out of thin air on the spur of
the moment.

Fortunately, everybody was watching him. That gave me time to
get my face and voice screwed back to normal before I had to use
them. I was even able to face Ben without flinching, when he turned
on me to back up Tom's story.

Maybe I made it too good. Or maybe he noticed the blood still
smearing Twister's feet, when we hazed the stock back to the river.
I'll never know. But he had the whole deal well enough figured out
in his mind that I had to admit the truth, when he finally sprung it
on me while we were feeding cattle one morning late that winter.
There wasn't much left for me to do but come clean about the whole
affair.

"I don't think you should pass any of it on to Betty, though," I
added. "Not after the way Tom hamstrung himself to keep old
Whiskers' dirty work from rubbing off on any more of her life."

Ben backed up against the hayrack, eyeing me like he'd just discovered me for the first time. Then he slowly shoved his hat back on his head and stuck out his hand.

"That's a bargain, Curly," he said. "The two months we've been married seem to stand out as the first real happiness she's had for a flock of years. And we sure don't want any sour notes to horn in on it now."

He hauled his hat down over one eye and scratched his head. "As for that Tom Little Bear," he went on, cracking a grin that made his ears jerk, "it wouldn't be really square to spoil his story, not after proving himself one of the whitest chunks of humanity in the valley. And more especially," the big grin spread out another notch, "since his battlin' to learn white man ways has made him the best doggone liar this side of Cheyenne."